Tracks

Sex. Drugs. Rock and Roll.

Sarah Biermann
Edited by Meagan Burgad

Contents

Prologue

Oh my God, this is it. I opened my eyes long enough to look down once again at the envelope in my hands, one on each side of it. It was a smaller envelope than I was hoping to receive, which made me even more nervous. I was visibly shaking. I even debated whether or not to run to the bathroom to vomit.

But there is a slight chance I may not have to vomit, so I figured I'd hold off until I knew it was necessary.

I read the name on the return address stamp in the upper right corner of the envelope for the fiftieth time. *Harvard University School of Law.*

The gist of my academic career, since at least the 5th grade, has led up to this moment. My whole life has orbited around my dream of Harvard Law. High school and college weren't as fun for me as it probably was for my classmates. I brushed off parties, barely dated, and had limited friends. My Saturdays were spent at home, studying. What if that was all for nothing?

I knew I received amazing grades in college, and a much higher than average score on my LSATS, but somehow I still didn't believe it was good enough. I didn't come from a well-known or well-to-do family. I didn't have any relatives that had attended Harvard. There were a lot of people who want to go to Harvard Law with all of these extra qualifications and more.

I sighed, frustrated with my lack of confidence in my hard work. *Get a grip, Dylan,* I mentally scolded myself. I placed a finger under the tab of the envelope. I pushed my finger along it, hard, so that it ripped away from the paper, revealing a white letter inside.

I dug the letter out, letting the torn envelope fall to the ground. With shaky hands I opened the folded note and began to read.

Chapter 1- Fresh Start

I hear a knock at the door to my room, once again. I am trying to be as understanding as possible under the circumstances, but I swear if he doesn't leave me alone I will never finish packing. It's stressful enough as it is.

I sigh, "Yes, Dad?"

"I was just making sure you still didn't need any help," my dad yelled through the door. Honestly, I probably do need some help with the packing. Even though I am 22 and had already gone through undergraduate school, I had never actually moved away from home. It saved me from having to pay dorm fees at my school, and usually my dad truly wasn't this overbearing. There was no need to be, really. I was pretty much a perfect kid on the outside. So since I had never moved out of this house or this room in my entire life, I had accumulated an enormous number of things since I was an infant.

Although the help is probably needed, the idea of my dad rummaging through my things and tinkering with them makes me cringe. I am an extremely private person, even from my dad who is probably the closet person to me, aside from Theresa.

"Still okay, Dad. But if you don't leave me alone, I probably won't be done to leave on time tomorrow and then Theresa will kill me."

"No, okay, yup, I know," my dad mumbled awkwardly. I hear a trace of sadness in his voice. My heart constricts a bit at this realization. My dad would never let on that it was hard for him to see me move because I know he wants the best for me, but I do feel guilty for leaving him alone in the house. I'm not exactly moving around the corner, either. Boston is quite a drive from Philadelphia.

Through my bedroom window, I notice the sun is quickly setting in the orange sky. I step away from the box I am haphazardly sticking office supplies in and walk up to the window, looking out to the horizon. I would miss my home. I would miss the backyard and the rickety brown fence that enclosed it. I would miss my old swing set that still sat in the corner of the yard. I had never known another home. I know that this would probably be the last night I ever spent here where it still was my official home.

It's times like these I wish I had a mother to talk to. I needed comfort and support that only a mother could give. I try to picture what my mother would have said to me, gazing at me with her kind, brown eyes. I remember what she looks like, but I'm starting to forget certain things, like her voice. The way she smelled...

I hug myself tightly around my chest as I walk away from the window and back to packing. I must admit, I will be glad to leave some memories behind in this house and start a new life away from the pain.

The next morning, my dreams are interrupted by a sudden, horrible noise. I open my eyes, still heavy from sleepiness. I slam my hand down on my alarm clock, shutting off the nasal, buzzing noise. Six in the morning. I groan. I understand why I decided to leave at seven, because we would get to Boston around one in the afternoon, which would leave us a lot of time to get the boxes into our home and unpack before it gets dark. I can't stand clutter, so I'd like to have everything pretty much unpacked today. But I certainly could use more sleep.

I smile, thinking of Theresa, who is also waking up right now. I know she's cursing me. She's not at all a morning person.

I somehow manage to get myself out of bed and throw on a pair of jeans and a basic tee. No need to look stylish today. After I get done with my morning routine in the bathroom, I run down the narrow stairway outside of my room, continuing through the living room and into the kitchen. I smell that my dad has already started the coffee, and I silently praise Jesus and pour myself a cup. I'm a little overly fond of coffee, some might even say addicted, but when you need to get a 4.0 through all four years of college, it's a necessary evil.

I hear footsteps quietly climbing down the stairway. I turn in time to see my dad entering through the doorway to the kitchen. I detect the black circles under his eyes. Guilt grips me again. It's obvious he didn't sleep well last night, probably because of the events of today.

"Morning," my dad grunts, stretching. I smile at him and turn to pour him a cup of coffee. I'm a woman of few words, but my dad never minded. We often sit in comfortable silences.

I hand him the steaming cup and he smiles at me gratefully. Taking a sip, he leans against the doorway. "Are you all set, then?"

"Yeah," I sigh. "I need some help carrying the boxes from my room to the car. Are you okay with that?"

He nods. "Of course, yeah."

After our nice healthy breakfast of coffee with extra sugar, we manage to load up my little red convertible to the breaking point with my boxes. Theresa and I had, thankfully, been able to buy an amazing townhome on a quiet street that came almost fully furnished.

For two poor law students with no furniture of their own, this was a life saver.

I said an awkward goodbye to my dad, hugging him tightly around his thin waist. My dad was a handsome man, tall and thin with high cheek bones. His hair turned grey in his early forties, but it gave him a distinguished look, and now that he's approaching sixties, it's almost as if he hasn't aged since. He often used his good looks to his advantage.

I released my dad at that thought, shaking my head as if to shake the reflection away.

After exchanging goodbyes and a promise to call when Theresa and I arrive, I head off to meet Theresa at her house so I can follow her to our new home.

I was extremely excited when I found out Theresa was also accepted into Harvard. I had been worried, honestly, as her grades had not been as good as mine. They weren't bad necessarily, but she wasn't on the Dean's list, either. Much of her acceptance can be attributed to the fact that her father is a well-known politician who had also attended Harvard Law. She knew she would probably get accepted based on this information, and she took advantage of that a little bit while in school.

Theresa was much more sociable than I was in high school and college. She had many friends and liked to frequent weekend parties and clubs. Still, we somehow had a connection. I was closer to her than I had ever been to anyone, and that's about as close as I'm comfortable with.

I think Theresa and I balance each other. In fact, we are almost direct opposites in every way. Where she is shorter, dark skinned, and thinner- I am annoyingly tall, pale white, and curvy. Her hair is a curly, full brown mane cut to her chin. My hair is brilliantly blonde and hangs straight to just below my shoulder blades. She is bubbly, outgoing, giggly, and loves attention. I am quiet, reserved, shy, and die at the thought of any kind of attention. Where she pushes me forward, I settle her down. We challenge each other, and give each other a sense of steadiness.

It was with this in mind that I decided, against the wishes of my father, to buy a house with Theresa and live with her while attending Harvard. To me, it made more sense to be investing in something and paying a mortgage than it would be to rent something for the same price and throw money out the window for the next three years. That makes sense, right?

God, I just hope we don't get annoyed and start hating each other. That would suck, because now we both own this home. I just imagine Theresa having parties all the time well into the morning; the cops showing up frequently and knowing our address by heart. I envision all of the men she'll parade in and out of the house, and what that might sound like on nights when I'm trying to study or actually get a good night's sleep...

Fuck.

I am really good at suppressing bad thoughts that have the potential to make me feel uneasy, so I continually push my fears down deep as I follow Theresa to Boston for the almost 6 hour drive. I'm confident I've composed myself enough to actually be excited as we pull up in front of our new townhome on Massachusetts Avenue right on schedule. Keeping to schedules helps my anxiety issues.

The home we managed to afford, thanks mostly to Theresa's parent's generosity, is beautiful. There's a stairway leading up to a massive, green door. The right side of the home is rounded, giving it an almost castle-like effect. There are flowers to the right of the stairs, and the red-orange bricks adorning the entire structure scream Boston. The best part is that since we put so much down on the house, the mortgage is actually semi-affordable. For the two of us combined, at least.

Theresa parks her truck in front of our home, with me parking behind her. I see her exit the car, her brown hair bouncing and blowing in the Boston wind, and turn to look at me through the windshield. She runs over to me as I exit my car, smile wide, and throws herself onto me with her arms around my neck.

"We're here!" she screeches in my ear. I smile at her enthusiasm.

"It's so beautiful!" I try to match her excitement. "Let's go inside!"

We run up the stairs and open the door with our brand new keys. Pushing the door open, we enter into the foyer of our completely furnished new home. Looking at all of the furniture and art, it was obvious that it had all cost a fortune, and I wondered why anyone would want to leave it behind. I concluded that the kind of people who could normally afford a home like this would probably want to buy all new furniture that "fit" their new home. Must be nice. Even when I graduate Harvard, assuming I actually acquire the position I want as a state prosecutor, I probably still won't be able to afford furniture like this.

After oohing and aweing at our new place and claiming our rooms, we begin the tedious work of unpacking. The hours seem to pass quickly, but we manage to get a lot done. By the time evening passes and the dark night falls over the city, we have unpacked everything and have it organized appropriately. We even have the phone and cable company out to set everything up. The only chore we really have left to do is go to the grocery store. Theresa is the cook between the two of us, so she graciously agrees to go for us tomorrow.

Exhausted, Theresa flops her skinny body down on our couch and reaches for the remote. The TV hanging on the wall in front of her is one of the rare items that didn't come with the home, but was a housewarming gift from my father. He went into detail about how nice the flat screen was when I had opened it a few days ago, saying a bunch of letters and numbers that I didn't understand. It just looks like a nice TV to me, and so I'm grateful to him no matter how many pixels it has.

I offer to grab Theresa a glass of white wine to celebrate, walking into the kitchen and looking through the already crowded drawers to find a bottle opener. Successful, I twist the opener into the cork, popping it with a loud sound as Theresa flips mindlessly through the cable guide.

"I have to get used to all the new station numbers..." she mutters, still flipping through the guide as I place two wine glasses on the counter and pour in the liquid. "Oooh!" Theresa exclaims excitedly, throwing the remote down on the couch in triumph.

I walk over to her, holding a glass out to her as I sit on the opposite side of the long couch. She takes it out of my hand while not looking at me, her eyes glued to the TV.

I notice she had put on some music backstory show.

I look at her, warily. She finally turns her head to make eye contact with me. "It's on Jeremy Mason! You know I love him!"

I snort, sipping my wine. I turn my attention reluctantly back to the television.

A serious woman's voice narrates as pictures flash across the screen, "…musical boy genius, turned heartthrob. Even still, for all of his talent and fortune, over the years he couldn't quite seem to stay out of trouble. Mr. Mason found himself arrested several times for assault, possession of marijuana and cocaine, and disorderly conduct…"

Pictures of him continue to fade on and off the screen. One was him as a boy, not older than 5, as he played the piano for an enormous crowd of people. The next showed him a bit older, dressed in a suit at Buckingham Palace in front of a piano. Another was recent, his hair tossed in all different directions on his head, sweat running down his bare, lean chest. He has a serious expression on his face in all of them; his eyes, although strikingly blue and beautiful, almost seems empty or devoid somehow. It's strange to me that a boy living this fantastic, exciting life would be so miserable looking in all of these photos.

I must have a puzzled look on my face, as Theresa says, "What's on your mind?"

I snap out of my trance. "Nothing," I said, sipping again on my wine.

I see Theresa smile out of my peripheral vision. "Isn't it awesome that we're seeing him tomorrow night?! Front freaking row!"

"Yeah. Awesome," I concur. It is exciting, I must admit. I'm not the kind of person that ever dreamed I'd be front row of any concert, especially the sold out concert of the year. These tickets were worth amazing money. Like, thousands. Each. They were a very gracious and thoughtful (I couldn't help but rolls my eyes) housewarming present from Theresa's parents.

"Don't start on the usefulness of the gift, buzz kill," Theresa scolds me, obviously seeing my eye roll. But I mean, honestly, what kind of housewarming gift was that?

Finally I decide I can't keep my eyes open much longer, exhausted from the long and eventful day. Standing up, I stretch and walk over to place my wine glass in the sink. "I'm off to shower, Therese," I say over my shoulder as I walk down the hallway.

She mutters something unrecognizable as I open the door to the bathroom, still fixated on her show. I shake my head and shut the door behind me, turning the water on before I undress. Next to coffee, showering was biggest addiction. I was convinced that any problem or sickness could be solved by a nice, long shower. In the shower, I was able to let my mind wander, and even when bad thoughts or memories arose, at least no one was around to see me cry. Or have a panic attack.

Sadly my shower has to be cut short, as my eyelids slowly begin to grow heavier the second I enter the white tub and close the curtain. I manage to wash my body and hair, at least, and step out to dry off. I walk over to the sink and brush out my hair and my teeth, wobbly on my feet. Throwing open the bathroom door, I stumble across the hallway into my new room.

The white bed with unfamiliar sheets looked more inviting than any bed I had ever seen. I barely remember opening the drawer to my new light wood dresser, grabbing shorts and a big t-shirt, and throwing them on myself before collapsing on the bed and falling into a deep, dreamless sleep.

Chapter 2- Unexpected Hero

I begin to stir as the light hits my eyes, an unfamiliar feeling as my window at home was in a different position in the room, blocking the morning light from entering so directly. I rub my eyes, still hazy with sleep. Stretching, I open them slowly and turn to look at my bedside table. Wow, 11:00 a.m. I'm surprised I'm still so exhausted.

I sit up just in time for my door to fling open. As the adrenaline rushes to my heart, I see Theresa scamper into the room. "Good morning!" she sings.

"Thanks for scaring the shit out of me!" I sing back. I'd ask her why she is in such a good mood, but that's how Theresa is pretty much all the time.

She ignores my snark, as usual, and sits on the side of my bed, smiling widely. "Are you ready to get up and get ready?"

"Ready? The concert isn't until six."

Theresa looks at me confused. "Yeah, and it's almost noon."

"Yeah?" I give her a confused look back. We sit for a moment in silence.

She rolls her eyes. "Anyway, time to get up and eat!" She pats my leg before getting up and loping back through the door and down the hallway.

Hopeful that Theresa means she cooked a nice, big breakfast, I manage to pull myself out of bed and follow her out the door. I walk to our kitchen, smiling when I see pans on the stove with eggs and pancakes in them.

"Already went to the store?" I ask her, plopping down on one of the wooden chairs of our new dining room set.

I hear Theresa grab the plates from the cabinet above her head. "Yes! I woke up early this morning. I barely slept last night. I'm so excited for this concert!" she said, as she plated food for me and sat in down on the table in front of me. After she handed me a fork, I gratefully began to eat, feeling ravenous due to not eating properly the past day or so.

Right, the concert. I mentally sigh, thinking about how I'd rather be at home in my sweats reading a book. What's the big deal with concerts, anyway? People spend a fortune on tickets to see someone so far away they probably could use a body double and no one would notice. You hear the same songs on the radio. Why not watch them perform on a talk show or something? You'd see better and save a bunch of cash.

Of course, explaining my opinion to Theresa wouldn't help in the slightest. Of this, I was sure. She reaffirmed my belief by relentlessly talking for the rest of the day about the concert. I tried to smile and play along with her enthusiasm, because that's what best friends do. I was really hoping she'd be able to stay sober and come home by herself tonight. I wasn't mentally prepared to handle Theresa coming home with a man yet. How was I supposed to drown that out? And seeing these men come home one night and be put out the next morning on the curb like a pile of trash was going to be more than awkward. Theresa, you see, is what some people would call a "player" if she was a man. Because she's a woman, a lot of people in our high school and college had another word for it.

Of course, they would never call her that to her face, or she'd make their social life hell, as popular as she was. They would never say it to me, either, or they'd get a fist full of my fingers in their mouth. I really am more of a lover than a fighter, but I'd be God damned before someone would bad mouth Theresa. In fact, I know she did the same for me after people found out how my mom died. No one ever bothered me about that at all, and I know I had Theresa to thank.

Although her parents had given her a strict talking to about protecting her reputation once she got to Harvard, I don't actually believe she will settle down. The one hope I have is that it is a Jeremy Mason concert, so at least 75% of the audience has to be women. Right? That puts the odds a bit in my favor.

Theresa had spent most of the day getting ready. She redid her hair, tried on many outfits, painted her nails, etc. I, on the other hand, did practical things instead. I looked up directions to the venue, ensured our tickets were in our purses, stocked our bags with things we may need, and did an ATM run for cash. That's why our partnership worked.

When I finally had time to get dressed, I had to do it quickly. Walking out of the bedroom afterwards, I look up to find Theresa standing in the hallway, looking at me disappointedly. She looked amazing in a short, plum colored dress.

"What?" I asked her, smoothing my shirt.

"Jeans and a blouse?" she asked me, dissatisfied.

I shrugged. "What's there to fuss about? It's a concert. I'll probably get thrown up on or something. I'm not looking to meet anyone or anything." I continued walking down the hallway with Theresa by my side. I could see her rolling her eyes out of the corner of my vision, but I decide to drop it. She knows me and I'm not about to suddenly change overnight.

Grabbing our things, we exit the front of our new home and lock the door behind us, running down the stairs. We hop into my little red car, and before we know it, we're off to the venue.

It wasn't a hard place to find, especially because there was a line of at a standstill trying to get into the lot.

After 45 minutes in line, we finally pull up to the entrance of the lot. I read the sign before we get up to the cashier. "30 dollars for parking?" I say, exacerbated. Theresa digs cash out of her wallet and hands it to me. I toss it into the cashier's hand and he hands me a ticket to put on my dash in exchange. I place it there as I begin to drive away, finding a spot relatively easily and pulling into it.

At this point, Theresa is bouncing excitedly on my seat like a fifteen-year-old girl at a boy-band concert. At least she's having fun. "Let's go!" I said, opening my door. We walk to the font of the venue and through the door, handing our tickets to the man stationed to collect them. When he sees our tickets, his eyes widen and he smiles at us. "Lucky girls," he says, waving us through.

Yeah. Yay me.

We enter and make our way through the crowded hall, with vendors selling t-shirts adorned with Jeremy Mason's picture as well as food and beer. After finding the door that leads to the floor seats, we enter it and hand our tickets to security, who lead us directly to front-row center. The only thing separating us from the stage is a big, metal gate. We're so close, I can see dust particles on the curtains. "Wow," I say, amazed despite myself. This is pretty neat.

Theresa is so flabbergasted she can't even speak. I think she mumbles something about how she can't believe how close he's going to be, but I can't be sure of her exact words.

I turn to look at the rows of people behind us. The venue is filled to the breaking point. I am relieved to see that my initial instincts were correct, and most of the crowd seemed to be occupied by women. The girls within the first few rows of us seem to be around our age, some younger and some older perhaps. They are definitely hard core fans like Theresa; they are already screaming and chanting. Some, I notice, are even crying. Crying! As if Jesus had appeared for the second coming.

I snort at them and turn back around towards the stage just as the lights begin to dim. The crowd begins to roar almost immediately, the arena once again blazing with lights from cameras and cell phones. I put my hands over my ears, the sound deafening. Especially coming from the left of me where Theresa stood.

Just as the crowd had calmed a little, a loud, long guitar cord rings out through the sound system. I jump at the unexpected sound, as do many girls around me. The crowd goes silent for a moment, also in surprise, and then once again roars in excitement.

Theresa grabs my arm. "Oh my God!!!" she screams. I wiggle out of her grip.

I can see movement behind the left side of the stage as a guitar riff starts to play. The sound is beautiful, unlike any sound I'd ever heard. The cords fade into each other effortlessly, without pause. A few men run on stage during this time, picking up instruments laid out on the stage. One man sits behind a set of drums.

After the band gets situated, they begin to play as well, complementing the melody of the guitar. The lights blaze on the stage and a man steps out of the wings where I had previously seen movement.

If the sound had been deafening before, it was earth shattering now. I put my hands up to my ears for a moment, and drop them once I'm used to the noise. The man struts- there's really no other word for the way he moves- across the stage and up to a microphone planted in the center, directly in front of where we're standing. His predatory smile is wide and gleaming in the stage lights, but it fades quickly back into his familiar serious expression. His body is not as slight as it seems on TV. He's tall and long, with wiry muscles outlining his forearms. Okay, he's attractive. I can appreciate that.

I feel the back of my chair hit the inset of my knees as it's pushed by the girls behind me and I step forward. The movement must have caught his attention, and he looks down at me. I'm immobilized, in shock of my sudden increased heart rate. His beautiful blue eyes are intense as he stares at me, piercing me through my soul. His face relaxes as he makes eye contact with me, seeming almost surprised himself. Meanwhile, his fingers continue to move effortlessly along the neck of the guitar, playing a beautifully loud melody.

We held each other's eyes for a moment, my mind blank. As suddenly as it had happened, he looked away from me and he fixes his previous expression back on his face. I'm still frozen.

Theresa yells in my ear, "He totally looked at you! Oh my God, awesome!"

"Yeah…" I say, under my breath. I don't even have a snarky comment to make.

The concert continues and I find myself enjoying it. As the songs go on, the crowd's excitement and fervor grow. I see girls run up the isle next to us and attempt to crawl over the fencing in front of the stage, but they are quickly snatched by the overly present security. Jeremy can dance, and he sure can perform. I even find myself smiling while watching him.

Strangely, throughout the show, I felt as if he was looking at me every few minutes. I guess that's part of the appeal of him, looking at all the women as if he's hunting them with his gorgeous eyes and sculpted face. I feel him looking at me again, and I see him step forward to reach his hand over the stage, into the crowd. It seems to come directly to me. Theresa reaches over and grabs his hand immediately. She's knocked away by security quickly. More hands appear in front of me, and he grabs them all. I look up at his face, close to me, and find him staring at me. I am again frozen under his stare.

More hands continue to find him, and I feel my chair being pushed against me again. I am knocked from behind as a girl jumps over my seat and hits me in the back. I stumble forward, releasing his gaze from mine and trying to catch my footing. Before I'm able to, I am knocked from the side by another girl, and then again from behind by yet another fan. I fall to my knees, catching myself with my hands. I feel feet step on my back hard, and I fall to my stomach so that I'm flat on the ground. Out of instinct, I put my hands up to cover my head. I feel more feet step on my legs, and I scream.

"Stop!" I hear a man's voice shout, loudly. Some of the music trails off. "Stop, stop, stop!" I hear again. The music stops dead.

"Help her. Now!"

I don't move, I still lay on the floor with my hands over my head, but I can tell the women are moving away from me. I look up just in time to see a man walking towards me, moving the women around him roughly.

The guard- a young, tall, dark as night man at least 300 pounds-throws me up into his arms. I gasp as I am suddenly whisked through the crowd, which parts like the red sea when they notice the big man coming towards them. He pushes through a heavy, grey metal door. It's pitch black when we first enter, and I hear the door shut with a bang as the man hurries down the hall with me still in his arms. It gets brighter in the hall as we approach five or six rooms on either side of the light green hallway. As we pass the first room on the left, smoke is pouring out in gray bunches and there is hard rock music playing loudly on a stereo. Seven or eight young people are sitting around a red couch smoking what looks to be cigarettes, but I'm not given time to investigate as we hurry past the room and into the doorway of the second room on the left.

The room is silent and empty aside from another old, red couch sitting in the middle. The couch has a few folding chairs surrounding it, and a small white desk with a mirror against the wall. The man sits me gently down on the couch and kneels next to me, thankfully blocking the bright light from the fluorescents above us. In a soft but deep voice, he says "Are you okay, miss?"

I look around the room in shock as I think for a minute. I mentally check my body. Yes, I believe I'm in one piece. "Yes," I stammer out. "I'm okay. I'm not hurt."

The man nods and looks away as he touches a button on a black microphone that hangs from his ear. "Got it," he says in his deep voice. He looks back to me. "The doctor on staff is going to take a look at you."

I sigh. I did just say I was alright. I hate this kind of fuss and attention. The fact that he stopped the whole concert just for me was enough to make me want to die. All of those people looking at me getting carried like an infant…ugh.

I suddenly think of Theresa. Damn, I left her out there all alone and she's probably worried. "Um…" I say as the man gets up from his knees in front of the couch. "I…I came with my girlfriend…and she's out there and worried…"

He nods. I can still hear the concert, which has continued, blaring from far down the hall and outside the steel door. "No problem, miss," the man says loudly. "I saw her next to you. I'll go get her and bring her back here."

I smile lightly. "Thank you," I say as he turns away. She'll flip knowing she's going to come backstage, even if there's not much to be excited about. I realize that I'd never myself been backstage at a concert- but I must admit I expected it to be much more stirring than this.

I wait a few minutes, lost in my thoughts, until I hear a light knocking at the doorway. I look up quickly and see a man with a light blue and white stripped polo shirt and black pants enter. He's older, maybe 50, with greying hair and gentle brown eyes. He carries a black bag and has a stethoscope around his overly tan neck.

He smiles. "Miss, um..."

"Ackhart. Dylan." I smile.

"Miss Ackhart. I'm Doctor Philips. I heard you had a spill," he says, as he kneels beside me and begins to take out his things.

I wanted to say, 'No, actually, a bunch of crazy fan girls knocked me down like a bowling pin and then trampled on me like a stampede of wild bulls,' but I decided to give my sarcastic side a rest, and nodded instead.

As the doctor looks me over with all of his gadgets, I hear another, fainter knock at the doorway. Theresa comes in, looking around the room with a worried look on her face. Relief washes over her as her eyes lock with mine. She runs over to me, crossing the couch from behind as to not disturb the doctor, and kneels beside him, close to my head.

"Dylan!" she cries. "Oh God I was so worried!" she grabs the hand that is hanging off the couch. "I couldn't get to you to help you up. I'm so sorry. Are you hurt?" she asks, as she looks at the doctor.

"No," Dr. Phillips smiles. "She's just fine. A few bruises here and there, maybe." He begins to put his things back in the bag. Theresa smiles at me. Dr. Phillips stands up and grabs his bag in his left hand. "Take care now Miss Ackhart. You can go whenever you wish, but take your time."

I look at Theresa as her smile widens with excitement. I thank the doctor again as he leaves the room and his footsteps fade down the hallway. "Ah!" Theresa shrieks. "Backstage!"

I wince as I sit up more. I admit I'm starting to feel that bruising. "Thanks," I mumble. "Glad to see you were so worried. Its girls like you who put me here."

She rolls her eyes. "I *was* worried. But, you're obviously fine and now we're back stage! At Jeremy Mason's concert! Oh my God, everyone will die when they hear. Let's go explore!"

I roll my eyes as I get up from the couch slowly, first sitting and then standing up. I feel a bit dizzy but I attribute that to being carried by the big man and the smoke pouring out of the room next store. Theresa grabs my hand as we walk out of the room and back into the dimly lit green hallway. We hear clapping and cheering from the stage down the hall.

"I think the show must be over," Theresa says loudly, above the clapping and music from the smoke room.

Suddenly, we hear what seems like thousands of footsteps coming towards us from where the concert hall is located. When I squint, I can just make out a wall of people walking in our direction. I pull Theresa up against the wall with me just in time for the people to pass.

There are men with huge digital cameras, beautiful women in business suits carrying microphones being followed by camera men, barely dressed girls slinking behind, and men carrying various pieces of stage equipment. Theresa and I watch silently. This is more of the pandemonium I expected from being backstage at the biggest tour in the world.

Behind the men with stage equipment come more photographers with lights flashing away. I see the big man that carried me backstage walking behind the photographers, with two more men who look like him walking behind him on either side, creating a V shape around a man in the middle. Theresa squeezes my hand in recognition as the men turn to a doorway just past us on the right side of the hall, the only one with a door, and push the man inside. The door closes behind him.

The photographers and news anchors stop to take pictures and talk to their cameras. I overhear one bubbly blonde anchor say, "That was Jeremy Mason after his show at the Wilbur Theater."

I turn and look at Theresa. She mouths, "Oh my God." Her dark skin looks almost pale.

I suddenly feel a tug at my right hand. I turn quickly and see one of the slinky girls from the crowd. She has a short leather skirt on with ripped up black fishnets and ankle length boots. She has a red halter top that bares her midriff and barely covers her large breasts. She has a pixie-like face and a pierced nose, with striking red hair. She leans closer to my ear. "Come with me," she breathes into my ear.

I hesitate and look at Theresa, who is oblivious. "Trust me," she whispers loudly in my ear. "It's crazy here."

I begin to follow, pulling Theresa with me. We enter the doorway to the smoke room. The girl lets go of my hand as we enter. The smoke instantly surrounds us and I identify the familiar smell as cigarettes. There are glasses all over the room. It looks like the one I was placed in except there's a small, brown coffee table in front of the red couch. There's a blue iPod dock on the white mirror desk playing alternative rock. A man and woman are currently having sex on the couch and not being shy about it. Neither are the two big breasted blondes making out shirtless on one of the folding chairs in the corner, one sitting on top of another, their hands all over each other. The other five or six people are standing around: talking, drinking, and some watching the, um, 'action.'

I must look like I'm in shock. I've never seen anything like this in all my life. As far as virgin eyes go, I'm about as virgin as one can get. When I look at slinky girl, she smiles a sly smile and rolls her eyes. "Rock and roll, Emeralds," she says, before she lets go of my hand and turns back to a group of friends talking. I beat my bright green eyes bashfully, embarrassed at my ignorance and inexperience.

I look at Theresa and she seems to have the same uncomfortable look as me. This is not where two girls about to go into Harvard Law feel at home. We both wordlessly turn for the doorway at the same time, when suddenly the big man that pulled me from the crowd appears, blocking the exit.

"Miss," he says, low with a nod. "Mr. Mason would like a word with you, if that's alright."

I feel Theresa freeze in her tracks. She noticeably tenses. Even I am taken aback. Why on God's green earth would he want to talk to me? Is he sure he meant me?

"Go!" Theresa says. "I'll wait here!"

I look behind my shoulder at the spectacle taking place behind me, and I feel uncomfortable at the thought of leaving Theresa here alone.

Then the big man grabs my free hand and I realize that I don't have a choice. I let go of Theresa as he starts leading me down the hall, towards the door I briefly saw the rocker enter through a short time before. The crowd had begun to dissipate, although I hear noise in the room I was in with the doctor before, and assume it must be the press room and reporters have gone there to wait for statements from him.

As I'm looking towards the room behind me, I hear a door creak open and the big man telling the people surrounding the door to "back away." He then pushes me into the room and closes off the brown wooden entrance behind me.

Wait! I'm not ready...I'm not ready!!

I turn toward the door frantically after it closes, debating whether or not to run. I'm still torn as I flip towards the room again. I realize that no one is in the dim room, only me. I begin to fidget, unsure of what to do. Do I sit? When will he come?

The room looks similar to the other two in the hallway that I have seen; only it is obviously nicer. The walls are red instead of white. A red couch is still there, only it's newer and leather instead of ripped up upholstery. There's a red area rug on the floor with a blue swirl-pattern under a brown coffee table. Against the wall in front of the couch is a big, flat screen TV, currently on a music channel, with soft rock music playing lightly. Classic rock, I realize, and bluesy. The desk with the mirror is there against the wall across from the door, but the mirror has big, white ball lights around it. Along the left wall is a door that's open and leads to a closet. Closer to the door I entered from is another wooden door that's shut.

As I'm looking around, I hear the sound of a light switch being flipped off and the door along the left wall begins to open. I jump and back away from the door, turning to face it.

A man walks through, wearing a black tank top and a white towel around his neck. He's running his hand through his multicolored dirty blonde hair that's messy and unkempt and sexy. His black jeans ride low, exposing a bit of his pronounced hip bones. He has black boots on, and the bottom of his jeans bunch around them. He peers up from under his hand as he enters the room, and his bright sky blue eyes widen in surprise when he sees me standing across from him.

When he looks at me, my stomach tightens. I had never noticed his eyes before I saw them from the audience, but the TV and album covers could never do them justice. My cheeks instantly flush. I feel like I'm intruding in his space. I'm intimidated in spite of myself. I realize there are a lot of girls who would kill to be in my shoes right now, and even though I don't normally get star struck, it's not every day I'm five feet from someone as famous as Jeremy Mason.

"Oh," he breathes, straightening up and grabbing the towel around his neck with both hands. His lanky body stretches long as he arches his back, and it presses his abs against his tank top. My stomach tightens further when he speaks. I'm dead silent.

"Hi. I'm um...well, I..." he stammers. I'm still silent, but I smile a bit. For someone so eloquent with lyrics, he's not so great with words. "I just, ya know, wanted to see for myself you were okay. You gave me quite a scare. I'd feel somewhat responsible if anyone were hurt at a show..." he trails off as he stares into my eyes, as if distracted.

He lets go of the towel and extends a hand as he inches towards me. I reach out my right hand to take his. As his hand enters mine,

I try not to tremble. His hand is so warm, so soft, but his fingertips are rough with wear from playing his guitar. He closes his hand gently around mine and I feel woozy. A charge flows through my hand, where we are connected, and up through my arm- all around my body. What's wrong with me?

"Jeremy," he says and smiles. He waits as he leaves his hand in mine.

I come back to earth after a few moments. "Sorry," I breathe. "Dylan."

"It's okay," he says, still holding my hand. "I think I'd be a little dazed after that if it'd been me."

Right, that's why I'm dazed. Sure.
Shit.

We stand in silence for another awkward moment. I start to feel uncomfortable. This is quite a vulnerable situation for a young girl to be in- alone in the dressing room with a rock star. Especially since I can't help but imagine his soft hand traveling up my arm to my shoulder and down my front...

"Uh," I speak to stop my wandering thoughts. "No I'm fine. Really. Thanks for stopping the show. I guess I should be going."

He finally lets go of my hand. He runs his fingers through his hair again. That really is very distracting.

"No, no. Please take a seat. I kind of hide in here for a while after a show. You know, to just relax. Before I go out to talk to the press and stuff." He holds his graceful hand out towards the red couch. Secretly I'm both pleased and upset that it's a larger couch and not a love seat.

I sit at the very end of the couch, straight up with my hands wringing nervously in my lap. Any closer and I'd be sitting on the arm rest. He drapes himself gracefully at the opposite end of the couch. He looks like he's doing a photo shoot for Vogue without even trying. I look down at my hands and around the room to avoid looking directly at him. I can feel his eyes- he's staring straight at me. He's suddenly very confident and comfortable.

"So *Dylan*," he purrs my name, putting emphasis on it. His voice is smooth and deep, but not low. I equate the tone to smooth chocolate, delicious and rich. "Are you from here?"

"Not originally," I say quietly, finally looking up at him. "I'm here because I'm starting Harvard Law in the fall."

His eyes widen, exposing more of his icy blue irises. Even in half light, they sparkle. "Smart girl. I'm impressed. Have you always wanted to be a lawyer?"

I'm beginning to wonder why he's interested at all. I feel like I'm boring him. I figure he's just making pleasantries. "Oh, yeah, sorta."

He looks confused. "Why? Money?"

I laugh nervously. "No, I want to be a prosecuting attorney. They don't make as much as most lawyers…" I unintentionally trail off as I look into his eyes. He raises his eyebrow at me, wanting more. "I guess," I continue, "I just want to fight for what's right."

"Ah hah," he says. "An 'idealist.' You know, punishing other people for their mistakes won't fix what's wrong with society in general. Or in your own life." He looks amused. His pink pouty lips make a wry smile.

I start to feel burning in the pit of my stomach. "Have a personal problem with prosecuting attorneys Mr. Mason?" I say, squinting my eyes. I try to make it obvious I'm referring to his often run-ins with the law.

He bites his bottom lip, trying not to laugh. "Touché, Dylan. And its Jeremy."

"Jeremy," I whisper, anger wiped away. I almost feel like it's a dirty word when I say it.

"You're awfully soft spoken for a lawyer," he comments, stretching his right arm along the back of the couch. I see the definition in his shoulder and upper arm, a tattoo of a snake running along the outside in dark contrast with his pale skin. "Star struck?" he says with his wry smile.

The anger burns again in my stomach. He doesn't have to be a jerk about it. "I'd say you seem awfully humble for a rock star but I'd be lying."

He chuckles. It immediately quiets the burning anger and I laugh in spite of myself. "Now there's a little spunk," he says. Sometimes even when he talks it sounds like a melody. His voice is sultry. He sits up a little and leans closer to me, resting his forearms on his legs. I shrug.

"What brings you to the show tonight? You don't seem like a drooling, screeching fan," he runs his blue eyes up and down my body. I fidget, uncomfortable at the way he's looking at me. I wrap my arms around myself, crossing my arms in an attempt to cover my body. Out of the corner of my eyes, I think he smiles. "At least, not a big enough fan to pay the kind of money to have front row seats at my show."

I talk quickly. "My friend Theresa and I just moved into a townhome on Massachusetts Avenue here in Boston. The tickets were a gift to her from her dad. As I guess like a housewarming gift."

He laughs loudly. I jump a little but then smile at his jovial laughter. "What a useful gift that is. You can definitely use this around the house."

"I'm sure Theresa will frame the tickets, so technically it counts as artwork."

He composes himself as he looks into my eyes. "Well, since I'm technically providing you with artwork, maybe you could give me some?"

I stare at him, confused, as he stands and walks over to the white desk with the mirror. His pants are running low, still exposing his amazing hipbones, but he doesn't fix them. He turns around and slinks back down on the couch and holds up a permanent marker. "I'm short on paper and my assistant has my phone. Write your number on my arm."

Chapter 3- Denial

My eyes widen. I look at the marker, and then back at him. He has a cocky smile on his face, his piercing eyes boring into mine. I must look as shocked as I feel. My cheeks begin to burn. Me?

Thankfully, before I can respond, there is a loud knock. I jump as he moves his head up toward the door. It flies open, hitting the wall behind it with a loud thud. The red-headed pixie, now swaying with a red cup in her hand, stumbles in. She's followed behind by one of the topless blondes I saw making out with another girl in the room I left Theresa in.

He stands and puts the marker down on the couch. The pixie red head stops as the blonde falls on her. "Oh," she says, staring at me. The topless blonde walks over to Jeremy and grabs onto his shirt, shoving her tongue down his throat. He kisses back for a moment and lightly pushes her away.

The pixie looks at him. "A third tonight Mr. Mason?" she says as she starts removing her top.

I stand quickly, making a disgusted sound in my throat. The pixie shrugs and I turn to walk out the door. I catch Jeremy untangling himself from the topless blonde. "Stay here," he breathes to her as I enter the hall. "Wait!" he says as I walk toward the steel

41

door at the end of the hallway. As I pass the room with Theresa in it, I see her and wave for her to follow me without stopping my pace. She looks relieved to leave and enters the hallway behind me.

I now hear two sets of footsteps behind me. "Dylan!" Jeremy's voice cries. I hear Theresa stop dead in her tracks, then speed up and catch my arm.

"Dylan!" she squeaks. "*Jeremy Mason* is calling for you!"

I stop, exasperated, and turn just in time to smack into Jeremy's chest. The smell of him- spicy, manly- is intoxicating. I look up into his face, thankful that the dim hallway keeps me from the full effect of his eyes.

"Mr. Mason, I thank you again for your help during the show. And for ensuring my safety." Ewe, I think. I sound old. "I see that you are *busy*, and I'm very not interested in staying for that, so I will get out of your hair. Good night."

I turn again and see Theresa standing just behind me, face stunned. Jeremy grabs my arm and spins me again. "Jeremy," he corrects, low and hard. "And we weren't finished with our conversation. I want to see you again. To know you." He slides his hand down my arm. I tremble, but not noticeably.

I sigh. "Look," I say. "The only thing you need to know about me is that I don't want to get caught up in all of…" I hear moaning from the room where I had left Theresa earlier, and see a bunch of naked bodies falling all over each other, some snorting a white substance off the coffee table. "That!" I almost scream, disgusted, when motioning to the room.

I hear him sigh.

"Goodnight," I say, more gently. I purposely trail my fingers along his hand before removing it from my arm, trying to delay our final parting. I turn, grab a dumbstruck Theresa, and continue to walk toward the steel door. I'm almost stomping. What did he think he'd get me to do, bringing me back here? Is that what he does: lures fans from the crowd and fucks them with his groupies in his dingy dressing room?

I push the heavy steel door open and walk out onto the floor.

It's amazing how the room has cleared since the end of the show- which was only an hour ago. I kick a few cups to the side as I continue to stomp toward the glass exit doors across the hall. Theresa is quick on my heels. I see a bunch of faceless stagehands in black shirts stare at us as we almost run past them.

My head is spinning. *What a pig. A womanizer. A...An...almost statutory rapist! I mean, that blonde girl must have turned 18 yesterday!* I'm trying so hard to be mad at him and dislike him. It does little to squash away the thought of his eyes running up and down my body. And to kill the nagging feeling of regret for not using the marker. I KNOW I did the right thing. I don't need to be getting involved in things like this.

When we finally get through the glass door and out into the cool Boston air, I stomp wordlessly towards the parking lot. I see a police officer directing the last of the traffic in the distance. Jeez, it's taken people an hour to get out of here.

"Ok, now, stop!" Theresa says breathlessly. I continue anyway.

Theresa grabs my arms and pulls back on it. I stop. "What?" I say, exasperated.

"What the hell was that about?" she says, trying to stifle her excitement unsuccessfully. She bounces up and down on her heels. "He wants to see you again?!"

"I guess. That's what he said, right?" I continue walking, but slower. Theresa walks beside me. I search my jean pockets for my keys.

"So, what happened?" she eyes me suspiciously.

"Nothing. We exchanged pleasantries. Really the proposal of him seeing me again came out of nowhere." I sound mystified, even to myself, as I pull the keys out of my pocket.

"Not 'nowhere'," Theresa says as we spot my beat up red convertible in the parking lot and head towards it. "You ARE gorgeous."

I make an appalled sound at her. "Righhhhttt..." I say as I open the car door and hop in.

She sits in the passenger seat and we buckle our seatbelts. "Well," she says. "You didn't want to see him again?"

I sigh. I'm going to choose my words carefully. It's not that I didn't want to see him again, but his lifestyle intimidated me. And it seemed wrong. And I need a one-night-stand with a famous rock star like I need a hole in the chest. But I can't tell Theresa that, because she'd make me feel guilty about what she would say was 'missing an opportunity.' To her, if I could have had a one night stand with him but instead turned him down, I'd be the craziest person on earth. She'd probably have me locked up.

"Two girls walked in the room pretty much naked and they asked if I wanted to join their, um," I look at Theresa and she's smiling a devilish smile. I turn bright red. "*Group*," I stammer out.

She laughs hysterically. "Oh I see, and that went over real well with YOU prudy pants!"

I smile. "Shut up, bitch." We both laugh and drop the subject. We speed away from the theater blaring music the rest of the way home.

At home we don't talk much about the concert, but as I suspected, Theresa pulls the ticket stubs out of her pocket and thumb tacks them on the wall above dining the room table.

"I'll get a frame for them later. This is a night I don't want to forget!" she yawns as she heads to her room.

I am torn on that statement. I wish I could forget the way his eyes trailed my body. The way his rough hands felt on my skin...

I finish cleaning the rest of the kitchen counter and put the dishes in the dishwasher before I finally decide that I should get some sleep. I appreciate my dad's offer on helping me pay my mortgage for the year so I don't have to find a job until January or so, but I honestly think I should look for a job anyway I'm going to have massive loans to repay after I graduate. So tomorrow will be a long day of job hunting.

I go into my bedroom, throw on a pair of shorts and a tank, and climb into my bed. The cool silk sheets feel good on my skin, and I silently thank God once again for our very well furnished townhome. I lie awake for a while, trying not to think of ice or blue or chocolate or music. I'm especially not trying to think of what he is doing right now, with prostitute pixie and well-endowed jailbait. I make a mental note to write a letter to Mattel for ideas for their next Barbie.

When I finally drift off to sleep, I dream of his fingers playing his gray, glimmering guitar. They slide up and down the neck of it, caressing it as if it's a body. The lights reflecting from the beautiful instrument is blinding, illuminating his perfect face. His eyes open and he looks at me, and he whispers my name, "Dylan…"

I wake up to the sound of our doorbell ringing. The sun looks a little too low in the sky. I stare at the clock. Holy shit, is it really 1 p.m.? What's up with me sleeping so much?

I stretch and yawn as I sit up. I hear the shower running, so I get out of bed to answer the door. I throw a silk white robe over my barely clad body, embarrassed that my shirt is so see-through. I run out of my room and open the door, but no one is there. I look down and see a box sitting by the doorway. I pick it up and bring it inside.

It's a cardboard box with flowers on it. I smile, wondering which one of Theresa's admirers they'll be from this time, when I turn the box around and see it's addressed to me. I stare at it, confused. I open the top of the box and pull out two dozen beautiful red and black roses. The vase is plain black, striking and heavy. I spot a card hidden amongst the roses.

In black permanent marker, it reads: "Bought you these flowers and called it a night early. Hoping you could give me another chance to get to know you- J"

I catch myself with a girly grin. How astoundingly sweet! I'm used to male attention to be honest, but it usually doesn't consist of sweetness. His handwriting is beautiful and elegant, bordering on calligraphy. His letters have swirls and curves in them. I can imagine what his original songs must look like when he composes: like artwork.

Suddenly I wonder if I shouldn't be creeped out. I mean, how did he know where I live? I ridiculously look over my shoulders, as if someone is standing behind me or watching me. I chuckle once under my breath. *Dylan, he's super rich with 17 thousand people working for him. You told him you just bought a town home on Massachusetts Avenue. Wouldn't be too hard for him to find you.*

I hear Theresa turn off the water I sigh and put the card into its stand. Placing the flowers on the dining table, I move them to the spot where the sunlight from the window is hitting the wood. I start walking into the bathroom as Theresa is walking out. She smiles at me and I smile back. "Morning sunshine!" she says, perkily.

"Hello," I say, getting into the bathroom and shutting the door. I turn on the water and steam fills up the room again almost immediately. I start to undress myself, letting my breasts free from my shirt and my shorts fall to the floor. I climb into the shower and let the warm water run on my skin. It loosens up my aching muscles. Sleeping this late really throws me off.

"Dylan!" Theresa cries. I roll my eyes. "Who are these flowers from?"

Oh boy.

"Can't hear you!" I cry. "Shower!"

A few seconds later, I hear Theresa's loud shriek. I giggle.

Of course when I get out of the shower, I'm ambushed. "How does he know where we live? Are you going to respond? HOW are you going to respond? Doesn't this freak you out? If YOU don't respond, I will!! You're going to see him again! You MUST!"

I'm literally in a towel in the middle of the hallway, dripping water onto the floor. Theresa stands 6 inches from my nose, practically bouncing as she talks. I hold my hands up. "Woah," I say. "At least come into my room so I can get dressed."

She steps aside so I can squeeze by her. Honestly, I hadn't thought about how I'd respond even if I wanted to. I hadn't thought of actually responding. I'm still in the shock stage.

"SOOOOO???" Theresa says and throws herself on my bed, as I pull out a pair of jeans and a blue and green wrap shirt from my closet. I walk over to my drawers and pull out some underwear and a bra.

"I don't know. I guess I would see him again. But I have no way of contacting him. I don't even know if he's still in Boston."

"He is!" Theresa screamed. "He's from here, you know. He's playing three shows here to kick off the tour. There's no show tonight, but Friday and Saturday he's having one. He's here until at least Sunday night!"

I surprise myself by being relieved. Strange… I shake my head as I fasten my bra. I'm losing it.

"I'm STARVING!" Theresa says. "I'm going to make something to eat. Ziti?"

"Ziti," I confirm as I throw on my shirt. I run over to my mirror to brush my hair.

After I dress, Theresa and I sit at the table for lunch. The roses sit in the middle between us, but off to the side a bit so we can see each other. I stare at the huge flowers. The black roses, I decide, remind me of him: beautiful and dark and lovely…

'And a big fat WOMANIZER,' my rational brain interrupts. I sigh.

"Why...so...silent?" Theresa says slowly. "Deep in thought?" She raises an eyebrow.

I tighten my eyes at her when I hear a knock at the door. I stand and put my plate in the sink before I answer it.

When I open the door, the big security guard who pulled me from the crowd is standing there. He has black jeans and a black shirt on, with black sunglasses on his big, bald head. I freeze.

"Hi, Miss," he says in a big booming voice.

"Hi..." I breathe in shock. Theresa has left the table and stands behind me.

"Can you come with me? Mr. M requests your company." He stands like a brick wall in front of my door.

I wonder if I really have a choice again as I turn to Theresa. Would Jeremy dare to have me carried there? Something tells me I shouldn't put it past him.

Theresa's eyes are wide and excited. She smiles at me and runs over to my bedroom. "What are you doing?" I say as she runs out with a pair of sandals and pushes me down on the floor.

"Wait!" I scream, falling to the floor. She shoves the first sandal on my right foot.

"You're going don't you even dare fight with me I'm not letting you blow this oh how exciting!" she says quickly as she shoves my other sandal on my foot and pulls me up from the floor. She grabs my purse from the couch behind her, slams it into my chest, and pushes me out the door toward big man. I turn back to her and give her a dirty look.

"Do your make-up in the car!" she says and waves. I try to get back inside. I need to think about this rationally before I actually go.

Theresa slams the door in my face. I was prepared to yell through the door, but big man grabs my right arm. "Let's go," he booms as he drags me down the steps and towards a black car parked on the street behind by red convertible.

He opens the back door to the black car and throws me down in it. I rub my arm as he shuts the door. Jeez, I'm getting sick of being manhandled like this.

He sits in the front seat, and before I know it, we're moving. After a few moments of getting my bearings straight, I try to decipher where we are. "Are you going to tell me where he's taking me?" I hope it's not to his place…I hope it is to his place…I mean, *not* to his place!

"He's at the record store right now, I'ma take you there."

I raise an amazed eyebrow. Not what I was expecting, but okay. I decide maybe it is a good idea to throw on some make-up. I dig through my purse and pull out my black make-up bag. I open my little mirror and immediately direct it at my hair. Thankfully, it's dry, long and straight. The summer sun has really lightened it. I throw on some concealer, blush, and shiny lip gloss. I skip the eyeliner. I almost never wear eyeliner. Why draw attention to things so obvious to begin with?

I zip up my make-up bag and put it back in my purse just in time. The black car pulls up outside a white building with records painted on it. It's sandwiched in between two abandoned shops. On the top of the shop, the dingy sign reads, "Hal's Records."

The door suddenly opens and a dark hand extends to me. I grab it as big man pulls me out.

"By the way," I say to him as we walk to the door. "Since we keep running in to each other, can I have your name?"

"Rich," he says in a booming voice.

"Rich," I say, looking at the huge gold R around his neck. "It fits you."

I think I get a hint of a smile when he opens the door and I step inside.

The store is huge, much bigger than it looks from the outside. As I walk in, there's one cash register at my left, the shelves behind it lined with band memorabilia. In front of me are what looks like hundreds of rows of records and CDs. They go vertically across the store from wall to wall, with another row behind the ones in front. There's a staircase in the back that leads to an upper loft.

I take a few steps, and it's so eerily quiet that my footsteps almost echo. I look behind me to see if big man- uh, Rich- is there, but he must have not followed me in. My heart beats faster. "Hello?" I say, my voice again almost echoes.

Quietly I hear soft rock music begin to play, a guitar solo that gets louder, as if someone was turning up the volume on the store's speaker system. I look around again.

From above me, I hear a smooth deep voice say, "Up here."

I stop walking and slowly look up towards the loft. I feel my heart hit my throat. He's there, leaning nonchalantly on the railing. He has a white, long sleeved, button down shirt on with some black jeans. The shirt is unbuttoned a little too far, exposing some of his chest. I can see green ink speckling part of what was exposed. I wonder how many tattoos he has.

He grips the railing with his strong hands, some fingers donned with black nail polish, and leans over a bit and smiles at me. "Dylan," he breathes my name. My whole body gets tight.

"Mr. Mason," I breathe.

He smiles a crooked grin and turns to the stairs. I still haven't moved. He slinks down the steps and walks gracefully towards me. He stops in front of me, but only a few feet. I smell his scent- spicy and intoxicating- and see the rosiness of his pink lips. I think I stop breathing.

"Jeremy," he corrects me. "I'm glad you came."

He stares into my eyes. His blue eyes are kind and calm, like the sky after a storm. "Sometimes," I choke out, "I'm not sure I have a choice with your security guard."

He smiles "I'm not sure you do either. He doesn't like to disappoint me. But I guess that's his job."

I smile and finally disconnect myself from his gaze. I look around the room again. This store is definitely an up and running store, and it's a Thursday afternoon, yet there's no one else here but us. "Why are there no people here?"

"The owner is a friend," Jeremy explains. "Sometimes I pay him to shut the store down for me. So I can come here and be alone. Browse the records." He walks over to the nearest row of vinyl. I turn towards him, but I don't move from my spot.

He picks out a record and holds it up. "Jimi Hendrix. This album is amazing."

I nod. "My dad has the CD."

He shakes his head. His messy, dirty blonde hair moves. "No, no. That ruins it. You have to have that on vinyl. The static in the vinyl is magic." He suddenly and gracefully runs up the stairs carrying the Hendrix record, and I hear the soft rock music stop. There's light movement during the silence, and eventually the new music begins. A guitar, sad and long, crescendos from the speakers.

Jeremy appears at the top of the stairs, gracefully descending towards me at the bottom. His movement reminds me of a cat. He slinks. Each step he takes down the stairs looks graceful. It reminds me of the old rock-and-roll singers: Mick Jagger or maybe Steven Tyler.

He walks up to me and stands, once more, three feet in front of me, smiling. I'm relatively sure he stands so close to me because he can somehow detect how it makes my heart race. "Do you hear the static?"

I must admit, I like the sound of vinyl. It's almost sexy in a way. "Yes. I like it very much." His eyes trail up my body again as his face turns serious. He has beautiful, black eyelashes. My cheeks flush red.

His eyes finally meet mine and, realizing that I'm blushing, he cocks a smile. He motions with his graceful arm towards the carpeted area in the back of the store. "Let's sit a while."

I nod and follow him onto the gray carpet and sit with him on the floor. He lays himself down on his side, like it was completely natural to him to lay here. I sit straight up with my knees bent, hugging them to me with my arms. I feel vulnerable with him, and I'm still not sure why. Feeling vulnerable really bothers me.

"So, let's see. I know you're in Boston for Law School. You never told me where you were from originally," he says, peering up at me with his blue eyes and playing with a pull on the carpet.

"I grew up just outside of Philadelphia. My Dad still lives there. Harvard has always been a dream of mine."

"What do you parents do?"

How is this possibly interesting to him? "My Dad's a college professor."

"Mom?" he asks.

Ouch.

"…No mom," I'm able to stammer out. I see pity in his eyes, but thankfully he doesn't ask further, sensing I'm uncomfortable.

He smiles. "I pegged you for a super-rich girl. How on Earth is he affording Harvard?" He adjusts his position on the rug. He stretches his arms behind his head and lies on his back, but turns his face toward me. His chest is super exposed this way, and I can see his abs, so defined and rock hard. I feel a tingling in my groin I haven't felt in a long time.

"Uh," I say, my eyes shooting back to his face. I don't think he noticed. "He can't. I'm paying for it." His eyebrows go up in disbelief.

"Sort of. I'm taking out loans. I was able to go to college for free where my Dad teaches, so I'm debt free as of right now. So I figure I'll get out of school with a normal amount of debt since I didn't have to pay anything for undergraduate."

"It's a damn lot of debt to pay back as a prosecutor," Jeremy says. My eyes narrow.

"Thanks. So encouraging."

He laughs. "No, I think it's good you're following your dreams no matter what. And hey, you could always meet some rich asshole trust-fund baby at Harvard and marry him. He could foot the bill."

The tingling in my groin is overshadowed by the burning anger building in my stomach again. He sure can play with my emotions unlike anyone ever has before. "Right, because I'm definitely the prostitute type. You really can be an ass sometimes."

He laughs so hard I jump a little. He covers his eyes with his left hand. His teeth sparkle in the light. He looks so much like a happy little boy, it's hard for me to remember I'm mad and not laugh with him. "What's so damn funny?" I snap.

He uncovers his eyes and composes himself. He lies on his side again and rests his head on his left hand. "I just like when I can get a rise out of you. It makes your pretty eyes burn. It's fantastic."

I blush. It's the first time he's really ever said anything romantic to me at all. I realized I'm relieved he may be looking for more than friendship. Oh jeez. I feel like I'm involved in a really bad car accident on the highway, and it's happening right now in slow motion. You know you want to stop it from happening, and it probably will end badly if you don't, but for some reason you can't make your mind or body to do what you need it to do to avoid it. And it's stupid, because this guy's a rock star, and I barely know him.

"How about your parents?" I ask, shifting the attention off of me.

He smiles. "My mother lives locally. I see her from time to time. Not very often."

"She lives locally and you don't see her very often?" I try not to sound too suspicious.

He smiles wryly. "It's so nice dating someone who doesn't know everything about me already. Or think they do anyway from the tabloids. Its…refreshing. It makes me feel kind of…normal."

I hope he doesn't think I'm so simple I didn't notice him side step the last question, but I figured I'd let it go, as he had let my mom issue go. Anyway, I was still allowing my brain to wrap around the word "dating."

"Is that what we're doing?" I say slowly, finally looking in to his eyes.

He shrugs. "I'd say so. I liked you the first second I saw you, in that crowd. I like your shyness. I like your spunk. I think you're special, unique. So I asked you out. And here we are." He says it so confidently, without fear. I wonder what it's like to be that confident.

"I appreciate that, Jeremy," I say, in a business way. I use that when I feel vulnerable. "But I don't understand why you think those things. You barely know me. How could you like me? Why do you like me?"

He looks confused. I continue, "I mean, you're a mega rock star. You've been with the most beautiful women in the world. You have big breasted naked bottle blondes in your bed nightly." He rolls his eyes.

"First of all, let's try to forget that portion of last night." I smile and nod, only too happy to oblige to that request. He sits up more and leans towards me. He speaks low and deep, resurrecting the effect he had on me the first night I heard him speak. "And I think *you*, Dylan, are the most beautiful woman I have ever seen. You're captivating. I can't take my eyes off of you."

My whole body feels warm.

Time freezes for what seems like hours. He is inches from my face now. Inside, I'm melting. My heart is on fire instead of my stomach. It's something I've never really felt before. I assume this is what desire feels like.

It's hard for me not to shake as he stares at me, looking into my eyes, then at my lips. I decide that I'm not ready for this, so I smile and begin to stand. He seems disappointed and confused, but only for a second and then it's gone. He stands up with me and grabs my hand. I feel the rough of his fingers curl around my soft skin. It sends a shock wave straight to my groin.

"Come on," he says and smiles.

We spend the next few hours looking through records, talking music, and listening to different songs on vinyl. I discover that his inspirations include Mick Jagger, of course, but also Carlos Santana and Mozart. "Mozart?" I say, shocked.

"He was a misunderstood child prodigy," he shrugs. "Sound familiar?" he cocks an eyebrow. I laugh.

Finally, after another hour or so, I look out the window. It's starting to get dark. My stomach rumbles. I put my hand over it.

"Oh," he says. "Hungry? I'm sorry we've been here so long."

I smile. I've had so much fun getting to know him I hadn't even realized I was hungry. "It's ok, but we probably should get out of here." And back to reality. I'm sad at the thought of leaving him, because in the back of my mind I doubt I'll ever see him again. And the memories of last night that made me want to run from him have faded.

"I'll take you home," he says, running his hand down my arm. It's a sweet gesture, not sexual, and I smile at him. He takes out his phone and sends a text. He waits until his phone beeps, pauses a minute to read, and puts his phone back in his pocket. He grabs my hand again and leads me to the back door.

"Why this way?" I question him.

He looks at me and shrugs as we walk. "Apparently, there's some press at the front. The back is pretty much clear." We reach the back white door. Jeremy takes a key out of his pocket.

"*Pretty much* clear?" I say as he opens the back door and we walk out into a sea of people and flashing lights. Jeremy holds my hand tighter as he turns quickly, locks the door with ease, and steps in front of me. I throw my hands up over my face to try and protect my eyes from the flashing.

"Jeremy! Jeremy!" people are screaming. Girls are grabbing at his clothes. Microphones are being thrown in our faces. "Jeremy, who's the girl? What's your name, Miss? Is this your new girlfriend? What about the girl you were seen with last week in Texas? Are you going back to her house? Any updates on the new album?"

We are pushing through the people. I hear a ripping sound. Hands are everywhere; all over me. I feel a hand tangle into my hair. The person pulls hard and I scream in pain and surprise. My head whips frantically as I try to shake their hand. Eventually, I'm able to wiggle out of their grasp and hop into the black car behind Jeremy. He leans over me and shuts the door quickly, but I'm in so much pain I'm not even able to enjoy his close proximity. The car speeds away and Jeremy sits back down in his seat.

I'm holding the top of my head where my hair was yanked. It hurt-really badly. Jeremy's eyes are wide with concern. "Dylan? Shit. Are you alright, baby?" he grabs my hand on top of my head and holds it as he strokes my hair with his free hand.

"Yeah," I whisper, still able to love his hands on me. "But I'm starting to think you're dangerous for my health."

His worry fades and his icy eyes smolder. His hand pauses on my head. "Yeah," he says deeply. We stay frozen like that, his hand on the back of my head, his other hand holding mine. Somehow, it's very sensual. I feel the electric charge between us increasing in power. Finally I can't resist and place my other hand on his leg, running it slowly up towards his stomach. He closes his eyes.

I look down and realize his shirt had been ripped completely open, the buttons torn off and a sleeve half gone. His chest, white and hard, inked with green tattoos, is inches from my touch. I almost want to salivate.

While I'm looking down at my hand and his chest, he leans closer and I tense, stopping my hand. Slowly, sweetly, he kisses my forehead. I close my eyes and love the feel of his warm, wet lips on my skin. His scratchy face rubs down my hair to the side of my face, so that we're almost cheek to cheek. My breathing speeds up. "Dylan," he whispers. His hand is still on the back of my head.

I know I'm now shaking, and I know it's noticeable. My mouth is completely dry. "Yes?" I whisper.

He breathes warm air into my ear. I sigh. "The car stopped…" he whispers again in his melodic tone.

My eyebrows come together. I open my eyes and look out the window opposite me. I see the sidewalk in front of my townhome illuminated by the street lights. I sit up straighter as he drops his hand from my hair and lets go of my hand. He turns and opens the car door. He steps out on to the sidewalk and I scoot to the door, stepping out behind him. As soon as I'm on my feet, he grabs my hand again, like it's so natural now. My heart is heavy. What happens from here?

He pauses on the sidewalk and turns towards me, looking down at our hands entwined. He looks into my eyes. "I'd like to come up."

Chapter 4- Sexual Encounter

I tense. I wasn't expecting that. I try to go through scenarios in my head. He waits, even seemingly becoming uncomfortable. "Um," he starts. "I understand if you don't want me to…"

"No," I interrupt. His smile fades a bit. He almost looks hurt. My eyes widen, panicked about his misunderstanding. "No, I mean, it's not that I don't want you to. It's just, I'm not sure I want to…I'm not sure I'm ready to do anything yet…"

His eyes darken with desire. "I wasn't necessarily implying that. I just don't want this night to end. It's only 9:00. And I actually have the night off. And I want to spend it with you."

How could I deny that? "Okay, come on." I pull his hand as I start walking up the stairs. We get to the front door and I walk inside. I hear footsteps come running from the hallway. Oh, shit.

Before she can see me, Theresa says, "Dyyyllannn! How was it? Was it amazing? Was…" she trails off as she comes into sight. She freezes and her eyes widen as she stares at him.

"Theresa!" I say, almost too loudly. Lord, please don't let her embarrass me. "This is Jeremy." I motion towards him. "Jeremy," I point to Theresa's frozen body. "This is my best friend, and *obviously*," I emphasize, "your biggest fan, Theresa."

"Charmed," he says, and extends his free hand to her, even though it's his left. I'm happy he doesn't want to let go of me. Theresa shakily holds out her hand to take his.

She seems to snap back to earth, looking at both of us. "Oh my gosh! I have such an important *thing* to go to!" she almost shrieks. She's wearing a ratty T-shirt and some gray sweat pants. She runs behind our couch and throws on some of my sandals. "Planning it all day," she says as she grabs her purse. She walks past us and to the door. "See you guys later!" she says as she opens the door and steps out. "Nice to meet you!" she waves and shuts the door. I hear her flip flops going down the stairs.

Subtle, Theresa.

I turn to Jeremy and give him a shy smile. "She's...perky," he volunteers.

I laugh under my breath and let go of him to put my purse down on the couch. The silence lingers. "So," I say. "This is my home."

"It's cute," he says, looking around. My stomach rumbles again.

I start heading toward the kitchen. "Is pizza okay?" I say, taking dough out of the refrigerator.

"Yeah," he says and smiles, sitting on the couch. I turn the oven on to preheat and turn to look at him before I reach down for the tray. I see him looking down at his torn shirt. He shrugs and takes it off.

I feel like such a jerk. "Oh, Jeremy, I'm sorry. Do you want me to get you a shirt?"

He puts his shirt over the back of my couch. "No, I don't mind being shirtless. Usually I perform shirtless."

I smile, secretly happy my ogling can continue into the night. "But what about getting home?"

"I'll have Rich bring me something." He pulls out his phone and writes a quick text. I continue to cook.

We make conversation as I finish the pizza and continue talking as we eat. Sitting on the couch across from this man, this piece of living art, draped so normally along the cushions seems like a dream. It's almost easy to forget that he's the bad boy on TV, the mega-star, the child prodigy. We talk about normal things; favorite movies and shows, what schools we went to, what friends we had. Jeremy tells me about traveling all over the world with his parents, playing the piano for the Queen of England, meeting Princess Diana and various U.S. Presidents.

"Your life," I say, smiling. "It sounds so amazing. You're very lucky."

He looks down at his empty plate and puts it down on the coffee table. "Yea," he says darkly. I look at the clock. It's after one in the morning already, my eyes watery and red from sleepiness. I think of Theresa and hope she's okay. I worry when I don't hear from her.

I stand, stretching as I do. He looks up at me and stands as well, his hard, shirtless body in plain sight. I wonder how his warm skin would feel against mine.

"Well," he sighs. "I better get going. I have a show tomorrow night..."

I know that it's best that he leave but I really don't want him to go. "Okay," I say quietly.

"Could I call you, maybe? Tomorrow?" He sounds unsure. It's very endearing.

"Sure, yeah. Of course." I try to hide my excitement.

His eyes meet mine, and they are smoldering. He slinks closer to me, prowling. I tense. If he comes on to me now, I don't know that I would deny him. "I am so happy you came to meet me, whether or not it was forced."

I squeak out a breathy laugh. I muster up some courage and walk over to him and into his arms, wrapping my arms around his bare chest as he wraps his arms around me. We hug for a moment before I realize he's shaking.

"Oh, are you cold?" I say, instinctively running my hand up and down his bare back. Weird, because it's about mid-August and around 70 degrees, even at night. "Let me get you a shirt."

"Oh," he lets go of me instantly. "No, no, I'm alright. I'll call you tomorrow," he says and heads for the door. He opens the door and stops at the top of the stairs. "Night," he says and smiles, but I think he doesn't look too well.

"Night," I say as he turns and walks down the stairs, getting into the back of his elegant black car. The car pulls away.

I stand there for another minute after I watch the car fade into the distance. I am a mix of emotions: confused about the shaking, worried about his sickness, sad to see him go, and excited about the thought of him calling tomorrow. I feel very unsatisfied at how the night ended. I am also unbelievably tired. I turn and go back inside, shutting the door.

I take off my green and blue wrap shirt as I walk towards my bedroom. Before I take off my jeans, I send a text to Theresa.

Me: Theresa, where are you? It's almost 2 am.

I throw on some shorts and a tank. I head to the bathroom and wash the make-up off my face with the lights off. I throw my long hair up in a ponytail and leave the bathroom as my phone blings.

Theresa: It's cool! Crashing at Miranda's pad. Have FUN!!!

I roll my eyes. Miranda is a friend Theresa knows from childhood who moved out here a few years ago. I'll explain everything to her tomorrow. I'm too tired to have the 'I'm not into being a slut' conversation.

I crawl into bed and fall into a dreamless sleep, finally too exhausted to dream- even about Jeremy. But at least it keeps the nightmares away, too.

I wake up the next morning to my bed shaking. I fly up in bed, alarmed. Theresa is at the end of my bed.

"Shit Terri!" I say, holding my chest. She looks disappointed.

"Did he leave already?" she moans.

I roll my eyes at her. "He left *last night*."

"Ewe, he just left after the action? That's kind of jerky."

What does she take me for? "No action, Theresa."

She scoffs. "You had him here ALONE and you did NOTHING??"

"Nope!" I say, proudly. "Not even a kiss."

She moans loudly and stands up from the bed. "Why is it YOU and not ME?? I bet he's FABULOUS in bed. The way he walks, his sexy voice..." I feel a tingling in my groin as she describes him.

"Allll right, Theresa. Let me get dressed. I'll tell you all about it when I get out," I say, climbing out of bed.

I quickly shower and get dressed. I put on a nice blue, short sleeve, silk blouse that has three buttons going down from the collar and light blue jeans. I can tell I haven't gotten enough sleep. It's only nine in the morning and I went to bed after two. I'm a solid eight hour sleeper, so I rarely feel rested since I haven't gotten 8 hours in a long time. Maybe that's why I've been sleeping so late lately. I silently praise God for Theresa when I walk out of the bathroom and smell coffee.

I walk into the kitchen and start pouring myself a cup. Theresa is sitting at the kitchen table, reading a magazine. "I put that on when I walked in the door," she says, flipping a page and not looking up. "I thought you would like some coffee because I thought you two would have been up all night."

"Silly you," I said, taking a sip and pulling a chair out from the table opposite Theresa.

"So," she said, shutting the magazine and looking up at me. "What DID happen?"

We spent the next hour talking about the previous night. Theresa did me an unasked favor by analyzing his every statement and movement. It was nice to talk to someone about it, I guess.

At one point we're laughing, and I happen to glance down at the magazine she was reading. There's a dark picture of Jeremy on the front with a familiar looking girl with her hands raised to the camera, blocking her face.

I stop laughing immediately and pick it up from off the table. "Theresa, where did you get this magazine??"

She looks confused. "From a little convenience store down the street where I stopped to get the bag of coffee. It's one of Boston's free daily gossip things I guess. Why?"

I'm flipping widely though the magazine. I find the article that says, "Jeremy Mason's New Mystery Blonde." There are pictures of him and me leaving the record store. There are also pictures of him leaving my house without a shirt very early in the morning. In the article, they suggest that we are having a passionate and sexy love affair. They even identify me by name, and say I'm off to Harvard Law in the fall!

I look horrified. "What??!!" Theresa stands up from the table in alarm.

"Didn't you see the fucking cover?!" I spit, looking up at her angrily. She's instantly taken aback. I almost never use the F-word out loud.

"I know Jeremy's on it, but he's almost always on the cover of everything."

I push the cover at her. "Does she look familiar?"

Theresa squints at the cover. Her face relaxes and she laughs. "Haha, oh shit! You're famous, girl." She puts the magazine back down. "No one can tell that's you."

"Yeah," I say exasperated, standing up and walking away from the table, pacing. "Except that they identify me by name in the article and specifically mention I'm attending Harvard Law in the fall."

"Oh my gosh! Everyone will want to know you!" Theresa says excitedly.

Oh God. Everyone will know me. Stare at me. Ask me questions…

I huff. "I do not want to be known as the party girl slut who sleeps with 'rock stars' at Harvard. I want to be taken seriously. How did they even get that in the paper so fast? He just left last night. Err, early this morning."

Theresa walks over to me and places her hands on my arms to stop my pacing. "It's okay. Breathe. It's in a local paper that probably no one even reads. This will blow over before school starts."

I look into her comforting brown eyes. I sigh and the burning quells. "You're right. I'm blowing this out of proportion."

Theresa picks up the magazine and throws it in the trash can in the kitchen. I go into my room, reach under my bed and pull out my laptop. I bring it out of my room to sit at kitchen table. Theresa is doing some dishes in the sink. I figure I'd do some job hunting to get my mind off things.

As I'm searching and applying for jobs, my mind still wanders to those pictures in the paper. I never even saw anyone standing outside my doorway. How scary, the thought people are watching your every move and you never know how to anticipate it. I feel a pang of sympathy for Jeremy, but in the back of my mind I wonder if he even cares, or maybe even likes it. He is a little bit of a narcissist.

I apply to a few jobs here and there. I have an undergraduate degree in political science, so I apply to a lot of courthouses and police stations. I'd really like to work part time in a courthouse so I could get my foot in the door with the lawyers who own law offices and the judges. If I don't make the DA office, I have to have a backup, right?

When I finally look at the time, it's one o'clock, and I'm hungry. I stand up and stretch, about to walk over to the kitchen, when I hear my cell phone ring. Theresa turns around on the couch where she's watching TV to look at the phone vibrating on the dining room table. I freeze.

"Go pick it up!" she half whispers.

I walk over to the phone and, without looking at the caller ID, slide the button on the screen over. "Hello?" I say as I put it up to my ear.

"Dylan," I hear in a silky melody.

"Hi Jeremy," I say as my mouth goes dry. I almost instantly begin to pant. Theresa silently claps her hands in a giddy way.

"How was the rest of your night?" he says. I can hear a lot of commotion in the background.

"I just went straight to bed. I was exhausted. Are you feeling okay?"

He's silent for a minute. "Yeah, I guess I was tired too...hey, you want to come here? Maybe watch the show tonight from the wings?"

My heart leaps. "Yes!" I blurt out, too excitedly. He chuckles. "Okay. Rich will be there soon."

"Alright," I sigh. Ew, am I actually swooning? I commit this feeling to memory for later consideration. "Bye."

"See you soon."

We pause. I wait for the other line to die, but I still hear him breathing. Obviously, he was waiting for me to hang up, too. He chuckles and I laugh.

"Bye," I say and hang up. I'm not one of those lovey-dovey "you hang up first" girls. Ew.

Theresa stands up and hugs me. I hug her back and laugh uncomfortably. "Um, why?" I say.

"I'm just so happy for you," she says in my ear. "I thought you were asexual for a while."

I laugh. "I am asexual."

She backed away from me and looks in my eyes. "Oh no, honey. That conversation you just giggled out...you're sexual."

I blush. Just a few minutes go by until I hear a knock at the door. Theresa walks over to open it, and Rich is standing at the top of my stairs. Again he's wearing all black with black sunglasses. I smile and wave. He nods at me in return. "Ready, miss?" he says in his big voice. I check myself in the mirror hanging by the door, running my fingers through my straight hair. I slip on the gold sandals that are next to the couch and grab my gold purse and throw it over my shoulder. It's really heavy. I'm going to have to clean it out ASAP.

As I'm walking down the stairs, I take a second to really absorb how crazy this all is. In just a matter of three days, I've had feelings that I would have sworn two weeks ago could never exist in me. I think it's probably easy to fall for him, though, even for someone as uninterested in love as I was. He's, for lack of a better word, perfect. I wondered idly if my parents had ever even once felt this way towards each other. I stopped that thought dead in its tracks. No, I'm not letting them ruin Jeremy the way they ruined all of my other relationships my whole life. Jeremy is special; someone I was pretty certain I could never find the equal to again.

Rich opens the back door to the familiar sleek, black car. I crawl inside and once again do my make-up on the way to meet Jeremy, back at the Wilbur. The drive is shorter than I remember, and we pull up to the stage entrance just as I'm putting away my lip gloss. I quickly spritz myself with flower-scented mist before Rich opens the door. I take a deep breath to calm the butterflies fluttering rapidly in my stomach before I exit the car and step onto the asphalt. Rich and I walk towards the steel door. He reaches it first and opens it for me and I step inside to the darkness.

We walk down a short way before I see the madness ensuing inside. People are running here and there, mostly in all black and wearing headsets, though some have business suits on. Some are yelling over the headset, some at each other, others are carrying heavy equipment. Rich and I walk slowly down the hall. "What's going on?" I yell to Rich above the noise.

"Getting ready for the show," he replies. His voice is so deep and booming that he doesn't need to yell. We continue until we make a right and come to the hallway that I recognize. I look behind me and see another steel door and realize that it's the door by the stage I was carried through the first night. It's nice to have my bearings straight. We pass the smoke room and I'm thankful to not see prostitute-pixie or bottle blonde in there, but there are a few younger people standing around, listening to music and smoking cigarettes. Some are pretty girls that are scantily clad. The butterflies in my stomach stop and are replaced by jealous knots.

We finally reach the wooden door to Jeremy's dressing room and Rich knocks loudly. I hear a smooth melody answer, "Come in!" Rich opens the door and puts his hand on my lower back, basically pushing me in. I stumble a bit and Rich closes the door behind me.

I see Jeremy draped on the couch. Beer bottles clutter the white desk with the mirror and the coffee table. I assume he had some people in here last night. The knots tighten and make me want to throw up, remembering the kind of activities he likes to enjoy with certain females.

I finally look directly at Jeremy and everything in my body turns to butter. I tingle with electricity. He looks astonishing. It's a hot day, and he has a sheen of sweat covering his body. His tight white T-shirt clings to his muscular chest. His dark jeans are again hanging low on his hips, exposing his hip bones. He's barefoot and sleeveless, so casual yet he makes it look so elegant and beautiful. He has his signature grey guitar on his lap and a cigarette hanging from his gorgeous pink lips. He's clean shaven today, which kind of disappoints me. I loved the way his face felt when it grazed against mine. I imagine for only a moment the way his stubble would feel against my inner thighs…

"Hi!" I say, quickly. He smiles around his cigarette and lets go of the neck of his guitar to remove it from his mouth.

"Dylan," he says, in what I now consider to be his usual greeting. He sits up straight and motions me to sit beside him.

I take a seat, but this time I'm a little more relaxed being close to him. I don't feel the need to sit almost on the arm rest. The leather feels familiar against my skin. I like feeling familiar in his space.

"It's fitting you should be here. I'd like to start fresh in this place," he says, with a serious look.

"My reaction was uncalled for," I said, even though I'm not sure I agree with that. I'm just in such a good mood. "I had no right to be upset."

He smiles wryly and takes another drag on his cigarette. His eyebrow goes up like he knows I don't believe a word I'm saying. I continue talking to distract him. "Where are your, um, friends today? Or do they only come after?" I start to feel a little bit of the burning again in the pit of my stomach. Jealousy is painful.

He laughs a little. "I got rid of them. They won't be around anymore."

I give him a confused look. It seemed like he liked them an awful lot. "Why? Seems like you were buddy buddy…" The burning builds. I feel my face being to scowl.

He sighs as he strums a few cords on his guitar softly, the cigarette hanging from his lips. The sound is beautiful from that beautiful guitar. I don't know instruments but I know that guitar is special. He pulls the cigarette from his lips and lets some smoke escape slowly. Watching him blow that smoke out of his mouth is so sexy, the tingling in my groin goes from zero to sixty.

"Because I knew they would upset *you*. And since they don't really matter to me and you matter to me a great deal, I got rid of them."

His eyes bore into me as he continues to strum his guitar. He doesn't even need to look at it to play. I absorb his message. He cares about me, which is good. However, he doesn't care about two girls he was obviously intimately involved with, which is not so good. I feel a sudden defensiveness for these girls. "In that case, I hope it stays that way and I don't get thrown out as easily as they did."

He stops playing and puts his guitar down on the floor next to him gently. He folds his hands and places them in his lap, with his cigarette in between two fingers. "What's up with you? Why are you so damn defensive?" He tries to sound angry but seems amused. His angry voice is rough and sexy.

With that I stand up off the couch. I don't understand why I'm angry. I obviously take him by surprise. His eyes widen and he looks up at me.

"I don't know," I answer honestly. I turn red. "I'm sorry. I honestly don't understand what I'm feeling." The words are spilling out uncontrollably. I try to scream at myself to stop but it just feels so good to get it off my chest. "I feel like an idiot. I've never felt this way. I'm just so damn jealous."

Jeremy stands up and places his soft hands with rough fingertips on my arms. He runs his hands down my arms slowly to grab my hands. We stare into each other's eyes for a minute. I start to feel ridiculous, and I laugh at myself. He smiles and laughs a low laugh too. We sit back down on the couch together. "Feel better?" he says, smiling.

"Yeah, actually." I'm somewhat embarrassed. He lays back slightly on the arm rest.

"So…" he starts. "You've never been in a relationship?"

I guess I opened myself up to this line of questioning. But I remember what I was thinking on the stairs outside of my house before I came. Jeremy is, quite possibly, one of a kind. I decide that I'm going to try to be as open as possible and let my guard down a little. That way, if it goes wrong, I can shrug my shoulders at fate and say, 'Hey, at least I really tried.'

I sigh. "No, I have. I've dated a few guys here and there. But I've only been in one serious relationship."

He puts his elegant hand up to his face and rubs his chin for a moment. He immediately puts his hand back in mine. "It was a bad ending, then?"

I shrug. "No," I answered honestly. "I just didn't love him. I was comfortable with him, and at the time I thought it would be enough. But I've seen that life, and it doesn't work out for anyone," I say darkly.

I look at him and he is listening patiently, hanging on every word. His bedroom blue eyes burn into me. "Don't you think sometimes comfort and stability should overcome passion?" he says pointedly to me.

Meaning what?

There's a knock at the door, and Jeremy yells for them to enter. A woman comes in, dressed in all black, and pulls in a food cart. Jeremy thanks the woman, and she leaves.

Over lunch, the most delicious seafood and pasta I've ever tasted, I tell Jeremy about my parents. It's hard for me to talk about, as only one or two people in my life have ever even known.

My life as a child on the outside seemed normal enough. My parents were very loving to me when I was younger, an only child, and I learned a lot from them. A lot of good things: how to focus in school, responsibility, and critical thinking. It's what got me into Harvard. However, I learned a lot of awful things from them, too. My parents were friends for many years before they got married. They worked together numerous times when they were organizing political marches and benefits for the Democratic Party in the sixties and seventies. My parents married for convenience, so they didn't have to be alone. They both wanted children but had thrown themselves into their work for too long to have met anyone, and they were approaching the age where it was too late to conceive.

They got along well enough. They never fought or argued, but they were never intimate either. They were just…nothing. They barely spoke. They never took me on family trips or took family pictures with me. It confused me so much as a little girl. I knew my family wasn't normal. Then one day when I was seven my mother took me to my father's college so she could drop a book off that he had forgotten at home. She walked up to the receptionist's desk and handed her the book, talking causally to her. I ran ahead of the desk, excited to see my dad. Mom told me to go to his office to say hi. I remembered running up to his office door, which was shut, and pushing it open.

There I saw a young girl, no more than 18, bent over the desk. She was naked from the waist down, and he, also naked from the waist down, was pounding her from behind. I immediately felt the blood rush from my young face. I heard the girl moan, "Professor Ackhart" before I snapped out of my shock enough to shut the door quietly.

I stood by the door for a minute. I didn't know what I had just witnessed exactly, but I knew I shouldn't tell my mother, and I never did. But I'm sure she eventually found out herself. I had heard through the years of many affairs my father had with his students, from various sources. I had even heard some of my old bubbly, idiot classmates from high school had run-ins with him. I hated my father for a long time, and I'm still bitter in many ways.

Not that my mother was innocent either. How I came to be was always a mystery to everyone. I had been asked on more than one occasion if I had been adopted. Here I am with two parents with olive skin, dark hair, and brown eyes. I had blonde hair, fair skin, and the strangest, biggest green eyes anyone had ever seen. My whole life all I had ever heard about were my eyes. They are definitely the most noticeable thing on me. I used to love it. Even when other kids in school used to say that I was weird looking, I thought they were so beautiful. How bright and amazingly green they were, and how they had specks of blue and gold, made me feel like I had a whole world in my eyes.

One day, however, that all changed. When I was finally going into 3rd grade, which was in a new school building for us, I was very excited because I knew I was going into my mother's class. My mom brought me in early the first day so that I could help her set up and welcome my new classmates.

Before the kids arrived, I heard a knock on my mom's classroom door. A man appeared, tan and handsome with light blonde hair, and walked into the classroom. He was wearing a brown suit and was straitening his tie.

"Patricia," he said, before he noticed me and stopped in his tracks. I heard my mother's breath catch. "Paul," she said, quickly. "This is my daughter, Dylan." She motioned to him as she put a hand on my shoulder. "Dylan, this is Mr. Horris. He's your new principal."

I stared up at this man in disbelief. Looking into his face, I saw myself- clear as day. Every feature had been identical. Our noses both curved slightly upward. Our cheeks were both high and our faces rounded. Most importantly, as he stared down at me, I noticed his glowing green eyes staring back into my own.

I didn't understand how my parents could do that to me, or each other. I found out later that my mom had been in love with my real father for a long time, but he was married, and wasn't interested in leaving his wife. She had been used by him, tormented. I started to question if true love actually existed, or just didn't exist for my parents. But these discretions are so common. All people in love seem to do is constantly hurt each other and the people around them. I knew from then on that I would probably never get married.

I guess it ended up being too much for my mother to handle. She began to act strangely. She would come home at all hours of the night, drunk and sloppy. She would randomly not show up to work. Eventually she was fired from her job, and those last months were where she really went wild. My Dad tried to protect me as best he could, but at nine, I knew what was going on. A few months after she was fired, I had come home from school and found her on the kitchen floor, cold with a needle still in her arm. In the note I had found, addressed to my father, she had said that she had hoped having me would help save her life and make her happy, but that it hadn't worked.

I can't bear to look at my eyes anymore. Because it just reminds me of everything; of the childhood realization that storybook love doesn't exist. Of my mother's affair with a man who couldn't give a damn. Of the fact that I wasn't enough to keep her alive. So I threw myself into school work, ignored the boys as my body changed and they began to notice me, and moved out of my parent's house as soon as I could.

After I talked for what felt like an hour, I paused and looked at Jeremy. He didn't say anything, but I could tell behind his eyes he was thinking. We were still on the red couch, but we had finished our lunches, and we were leaning against the back of it, only our knees touching as we faced each other.

Finally, he spoke, "You know, that story is kind of beautiful." He takes a sip of the beer he's drinking.

I try to make my face still as I process that information. Emotions wash over me: shock, confusion, anger, and wonder. I decide to go with confusion. "Huh?"

"People who don't experience pain like that- they don't turn out to be people of substance. You know, people who make a difference," he says as he sits up.

I make a disgusted sound in my throat. "I am totally fucked up by what my mother did to me," I say, still aghast at his reaction to my story.

"Fucked up?" he questions, confused. "Why? Because you're shy? Because you're private? Because you don't like to be vulnerable? Because you strive to achieve great things to prove you're good enough to be worth something?"

The way he instantly knows me makes me very uncomfortable. I freeze, wide eyed and unable to speak for a moment. How could he see me so clearly? How did this connection between us go so deeply? It was disturbing to me, the understanding between us. It's deeper than even the physical pull between us, as if the air that separates our bodies is electrically charged. I had worked my whole life to push people away, building up this wall of protection. And yet here is this man, tearing it down and seeing who I am through all the bullshit.

"Yeah," I finally muttered. "Those reasons are pretty much why."

"It makes you beautiful. The things you say it created in you… are what attract me to you in this unbelievable way. You're timid, shy, brilliant, and completely unaware of how amazing you are."

I go statue still. My heart feels like it's going to explode at his words. How did our conversation change course so quickly? I don't know if I'm prepared for this. "Amazing?" I repeat in disbelief.

He smiles a catlike smile, like he's a hunter again. Immediately, my breathing increases. "Oh yes. When I first saw your eyes from the stage," he leans closer to me. I want to both back away and lean toward him at the same time. "I wanted to make them roll back into your head. I wanted to grab your round hips and pull you close to me." He crouches on the couch, one leg on and one leg off, leaning over me. With his face against my cheek again, he whispers in my ear, "You. Are. Breathtaking."

His hot breath in my ear is almost too much. I am audibly panting. He places his hands on my shoulders and pulls his head away. His face is inches from mine. He searches my eyes with his, looking for permission. I nod slightly, and he leans in to kiss me. When his mouth reaches mine, I inhale sharply through my nose. His lips are so warm and soft and delicious. He kisses me sweetly at first, moving his right hand from my shoulder to my face, resting it on my cheek. Slowly, he runs his hands down to my chin and grabs it roughly, opening his mouth. I gasp but open my mouth with him, allowing his tongue to caress mine. He tastes like cigarettes and beer, but it's a sexy taste- the thrill of the bad boy I'd never gotten to date in high school.

He pushes my face back a little so that I'm lying on the couch and he is almost on top of me. I want to wrap my arms around him but I'm frozen, unable to move and nervous. He lets go of my face but we continue kissing. I can feel his erection against my thigh as he lays closer to me, making me moan. "Yes," he whispers, a rough song under his breath. He runs both of his hands down the outside of my arms and across my waist. I feel like if I don't have his hands all over me soon, I'll combust.

His hands continue to move under my shirt, slowly, and up to my bra. He kisses me harder as his fingers begin to run over the outside of the cups. I feel a light movement against my nipples as he pushes my bra up and over my large breasts, freeing them. He makes a guttural sound in his throat, grabbing them roughly with both hands.

I release from his kiss and throw my head back, squirming and whimpering. He pinches my nipples and rolls them gently. The tingling in my groin is utterly unbearable. He kisses my throat, starting at my chin and working down to the collar of my shirt.

"Baby," he says, releasing my breasts and grabbing the bottom of my shirt. He pulls it up, and I sit up a bit and raise my arms so he can pull it over my head. He pulls my bra off just as quickly. He throws both onto the coffee table, pausing as his blue eyes look at my exposed body. I should be self-conscious, but he looks so amazed and hungry. It makes me feel…sexy.

"You relax," he says, staring into my eyes with a smoldering look. "Because I'm going to make you feel so good." His voice is rough. I take in his beautiful body, now glistening with sweat. He looks glorious and triumphant.

My breath is shaky as he leans down and puts my right breast in his mouth. I moan, squirming under his body. He could make me cum just like this, and I have never, ever finished during sex. He bites down on the nipple and then moves his tongue quickly back and forth over it. "Ah!" I scream, and put both hands over my mouth.

He looks up from my breast at me and grabs my arms with both hands. "No you don't," he says, angrily throwing my arms away from my face. "I want to hear you. I need to hear that I make you feel good."

"Oh God!" I scream, as he takes the other breast in his mouth and bites and licks the same way. "You do!"

He releases my breast and travels down my stomach, kissing the whole way, as he uses his hands to unbutton my jeans. I thrust my hips upwards so he can pull my pants and thong down more easily. "That's it," he whispers, looking into my face. His head is now between my legs, right above me. He takes his hand and, still looking up to stare into my eyes, rubs me with two fingers. I close my eyes, moaning for him. He starts slowly, in a circular motion, and then picks up speed. I moan louder. I open my eyes to look at him. His gaze is steady, never looking away from me. I feel uncomfortable, but I like that he seems pleased by looking at me. His hand moves faster and faster. I moan louder and louder. And suddenly, he stops. I open my eyes and look down at him, upset and confused. He smiles wickedly when he sees the disappointment on my face, "You're going to finish, but I want to taste you," he says, making my stomach muscles tighten.

He places his tongue where his fingers just were. I immediately, without control, bring my knees up towards my chest. He moans and moves his tongue faster. He sticks three fingers in me as he goes, and I am dripping wet for him. I finally feel his smooth face against my inner thighs.

I'm screaming, and I feel like I should care that I may be scaring the stage hands outside the door, but I don't. I'm trying to grasp at the leather on the couch, but I feel myself building and building, and I know I'm close. I throw my hands into his messy blonde hair and pull. He moans louder and continues faster.

I finally release, shaking and screaming. He grabs on to my hips tightly and holds, pulling his fingers out and sticking his tongue in me to taste me. When I collapse on the couch, breathless, he sits up and pants, leaning against the opposite arm rest.

"Shit," he speaks, gasping. He throws his head back and closes his eyes.

I'm still shaking. He turns his head and looks at me. He smiles crookedly, and I smile a dumb grin at him. He laughs under his breath and crawls on top of me. He places his cheek on my chest, resting his head. I hug him to me and I still feel his erection against my legs. I'm not sure where we're supposed to go from here, but he's not making any attempt to get up from where he's lying on top of me. Am I supposed to do something? What am I supposed to do?

There's a quiet knock at the door. My head flies up from the arm rest, but Jeremy doesn't seem alarmed. "Jer-" a male voice says. "Sound check, buddy."

Jeremy puts his head down, forehead first, on my chest. "Alight," he says, low and sexy. I hear the man's footsteps walk away.

Jeremy raises his head and looks into my eyes again. His eyes are calm, almost serene, and strikingly aqua. He smiles and moves up to my lips. I close my eyes and he kisses me, soft and sweet, on my mouth.

Jeremy stands up from the couch and quickly adjusts himself. I grab my jeans from the floor and slide them on, curled to try and hide my body. It seems silly with everything that just happened, but I still try to avoid him seeing the full view of me naked.

Jeremy walks over to the mirror and runs his hand through his hair as I put on my bra and blouse. We're in a comfortable silence, trying to absorb what just happened. I kind of feel like a teenager who just had sex for the first time in her basement while her parents weren't home. It's all exciting and new. At least to me.

I stand and face him as he walks away from the mirror. He smiles, showing his teeth, and looks at the floor. I flush red, both of us embarrassed. He looks up again and slinks over to me, causing my muscles to clench throughout my body. He puts both of his hands on my cheeks, and I wrap my hands around him. The muscles in his back are fantastic. How can someone be so muscular, but so long and lanky? His white shirt sticks to his skin again.

He leans in and kisses me once more, a little harder this time. I bravely push myself against him, but he pulls away with a chuckle. "Do you want to come to the sound check?" he breathes, quietly.

I think I need to sit down and think a minute. All of this happened so fast- between me opening up to him and that somehow leading into our first sexual encounter- that I'm confused, almost dizzy. "You go, I'll catch up."

He smiles and runs his fingers through my hair. He releases me and walks over to the end of the sofa to pick up his silver guitar, admiring it with love before putting the strap around his neck. He walks over to the door and opens it, pausing to turn to me again. I'm still frozen in my place with my arms wrapped around my chest.

"See you out there," he says low toned with a smoldering look, his eyes piercing me.

I tense. "Break a leg," I say, breathy.

He turns and walks out, shutting the door behind him.

Chapter 5- Our First Night

I head over to the couch and plop down. My body feels like jelly. So that's what an earth shattering orgasm feels like. I smile silently. I pick my head up and look around the room. There are so many empty bottles scattered haphazardly everywhere that I wonder how many people he had in here last night. I almost feel sick again with the thought. It feels wrong that our encounter happened on this couch, and I wonder how many women he's had on it. He has "performed" here several times before. I look down at my hands, considering it. Did he just use me? For someone who doesn't want to be a slut, I certainly gave a lot up to him within only three days. I put my head in my hands.

Remember, Jeremy is one of a kind. Don't taint this memory. Just have fun. I am so uptight all the time, maybe it'll do me good to let loose.

I shake the thoughts away and get up. I throw on my sandals and walk over to the white desk with the mirror. I adjust my hair which surprisingly isn't too messed up. I smooth it with my fingers. It lies effortlessly to the middle of my back. My cheeks are rosy, my skin glistening. I'm happy with what I see.

I smile and turn to exit through the wooden door. I enter into the dark hallway and pass the smoke room. No one is in it this time. The hallway is eerily quiet as I continue towards the steel door. I push it open and see a bunch of people running around, playing with cords and sound boards. A group of young people, some I recognize from the smoke room, are standing on the far right of the room near the stage. A few girls are sitting on folding chairs in front of the first row, whispering to each other and giggling, all with lanyards around their necks. Most of the girls are young, maybe around my age, but some are older women trying way too hard to relive their glory days. I shut the door quietly and see Jeremy up on the stage, wearing a long sleeved, sheer grey shirt and black jeans. He's barefoot and sweating; his dark blonde hair glistens in the stage lights. He's talking to one of the male stagehands. The man says something in his ear before Jeremy nods and the stage hand walks away. I stand beside the row of folding chairs with the girls in it.

Jeremy turns towards the front of the stage where there is a single microphone on a stand. He struts up to it, the grey guitar slung around his neck. He looks down at the girls and sees me there. He gets a delighted, boyish smile on his face and his eyes glow. My breath catches as I shoot a coy smile back.

"Dylan," he breathes into the microphone. My name echoes all over the large theater. Everyone turns their heads to see who he's looking at. I freeze and blush, embarrassed.

"Come up here," he says. He walks away from the mic and extends his graceful arm out to me. I reach out to his hand and grab it, walking up the stairs leading to the stage.

He pulls me close to him, throwing his hips against me. "My girl sits on stage with me," he whispers, kissing me softly. The girls in the front row gasp when he kisses me. My face burns. He points to the wing behind the left side curtain, and I detach myself from him and stumble over to my seat, gladly escaping the attention.

Ok, so he pretty much just publically acknowledged me. Am I ready for that? What does it mean?

I look at Jeremy on stage as he strums his first cord. The sound sends shivers down my spine. His hand comes up above his head and he arches his back. He is a liquid sex rock star. I decide, in a 12-year-old girl kind of way, that he can acknowledge me whenever he wants… just as long as I get to touch him.

His hand returns to his guitar and he begins to play fast. His fingers move like lightening against the neck, holding down the strings. The sound echoes beautifully throughout the theater, loud and jolting. His eyes are closed as his head moves to the music.

His guitar sparkles slightly in the stage lights. He lets the rapid sounds pause for a moment, and the crowd of young people whoops and claps. He doesn't acknowledge them in any way; his eyes stay closed as the music changes and he strums a slow, sad tune on the guitar. He raises his lips to the microphone, almost softly kissing it. I blush, thinking of where his lips were only a half hour ago...

He opens his mouth, "Oh darlin'...how could I ever let you go, now..." he croons. His voice is so bluesy and painful. Mick Jagger plus Ray Charles and an Italian model all rolled into one. He is spectacular.

And he could be yours.

He plays grace notes, his fingers moving quickly on his guitar again. He raises his lips again, "Oh oh oh oh, darlin'. How could I ever ever let you go. I'm bringing you back, bringing you back. I want you to come on home." He drops his head and strums his guitar. The girls in the front row are screaming. "I love you!" one screams. "I want you!" screams another.

He stops playing and looks out towards the back of the stadium. "We good?" he says into the microphone. He nods, obviously seeing some kind of sign, and throws his guitar on his back. He walks off stage towards me.

I stand when he comes over to me, and he gives me a confused look. I realize my mouth is hanging open. I look down in embarrassment. "You did great," I say, picking my head up to look at him. His blue eyes catch me off guard and he puts his hand on my arm, stroking it. "Amazing…" I say in wonder.

He laughs like a little boy again. "You were at the show last night, but you look like you've just seen me play for the first time. And this was only a sound check. Was I that bad yesterday?"

He's still smiling but now I think I've offended him. "No, no it's not that," I say, putting my hand on his lower chest. His eyes smolder. "I just haven't seen you play before we were…before you were…"

"Yours?" The word purrs out of his mouth.

"Mine?" I say as a question.

He sighs. "Well I'm definitely committed to being yours for at least the next two weeks that I'm here. All yours." He kisses my cheek, moving his lips to my chin, and back up to my ear lobe, taking it in his mouth. I moan quietly. It feels amazing.

"Jeremy," a stagehand calls. "Can I use you to work on the lighting?" Jeremy drops his head, surprisingly breathless. I'm panting.

"Yeah," he says without turning around. The stagehand walks back onto the stage.

He pulls away and looks at me, apologetically. I'm still panting and my whole body tingles. My body feels amazing with all of these new sensations. I decide that *this* is probably going to happen tonight, because if it doesn't, I might burst. I'd feel ill. Maybe I should take this opportunity to privately freak out at home. I need Theresa.

"It's okay," I say, putting my hand on his face. He smiles. "I'm going to go home and freshen up for the show. I have a few hours, right?" I pat my pockets, looking for my phone. I pull it out and look at it. "It's four o'clock."

"The show starts at eight o'clock. I want you here, on stage." It's a demand and not a request. I'm okay with that. It's better than being trampled on by the stampede of wild girls. "I'll get Rich. He'll bring you home and pick you up later."

I smile. He walks over to a man standing behind the stage. "I need Rich," I hear him say to the man, who in turn taps on the headset he has in his ear. The man says something and almost immediately- I hear the creek of the metal door by the stage open. I poke my head out of the curtain and see Rich, a wall in a red T-shirt and jeans, stalk in front of the stage. Either he moves really fast for such a big man, or he's never too far off.

Jeremy walks past me onto the stage. The girls talking in the front row freeze and look up at him. "Richie," Jeremy says. "Take Dylan home."

Rich nods and I appear from behind the curtain and walk down the stage steps. Rich gives me his huge, dark hand. I take it as I come off the last step.

I stop and turn my head over my shoulder, looking up at the stage where Jeremy stands. The girls in the front row are still quiet, but I hear them shift nervously in their seats. Jeremy stands, still as a statue, with the guitar still thrown around his back. Sweat drips off his forehead. I tremble.

"See you soon," I say, quietly.

He nods. I smile and turn back towards the steel door, allowing Rich to open it for me. I am jovial.

Rich and I walk quietly through the green hallway. We make a right and go down another corridor towards the steel door I had come in earlier. I look up at Rich. His face is stern, as usual. I wonder what he thinks about all day.

"So," I say. He turns his head slightly to peer down at me. "Have you worked for Jeremy long?"

"Twenty-one years," he says, in a low voice. Wow, I wasn't expecting that. I did the math in my head; that would mean Jeremy was seven when he met Rich.

"You don't look that old..." I say in amazement. I see a hint of a smile on his face.

"I'm forty-two." He says in his booming voice.

"Wow. Wife? Kids?" I say as he prepares to open the steel door.

"No, thank God."

I laugh. I guess he doesn't seem like the wife and kids type to be honest.

As quiet as it was in the hallway, when Rich pushes open the steel door, I'm immediately surrounded by people screaming and pushing me. I stumble back a few steps, completely surprised, while lights blind me. I feel Rich grab me around the shoulder. I steady myself, and feel my pulse quicken. I feel trapped and claustrophobic. Where the hell did they come from?

I put my hand over my face to block the bright lights as Rich moves me forward through the thick mob of fans and reporters. "Back!" he yells towards the crowd. "Back away!"

"Dylan!" I hear a man say. I try to look at him, but it's so bright and I'm being pulled in a hundred directions. "What's it like to be Jeremy's latest girl?" I feel a microphone being shoved in my face. "Um..." I say, but Rich smacks the microphone away.

"Dylan! Over here!" I hear people yelling. I am overwhelmed. There are people everywhere, hands all over me, pushing me and pulling me. "Bitch! I fucking hate you! Die! You ugly whore!" I hear girls screaming. Instinctively, I drop my hand from my face and try to look around. They couldn't possibly be talking to me, could they?

I turn towards the car again, looking up just in time to see a girl's hand above me, open palmed. Before I can grasp what is happening, the hand comes down towards me, hitting me hard in the face. "Hey!" Rich screams, pushing the girl backwards. "Don't touch her!"

I hold my cheek as I scream. It felt like something stung me. I can feel the blood rushing up to the surface of my skin. The girl hit me so hard- I almost blacked out, and I'm slightly dazed. I blink my eyes a few times, the blackness fading away. The only thing that keeps me moving forward is the pull of Rich's hand.

Finally, after pushing and pulling a few more seconds, we reach the car. I hear Rich open the back door and push me in. He gets into the front seat and I hear the locks click. People are banging on my window, the rear window, even the windshield. Rich starts the car and begins to drive. People seem to get the hint and get out of the way.

We speed out of the parking lot as soon as the car maneuvers its way out of the crowd. "You okay?" Rich says, with as much worry as his voice probably can have.

My hand is still clutching my stinging face. I have tears in my eyes. "Yes," I say shakily. A tear escapes and runs down my cheek. *Hold it together, Dylan. No crying.*

I'm relieved to be away from those people. Their mean words stung my already wounded self-esteem, maybe more than the slap did. I don't understand how they knew I was even there, or why they care about me? I'm not anyone important.

Just when I think I can breathe, Rich hits the accelerator hard. Before I can ask him what's wrong, I turn around and see three or four cars with people hanging out of the passenger's window. They are holding cameras, clicking away as they follow us very closely. "Oh my God," I say, ducking below the window. "Are these people serious?" I say to Rich.

He slams on the breaks, and I peak out of the side window and see the familiar sidewalk in front of my house. To my horror, there are at least forty people camped outside of my door. Their cameras immediately start flashing and they stampede around the parked car. Rich jumps out of the front, pushing people away from my side of the car as he goes around. He opens the passenger's side door and practically scoops me up and places me on my feet. I walk under his arm up the stairs as the cameras flash. When we reach the door, I pat my pockets to find my keys, but instead the door flies open and Rich and I almost fall inside. Rich turns around and shuts the door behind him, locking my padlock immediately. He turns and stands with his back against the door and takes out his cell phone, pushing a button before raising the phone to his huge ear.

I feel warm arms slide around me. I hadn't realized I was trembling so badly, on the verge of breaking down. I want to cry. I almost never cry.

"Dylan!" Theresa holds me. "It's going to be okay."

I feel insanely embarrassed and terrible for pulling her into this. "Oh Theresa, I'm so sorry."

"It's okay! I think it's kind of exciting! What's wrong?" She pulls away from me and I look at her from under my lashes. Her eyes are light and happy. She *is* actually excited.

I move my head completely back to look straight up at her. When she sees my whole face her smile disappears and her eyes show fear. "They are horrible," I cry out. "They're mean. They're like vultures."

"Dylan, your face," Theresa says, putting a soft hand on my cheek. "I'll get you some ice." Theresa walks towards the kitchen.

Rich hangs up the phone. "Miss Dylan," he says, softly. I turn to him. "I called the local police. They are going to clear the front of your house. I also asked them to have more officers at the show. I'm really sorry about this." He looks guilty.

"Oh Rich, it's not your fault," I say shakily. I sniff and stand straighter. I know he needs to get back to control the group at the show. "See you at seven-thirty?"

He smiles. "Of course."

He turns and opens the door enough to get himself out. After he manages to squeeze through the small opening, he slams the door behind him. I lock the top lock. I can still hear people outside, screaming and clicking.

I turn with my back to the door, sliding down to the floor. I feel overwhelmed and exhausted. Theresa walks in with ice wrapped in a towel and hands it to me before she sits down on the floor next to me.

We sit in silence for a few minutes while I hold the ice on my cheek. We don't look at each other or speak. Theresa has always been like that. She could always read me, and she always knows just when I need a minute to rest or collect my thoughts. I'm lucky to have a best friend that's so in tune with me. The thought calms me a little bit.

Finally, she turns her head. I feel her eyes on me, and I turn my head to look at her.

She gives me a slight smile. "Is it worth it?"

I look ahead of me for a minute. *Is it worth it?* Considering the last half hour or so, it's a valid question. Not to mention I have absolutely no idea what direction this relationship is going. And I know I'm failing very hard, very fast.

I close my eyes, and in my mind I see Jeremy with his hand above him, back arched, holding his guitar on stage. Eyes closed and sweat dripping down his perfect face. His hand comes down on his instrument and he strums, the noise filling my ears. The memory sends shock waves through me.

I turn back to Theresa, unable to control my smile. "Oh yeah, totally worth it." My voice is steady now.

We both laugh.

She gets up from the floor and holds out both of her hands towards me. I grab them as she pulls me up. "I have to go to the bathroom," I say to her. "Be right back."

"Okay," she says.

I walk down the hall and into the bathroom. I shut the door and look into the mirror over the sink. I'm taken aback by how I look. My blue blouse is disheveled. My hair is a mess. I have streaks of tears down my cheeks, one pale and one rosy from the slap. I sigh and decide I just should get in the shower. The warm water will help me calm down.

I pull my blue blouse over my head and slide off my jeans. I turn the water on and test it with my hand, allowing it to get hot. I slide off my underwear and bra and slip into the shower, shutting the white curtain.

I let the warm water run over my face while I think. I meant what I said, I think it's all worth it, but I don't know if this is something I could ever get used to. I'm hoping that maybe they are just following me around because I'm new- and within a few days they'll leave me alone. There's even a good chance, I think as my stomach knots, that after a few days *he* will leave me alone. As the press has said, he's with a lot of women. I wonder if he says the things he said to me to all the women he's with.

I hear a light knock at the door. I sigh. "Come in," I say. I hear the door open and someone sit on the toilet seat.

"Sooooo?" Theresa asks. "Before all of the madness with the press?"

I pull my face out of the water stream. "Sooo amazing!" I say. We giggle.

"Did you do anything?"

I describe in embarrassing detail my day.

"Oh my God, Dylan," Theresa says, shocked. "I am so jealous! So you're going back tonight?"

"Yes," I say. I feel myself blushing. "Theresa, I think this night might be it."

Theresa gasps. "Girl, get out of the shower. We're going to get you ready."

"Well get out of here and let me finish in the shower."

I hear Theresa stand.

"By the way," she says as she opens the door. "I got us a job."

I gasp. "No way!" I squirt the shampoo into my hands and lather up my hair. "Where? How?"

"At the college bookstore. We start early September. I met someone at Miranda's party when I crashed there last. He was able to pull some strings."

I run conditioner through my hair. "Another one-nighter?"

"No, actually, I'm going out with him tonight. Dinner," she says, nonchalantly.

"You? A date?" I say, in mock horror.

"You? Sex?" she says in the same voice. I laugh as she shuts the door.

Left alone in the shower, my mind starts to wander and I feel myself slowly begin to panic. I've never been self-confident. How am I supposed to pull this off? It's been over three years since I've been with anyone. And he was just an average boy, literally the boy next door. Not to mention every time I've had sex it's never lasted more than five minutes. Plus it's always seemed more like a chore than something that's supposed to be so enjoyable. I've never been with someone this experienced, or sexy, or a rock star…obviously.

I spend way longer than normal in the shower. I'm trying not to hyperventilate as I rub my body down with soap, twice, and then shave almost every inch of my body. Then I rub my body down with soap twice again. As I do, I examine myself. My hips look abnormally huge, my stomach bulges more than I remember. I have faint white stretch marks on my thighs that I swear weren't there before. Then again, I've never felt the need to examine myself like this before.

My breathing is short and fast. I certainly don't look like the girls in the magazines. Suddenly I'm not sure if my size ten is skinny enough. I secretly wish to be a size zero for the first time ever. I've never been obsessed with being thin or beautiful, but now it's different. What if I don't turn him on?

I get out of the shower as I try to calm my breathing. *Coward. You can do this.* I wrap my hair in a towel and wrap another one around my body. After I rub myself down with lotion, I turn off the light and walk into my bedroom. I see Theresa rummaging through my closet.

"You have nothing in here that's sexy," she says, still staring at my clothes.

"Never had a reason to." I plop down on my bed.

Theresa turns and looks at me on the bed. I stare back at her as she assesses me.

"I have a really awesome dress from college that would look amazing on you. And it was big on me..."

Theresa is a size six. I'd be amazed if it fit, but I think I'll humor her.

Theresa goes into her room for a minute and runs back in with something thrown over her left arm. She stops and holds up a spectacular dress. It's a dark gold color, with tiny sequins covering every inch of the fabric. It's strapless and very short, with a silver zipper showing down the back. I smile, watching as it sparkles in the light of the bedroom. It's very rock-and-roll.

I sigh, "It's perfect. I just don't see how it's going to fit." But I want it to. Bad.

I stand up from the bed and walk over to my dresser. I pull out a black thong and a black strapless bra. They are very plain but I don't have much in the way of sexy underwear. I never thought I'd need it before.

"I really think it will fit. Here," Theresa says, holding the dress down low. "Step in."

114

I carefully step into the dress as Theresa pulls it up over me. Wow is it short, but my legs look good since I've shaved and soaped and moisturized a dozen times. She pulls the dress around me tightly and I hear it zip in the back. Wow, I guess it must fit.

I turn around to look at Theresa. She has a funny look on her face. Her eyes are wide and she's smiling. "What?"

"Dylan, you look amazing. Go look in the mirror."

I step around her and shut the door to my bedroom, exposing the full length mirror behind it. I'm shocked at my reflection. My legs do look good, and when I have heels on they'll elongate even more. The dress really shows my hourglass shape. Because Theresa's chest is smaller than mine the top is tight, exposing a good amount of cleavage. It's as if the dress was made for me. I sparkle as I move. The gold makes the gold specks in my eyes stand out and I'm shocked they look so different.

"I love it, Theresa. Thank you," I say, quietly.

"He'll love it, too. I am so…freaking…jealous," she says and smiles. She sighs. "Get out of the dress; I have to do your hair and make-up."

As Theresa begins the tedious task of trying to make me sexy, our home phone rings.

Theresa hops over to my night stand and picks up the portable phone. She looks at the caller-ID and hands the phone to me, whispering "Dad."

I answer the phone, "Hey Dad."

"Hi Sweetie. I have some questions for you," he says, in an almost disappointed voice. Uh oh.

Theresa starts work on my hair, pulling on it with a comb. I switch hands and put the phone back up to my ear. "What's up?"

"I can tell," he begins, "that already you are distracted out there in Boston. Maybe you should have moved into a dorm. Maybe it's not good to live with Theresa. I mean, out all night with shirtless musicians? Not very becoming of a Harvard Law student. What will the other students and professors think?"

I sigh. "Where are you seeing this?"

"Honey, you've been on the news for the past two days."

My stomach knots. I feel the burning starting in my stomach. Who is he to judge me? Especially with his history? I don't think so. "Dad, listen. I have to go. I'm busy and I don't have time to defend myself against this ridiculous media frenzy. We're friends, just having fun. Starting slow. Relax. I love you," I say and hang the phone up.

I look up at Theresa. She winces, but continues her work.

Theresa really is a wiz with the straightener, hair spray, and eye-liner. By the time she's done, my usually lifeless blonde hair is sleek against the sides of my head, while the middle comes up in a poof and an arch, creating something like a chic mohawk. She's done my eyes so it looks like they're' surrounded in black smoke. It makes them pop even more. My skin is flawless, and I have a faint glow. You can't even see the mark from the slap anymore. My lips have just a hint of shine. When I smile, they sparkle like my dress.

After I stand up from the bed and put the dress back on, I do a little twirl. Theresa claps. "Perfect! I am a genius!"

I hear a knock at the door. I slide my gold high heels on, also compliments of Theresa, and head for the door. I decide not to take a purse and to store money in my bra instead. One of the many perks to being big breasted. It's a perfect August night, so thankfully I don't have to wear a jacket.

I check my watch. Seven-twenty. *Good thing I was prepared.*

I put my ear to the door, straining to hear if there are sounds of flashing cameras or news reporters. This is where a peep hole would come in handy. I don't hear anything, so I unlock the top lock and pull the door towards me.

I stop in shock. My mouth drops open. Jeremy is standing in front of me, with six police officers and three big African American men, including Rich, behind him. I hear Theresa behind me whistle. "Holy shit," she says, under her breath.

Jeremy's eyes widen for a minute when he sees me. His eyes trace up and down my body. I blush immediately, pleased that he seems to like what he sees. But his face quickly goes back to stern, almost angry. Of course even his scowl is hot. The blue of his eyes burn into me, his lips almost pouting. His stubble is dark, making my heart flutter. He has on red plaid pants and black van sneakers. As a shirt, he wears a plain black vest, with nothing underneath. His muscular arms are crossed in front of his chest. I see the snake tattoo crawling up his right arm.

"Dylan," he says, low and husky.

"Jeremy," I say quietly, a little afraid of his coldness.

I turn around and wave to Theresa. She gives me a little wave. "Good luck on your date tonight," I say. She smiles again, obviously intimidated by the entourage, too, as I walk out onto my doorstep and shut my door. I can feel Jeremy standing next to me. I turn to him so that we are face to face.

I look into his eyes, first stern and cold, and then they begin to soften. I smile at him.

He finally unfolds his hands and puts his hand on my left cheek. "How's your face?" he says, low.

"It's fine, really," I say, grabbing the hand he has on my face. "Is that what you're upset about?"

"Yes," he says, almost growling. "I'm so sorry you were hurt. I came to make sure you were okay."

"Rich took good care of me."

"I won't let them hurt you ever again," he vows. His face is very serious. We stare for a moment.

"Sir," one of the big men says. "We have to get back, quickly."

All of the policemen and security guards turn and walk in front of us down the steps. We walk up to his black car and he opens the door for me. I scoot all the way over, leaving him room to sit by the door. The policemen and one of the big men get into the three police cars parked randomly around the street. Rich gets into the driver's seat, and another big man gets into the passenger's side. I see the police cars' lights turn on.

Jeremy grabs my left hand, putting it to his lips and kissing it. He looks up over my hand into my eyes. "You look so sexy," he says. "How am I supposed to concentrate on stage?"

My eyes widen. "Oh, will I be distracting?" I say, feeling self-conscious.

He laughs his little boy laugh, loud and choppy. He puts our hands down on the seat, still connected. "Yes," he says. "But not in a bad way. I'm just not sure I'll be able to keep my hands off you tonight." His eyes smolder.

"I'm not sure I want you to," I say bravely.

I lean closer to him. He takes my chin in his free hand and grabs it hard, pulling my face to his. His lips press against mine, and he opens my mouth with his and licks my tongue. He tastes amazing. I feel my insides tighten.

The car suddenly stops, and we break from the kiss. Looking up, I once again see a steel door. I see a lot of policemen, but thankfully, no fans or reporters. "We sent a decoy car to another door," he explains, seeing my relief when staring towards it.

I smile, and he returns the smile as he leans over. He presses his cheek against mine, blowing into my ear. "That dress is going to be fun to peel off of you," he breathes. I pant instantly. I run my hands along his bare arms. The door opens and all of the police officers and big men are back, standing in front of the car and making a line to the steel door a few feet from us. Jeremy hops out and pulls me with him just as quickly. We run as fast as my six inch heels will allow into the green hallway.

Immediately, Jeremy is caught in a storm of stagehands and men in business suits. They are all talking at the same time as we walk towards the stage area. There is a younger guy who walks behind me, about Jeremy's age, dressed in jeans and a T-shirt. I wonder who he could possibly be as we almost make it to the stage. Instead of going through the steel door that leads to the floor in front of the stage, we make a left and go up a small flight of black stairs and through a wooden door that leads to the stage's right wing.

Most of the stagehands scatter when we reach the stage area. The three men in business suits take seats in the way back of the curtained area. They try to continue their conversation over the deafening scream of the fans. Jeremy leans over and says into my ear, "I'll be right back. Have a seat," he motions towards a chair set up in the wings.

I sit in my chair but peer over my shoulder at him. He walks into a room in the very back next to where the men in the business suits are sitting. It looks like it's probably a quick change dressing room. He's followed by the boy in jeans that I noticed earlier in the hallway. I already don't like that kid. There's something about him- he reminds me of a weasel. Maybe it's because he's short and has a tiny pinched face but he seems sneaky all the same. They shut the door behind them and are in there for at least ten minutes. When Jeremy comes out, he's smiling and holding a beer. The boy follows out behind him, carrying a little plastic bag that's tied at the top.

Jeremy waves to the boy and the boy turns and leaves. Jeremy makes eye contact with me and struts over. The fans are going wild, chanting for him and screaming. It's almost show time and they are getting antsy. I want to ask him about the boy, but I'm still getting to know him and we're only just dating. I figure it's none of my business and decide to let it go. He kneels next to my chair. "You ready for this?" he yells and smiles.

I smile and nod, noting that his eyes look different. The blue looks darker somehow, and they are...teary? Almost like he's going to cry, but he doesn't seem sad. "Is everything okay?" I say, concerned.

He takes a swig from his can, downing the rest of the liquid before crumpling it in his hand. He looks down, almost guiltily. "Just nervous!" he yells, looking quickly back up at me. I chuckle but I don't think he can hear me. I hope he doesn't expect me to believe that a man performing since before he could talk is nervous. Then again, I guess it could happen...

A staghand walks over with the guitar, and Jeremy stands up to receive it. He grabs gently, like it's precious or fragile. He throws the strap over his head, letting the guitar hang in front of his exposed chest. A woman is suddenly standing behind him, trying to comb through his long hair. I look up at him, watching the guitar shimmer in the faint light. He closes his eyes and takes a deep breath. The woman behind him steps away, satisfied with his orderly yet messy hair. He peers down at me and gives me a wry smile. I melt.

As he stands next to me behind the curtain, he raises his hand and strums hard on his guitar. The sound is loud- even louder than the crowd. It makes everyone backstage jump. The crowd goes silent at first, and then collectively begins to scream. Jeremy closes his eyes again, sweat starting to bead on his forehead. He begins to strum fast on his guitar, moving his fingers along the neck extremely quickly, up and down. The sound is sultry, making me shiver.

He sways his head to the music as he plays. The blue stage lights hit his face, and he looks like a beautiful, fantastic, other-earthly creature. I hear girls screeching from the crowd. I am overcome with emotion. I can finally say I can relate to his crazed fans.

He walks out on stage as he starts playing cords on the silver guitar. It shimmers wildly in the bright stage lights. The drums kick in and then the whole band begins to play. It's amazing to watch his show up close like this. There are girls crying, trying desperately to clamber onto the stage. It's madness. The girls sing along to all of his songs. There are pyrotechnics, bright white lights firing from the ends of the stage. At one point, Jeremy takes a bottle of water and pours it on himself, the girls scream. *I* almost start to scream, watching the water fall down his body. He jumps and shakes and twists, losing himself in the performance. He's so different on stage; uninhibited. No pretenses. It's pure magic.

I peer out into the crowd midway through the show and see girls lifting up their shirts, exposing themselves to him. Unfortunately, these girls are attractive and have a lot to show. I flush in anger and feel the jealousy building again in my stomach. I decide not to look out anymore.

When the show is almost over, Jeremy sits on a stool that was placed in the middle of the stage. He brings the microphone close to his face as the band exits the stage on the opposite side of where I sit. I can see them grabbing water and wiping themselves with towels.

The stage lights turn dark. Jeremy wipes his forehead with the back of his hand. Breathing heavily, he says, "Hello everyone."

The girls in the crowd scream, "I love you Jeremy!"

He laughs. "I'm going to cover a song by Peter Gabriel. I'm sure you know it. I've always loved this song and now it has a special meaning to me," he looks over into the wings at me, and shoots me a dazzling smile. I blush, frozen.

He exhales lightly into the microphone. "Love," he croons and plays a note. His voice wraps around the word like liquid. The crowd screams.

He sings a slow, almost sad version of "In Your Eyes," strumming his guitar slowly, gazing at me every now and then. It's bluesy and beautiful. I'm in awe of this man and overwhelmed by his gesture. I don't feel like I'm worthy of his time or affection- this genius, this beautiful man. My stomach aches as I yearn to touch him, to know him, to be with him. It is really the first time I recognize how strong my feelings are becoming.

When he's finished, the crowd goes crazy. "Have a good night!" Jeremy says, breathlessly. He stands, flings his guitar onto his back, and runs off stage. I stand up and he runs immediately into my arms.

"It was wonderful!" I scream, running my hands through his wet hair.

He pulls away and looks at me. Both of our faces pale for a moment. We stare in each other's eyes as awareness comes over both of us. The show is over, and now we have the night.

The stagehands and men in suits come up to Jeremy, patting him on the back. He lets go of me and turns around and shakes hands with his crew. He smiles and thanks everyone. A stagehand throws him a beer, and he drinks it immediately, like he was famished. He leans over to a man in a suit and says, "No press tonight man, tomorrow." The man nods and everyone starts to walk away.

A big man comes up behind Jeremy and says loudly, "See anyone you want to bring back?"

It takes me a moment to understand the question. As I slowly figure it out, the anger in my stomach hits me full force. What he meant to say is 'did you see any trashy chicks in the crowd you want to bang'.

The only person he'll be banging tonight better be me. I wait impatiently for his response.

Then again, am I sure I want to do this? Obviously, bringing girls back stage to woo them is something he does often. The bad memories of the night I first met him creep back into my head. 'Womanizer,' my subconscious mocks again. I tell it to leave me alone.

"No, not tonight," he says to the man. I relax immediately, my anger satiated by his quick denial. He turns around quickly and smiles at me. His smile is so happy, so light. It makes him look so innocent. I don't think he realizes I heard their exchange. I smile back shyly.

He slinks up to me, grabbing me around the back. The crowd is still loud, some still screaming for him, the rest making their way out of the glass doors to the theater. He puts his lips up to my ear. "I love when you blush," he croons. "Do you want to get out of here?"

I'm a little disappointed. To go where? I thought we'd just be in his dressing room most of the night. Actually, I'm a little happy to not have to be back there. I don't have to be on that couch, where I'm sure so many other women have been.

"Okay," I whisper back in his ear.

He pulls away and grabs my hand. We walk over to Rich, who's standing in the corner by the door that leads down the steps into the hallway. "Take me and the lady back to my house," he says, letting go of my hand for a minute to lift his guitar off of his back. Rich takes the guitar and nods, almost looking surprised. He hands Jeremy a black T-shirt that he throws on over his bare chest. He turns and we follow him down the steps as much stomach twists in on itself.

His house?!? I'm trying not to lose it right here and now. I feel the color run out of my face. I concentrate on taking steady breaths in and out, trying to convince myself that I'm ready for this.

Midway down the green hallway, Jeremy looks at me. I look up at him and see a concerned look on his face. "You okay?" he says.

No. I don't know. Maybe? "Yes," I whisper, unconvincingly.

Rich opens the steel door for us and we quickly run into the car. The police and security are finally doing their job because there's no sign of any fans or press. But as soon as we get into the car, Rich locks the doors and speeds away. Better safe than sorry.

Our hands are still locked together as the limo drives through the streets of Boston. My house is very close to the theater, but his house seems to be more on the outskirts of the city. Fifteen minutes of silence later, we still aren't there.

Jeremy breaks the silence. "Almost there. See that lake? I live right behind there."

I peer off into the distance and see the moon reflected in a little pond. We turn down a street beside it and finally up to a beautiful, old apartment building. It's very classic Boston, red bricks and vines growing up the side. I turn and smile at him. "Not what I was expecting."

"Why? I know it's not very grandiose, but I'm a very quiet, low key person. I just wanted a place to sleep. Most people around here are rich and older, so they tend to leave me alone." He shrugs.

"No! I love it," I say. I actually think it looks very much his style, now that I think about it. I can see the classical composer side of him choosing this place.

The car parks out front and we open the door and step onto the sidewalk. Jeremy walks around to the front passenger's seat, opening the door and getting his silver guitar out, throwing it onto his back. We both say goodbye to Rich and he drives off as we start walking towards the door. It's still warm out and it feels nice. The doorman opens the glass door and says, "Hello, Mr. Mason." Jeremy nods at him and leads me inside.

The lobby is beautiful. It has black marble floor with a matching marble desk on the right. It's a small lobby that was obviously redone, but it's very simple and elegant. Behind the black marble desk is a gold elevator. We walk over to it and push the button to go up. It opens instantly and we walk inside. There are buttons for four floors, and a place to insert a key. Jeremy pulls keys out of his pants pocket and turns it to the right. The elevator begins to move.

"This is how you get to the penthouse," he explains.

"Very classy," I say. He laughs.

When the elevator stops, the door opens and we step out directly into a living room. The living room is large, but barely has any furniture in it. The walls are black, and there is a white couch in the middle of the room facing the right wall, which has a huge TV hanging from it. The wall straight in front of the elevator has a fireplace with white marble outlining it. The left side of the room has a black bar with many bottles of liquor on the glass shelves behind it. Directly on my left, there is a hallway leading to more rooms.

He looks at me. Ridiculously, I think he almost seems nervous. "Do you like it? I don't have much. But I'm not really here all that often I guess," he explains.

"I love how simple it is. It's very elegant," I complement quietly. I turn my attention down the hallway again and my stomach flip-flops.

I turn to look at Jeremy, and am surprised to see the look in his eyes. They are bright blue and smoldering, and his face is serious. My breathing picks up and becomes uneven.

"Do you want to see the rest of the place?" he says, his voice low.

"Sure," I whisper.

We stand staring at each other for another moment. With our hands clasped, he turns and leads me down the hallway. The walls are still black and there are four rooms: two on the left side of the hallway, one straight ahead, and one on the right. He stops at the first room on the left and turns the knob to open the door. Inside, there's just a plain white bed, crisply made, and a black dresser against the wall. The walls are red and there's a black closet on the right.

He clears his throat. "This is the guest bedroom," he says quietly. There's no reason to whisper, except that the silence in the house is almost deafening, especially after leaving the theater. The quiet is welcome, and neither of us wants to disturb it.

I look around the room and then back at him. He's staring at me. "It's nice," I say, blushing. He smiles wryly and leads me to the next room on the left side of the hall. He turns the knob and opens the door again, flipping on a light.

"This is my music room," he says, stepping into the room. There are instruments absolutely everywhere, and it's a decent sized room. In the center of the room sits a beautiful baby grand piano. The lid is black, but the sides and legs are silver. along with the bench. It shimmers in the faint light. It's breathtaking. "Oh," I sigh.

He smiles. "You like it? I had it made at the same time as my guitar."

"Yes," I say, continuing to look at the room. There is a gold drum set in one of the corners, along with about seventeen guitars. Some of the guitars are electric, some are acoustic, and some bass. They are all in various colors, some more worn than others. One acoustic guitar hangs like a trophy on the wall, the only thing I've seen hanging on any walls so far besides his TV. It obviously must mean something to him. On the other side of the room are flutes, saxophones, trumpets, and all kinds of other random instruments. There's even a French horn.

As I walk around in amazement, I hear my heels clicking on the hardwood floors. I stop walking and turn around, smiling at him. He's standing tense and awkward. "Do you play all these?"

He shrugs. "Yeah,"

I reach out and touch the saxophone. Its shiny and cold to the touch. I look up at him again. "You took lessons for all these?"

He shifts uncomfortably. "No, I've never taken a music lesson."

My mouth drops. "Ever?"

"Nope," he says and gives me a smile. I turn away from him for a minute and do a mental inventory of all the different instruments in the room. I stop at twenty-five. I

132

am overwhelmed with the pure talent this one man could possibly possess. He's a savant; a true virtuoso. My heart clenches with just the thought of being in the same room with someone like him- a miracle.

Filled with amazement, I forget to be bashful. I want this man. Now. Bravely, I try to slink up to him like he walks up to me, attempting to make him feel the way he makes me feel. There's a hint of a sly smile on his face. I stop, standing a few inches from him, and grab his hands. I can see my dress sparkle against his black shirt. "What's wrong?"

He looks down at the floor. "I just never brought anyone here, aside from employees and family."

I blush. I had no idea, and I'm flattered. "Really?"

He looks up at me. "Really. I just wanted you to be comfortable. You don't seem like the, um, girls who I usually…pursue…"

I giggle. Seeing this man, a God, lost for words over me is just ridiculous. He laughs at himself.

"You've been with all of those women and never had any here?" I say, still laughing.

"No. I didn't want those women in my life. They were just to pass the time. To keep me from feeling…as lonely as I do…" He trails off.

We look at each other and the mood shifts. Our eyes are connected. I begin to breathe heavily again, and to my amazement, so does he. "You look so amazing in that dress," he says, looking me up and down.

This poor lonely, genius man. I want to make him feel good. I put my hand on his face and bring him back to my eyes. "Where's *your* room?"

His eyes burn. "Over here," he says. He drops one of my hands, still looking at me, as we exit the music room and arrive at the door at the very end of the hallway. He looks away from me and opens the black door to his bedroom. He holds out his hand and motions me inside first. I let go of his hand and walk in.

The room is huge, but again there isn't much in it. The walls are plain white and bare of artwork. There is a bed against the right wall that juts out horizontally into the middle of the room. The bed is a California King, with a black leather padded headboard and black sides. The sheets are black silk and look very expensive. On the left side of the room are two big windows with black curtains. There is a black dresser against the wall by the door. On the wall across from the door is a big closet with black doors. Next to his bed is a night stand with a mini fridge underneath.

I turn to him, and I see his lanky body leaning against the doorway. My stomach tightens. "A mini fridge?" I ask curiously.

He shrugs, "I get thirsty at night. I'm lazy," he says in his melodic voice. He grabs the strap from across his chest and raises the silver guitar over his head. He sets it against the doorway. He walks gracefully past me and opens the fridge, removing an exotic beer. "You want one?"

I'm so nervous that I'm scared I'm going to throw up as it is. "No thanks."

He sits down on the bed. He motions for me to sit next to him. He opens the beer with a pop and drinks a few gulps from the can. I put my hands in my lap as he puts the beer on the bedside table, and turns to look at me. We sit in silence for a moment. His eyes search mine, soft and light.

"I don't understand what you do to me," he says quietly. "I've never been...nervous. I've honestly never cared about making someone uncomfortable. I've never been with someone this...inexperienced."

My anger peaks a bit. "I'm not THAT inexperienced," I say, curtly. He gives me a doubtful look. He looks so amazing that I can't be mad. I smile. His face turns serious again, and I blush.

135

"I don't want you to do anything you're not comfortable with. But I can't resist you anymore. The way you walk, Dylan. The way you sparkle in that dress. The shape of your body. Your pretty face. The way you look at me, like you actually care for me. I need to have you." He leans over to me on the bed. His eyes are inches from mine. My breathing is fast and short, pushing my breasts up and down in the dress. "Don't say no. Please," he says; a sexy, low whisper.

That did it.

I practically leap for his lips. Our mouths meet and he lets out a low moan in his throat. I climb on top of him as he sits back on the mattress, my legs straddling him with my knees on the bed. I feel his erection against my groin. I grind into him. "Oh, God," he whispers, pulling away from my mouth. I smile devilishly. I like that I can do this to him, a man who can have- and has had- anyone he wants. I kiss him harder and slide his black T-shirt off, exposing his amazing chest. I rub my hands down his arms and then up his chest, grinding him still.

He pulls away from me. "I want you to do something," he says, short of breath. His eyes are overwhelmingly sexy.

"Yes?" I say. At this point I'd fly to the moon if he asked.

"Dance for me?" he kisses down my neck.

It takes me a minute to comprehend that. Again, not what I was expecting. "Dance. For. You?" I say, slowly.

Jeremy grabs my hips and lifts me, sitting me beside him on the bed as I let out a surprised giggle. He stands and walks across the room to the doorway. He turns the lights down with the dimmer on the wall and leans down to pick up his silver guitar. He walks over to the bed and sits beside me again, putting his guitar on his lap. He nods his head towards the empty floor in front of him.

"Over there. Dance for me. Undress yourself." He's breathless.

I stand up, unsure, and walk over to the middle of the space in front of his bed. I have no idea how to be sexy. I'm a deer in headlights. He smiles devilishly and starts strumming his guitar, a slow sexy rhythm. The music helps me, and I start to sway. I move my hips back and forth and I whip my hair quickly once. I run my hands up and down the dress. "Mmmmm," he moans.

I twist my hips so that I'm facing my back towards him. I slither down towards the floor. "Oh yes," he says, still strumming his guitar.

I stand up again and reach behind me to the silver zipper, grabbing it and pulling it

137

down to my lower back. I face him and run my hands down my body again, taking both my strapless bra and the dress down with me, exposing my breasts and black thong. The dress falls to the ground.

The music makes an ugly noise, and I look up to see Jeremy struggle to play the right cord again. I giggle, knowing he must really be distracted to screw up. I run my hands back up to my breasts and grab them, throwing my head back. He messes up again.

He suddenly gets up and passes me, putting the guitar back by the doorway. I stand still with my arms at my side, uncomfortable, watching him. He walks quickly over to his dresser and turns on the silver iPod dock that sits on it. Soulful music begins to play. He turns and nearly runs back towards me, grabbing my hips and flinging me around backward, so that he's pressed up against me from behind. He grabs my neck and pushes my head back against his cheek, and his lips are at my ear. I gasp. He's rough, but instead of being afraid, I'm electrified.

"You better not like this underwear too much," he growls, removing his hands from my neck and hip, grabbing the side of my underwear with his hands. I'm confused at first, but then I feel his body tighten and hear the underwear rip, and they fall to the ground.

I carefully lift my high heels to step around them.

I hear him unzip his pants and they hit the floor. I walk over to the bed and bend over it, placing my hands on top of the comforter.

He comes up behind me and rubs against me with his body. I feel how excited he is, and I moan. He inhales a shaky breath. "No," he says, leaning over to grab my wrist and flinging me around to face him. I take in his naked body for this first time and it's fantastic, like artwork. But my eyes are still drawn to his handsome face. His eyes are a bright, excited blue; his face partially flushed. "I want to see you."

He lays me down on the bed gently and wraps his arms around my back, lifting me so that I'm lying on the bed and my feet no longer dangle off of the end. His body is amazing, long and lean and muscular. His face is even more magnificent when he's excited. I realize my heels are still on, but when I go to kick them off, he stops my feet and shakes his head.

I'm shaking now and breathing heavily, some of the braveness melting away. My whole body yearns for him. Every touch burns me. He runs his hands down my legs and grabs both of my ankles. He lifts them and puts my heels on the bed so that my legs are bent and spread. He kisses up my left leg, to my knee, and upper thigh. I squirm and moan. Finally, his tongue finds me.

I grab his fantastic hair, pulling it. He keeps going, stopping when I get too close. I sigh angrily, until he starts again; stopping a second time before I release. It's incredibly torturing.

"Don't!" I pout. He looks up at me and smiles. "Not yet," he whispers.

He climbs onto the bed in between my legs. He leans over and manages to reach his night stand, opening the drawer and pulling out a condom. I give him a wry smile as he opens it and puts it on. "I thought you never have girls here?" I ask, touching his chest.

He leans down and kisses my lips tenderly. "I was hopeful about tonight."

He touches my breast with his right hand and runs my nipple between his fingers. "Do you want me?" he says, as I squirm.

I open my eyes and look into his face. He looks down at me sweetly. I raise my hands from his chest and touch both sides of his face. "Yes," I manage to whisper.

He rests himself on top of me, holding himself up by his forearms. I feel him everywhere. "My sweet Dylan," he says, as he enters me. I gasp. He fills me so fully it almost hurts.

He goes slowly at first, moaning loudly. His voice is deep and guttural, and it makes me want him more. I grind against him, urging him to go faster.

He picks up the tempo, leaning his head against my cheek. "Oh, god," I cry out. He leans over to his right forearm and puts his left pointer finger in my mouth. I suck it hard. "Oh shit," he says. I grab his hand from my mouth and hold it above my head. His warm skin feels so good on mine. I try to grab his other arm with my other hand, but he shakes his head. "I don't want to crush you."

I look into his blue eyes, grabbing the other hand. I want to feel him all over my body.

"Drown me in you," I say. His eyes sparkle, and he leans down to kiss me as he moans. He sets himself completely on me, still going, and raises his other hand above my head.

He starts to pick up tempo slowly, working up to a fast pace. I'm panting and biting my lip, almost ready to release. When he notices, he slows his rhythm. "Jeremy!" I protest angrily.

"Not yet," he says.

Finally, he moves faster than ever, pounding me hard. He gets up onto his hands, sweat dripping off his forehead onto my chest. The look of pleasure on his face, his eyes closed tightly and mouth open, sends me over I feel my release, hard and pulsing, squeezing him deeper. I throw my head back and scream.

"Damn!" he shouts. He grabs me around the waist and, exiting me, flips me around so that I'm on all fours. He enters me from behind, grabbing my hips hard. I tense at the sensation of this new and different position. He continues thrusting into me and I never want him to stop He brings me to release once again, but this time I feel him squeeze my hips harder. His body shakes and he moans loudly as he stops moving and then collapses on my back.

Chapter 6- The Blue Haired Girl

We settle ourselves under his black silk covers. He lies on his back, smoking a long cigarette with his left hand and holding me with his right. I lay with my head on his hard chest. Even though I'm exhausted, I don't want to fall asleep.

We sit there in silence for a while. I trace pictures with my fingers on his exposed abdomen. I'm starting to feel uncomfortable with the silence, and I'm hoping everything is okay. Just when I'm about to ask him, I feel him sweetly kiss the top of my head. I smile. *I could really end up with him. This could really happen.* I've never felt this way before about anyone.

I never wanted a man. I didn't feel I needed one; I was content on making my life complete with just myself. I wasn't interested in that kind of companionship. I had thrown around the idea of kids, but I assumed I could always adopt. But now, here with him, I'm not sure how I ever thought I wouldn't want this.

I pick my head up and turn to look at his face. He turns, his head rising from the pillow to look into my eyes. We smile at each other, and I bashfully look down at his chest. I see a tattooed circle on his right upper chest that looks like it has a spider web in the middle. "What's that?" I ask, running my finger over it.

He looks down at his chest for a second and then back up to my face. "It's a dream catcher. It's supposed to catch bad dreams. I used to have them a lot as a kid, so my little brother made me one in school. I had it above my bed when I was little."

"Oh," I say and smile. I didn't know he had a brother. On the left side of his chest, horizontally on his ribcage, there is a name. "Jonathan? Who's that?" I say.

"My brother," he says sadly. The name has "2001" written underneath.

I bite my lip. "I'm so sorry. What happened?"

Jeremy leans over to the bedside table. He puts his cigarette out in the ashtray after taking a long drag. He takes a drink of his beer and sets it back down. He sits up more in the bed, leaning back on his hands.

"He was born with a genetic disorder. It eventually made him get tumors around his heart, and he died."

"How old was he?" I rub his arm.

"Fourteen. I was sixteen when he died."

"Do you have any other siblings?"

"No."

I sit and think for a minute. "That must have been really hard on your parents."

He chuckles a dark laugh. "You have no idea."

I decide to change the subject.

"You said your mom lives locally? How about your dad? Are they still together?"

He leans over and takes another swig of beer. He's had a few tonight but he doesn't even seem tipsy.

"No, my dad is dead." He turns back towards me and leans on his hands again.

I feel stupid. "Oh wow, I'm so sorry."

He shrugs. "It's okay. We didn't really get along."

I pause, but my curiosity gets the best of me. "Why not?"

Jeremy sighs.

"You don't have to talk about it if you don't want to," I say quickly.

He closes his eyes. "No," he says, opening them again. They are deep sea blue. "It's okay." He runs his hand down my cheek and puts it back behind him. "I want you to know me, but it's just not something I ever really talk about."

He clears his throat. "My dad died in 2001 as well. After my brother died. He tried for a few months to pretend he really could get over it, but in the end it was too much for him, so he killed himself."

I look down at my hands. "I'm sorry."

He shrugs. "Like I said, we weren't really that close."

I look up at him again. "Why?"

Jeremy looks up at the ceiling. "Well, when Jon was born, everything about him was precious and special because my parents knew he would probably die," Jeremy explains. He looks at the wall across from the bed. "The very simplest thing he did was amazing. When he drew a picture, my parents nearly died with excitement every time. I'm not saying they shouldn't have, but they could have at least given me some..." He pauses and begins again. "Nothing I did was good enough. They always wanted me to do more. Even when I was playing Beethoven symphonies at age three on the piano for the Queen of England, it wasn't enough for them. It was like I had to do everything a hundred times better because Jon could only achieve so much in his short life, you know?"

He looks at me again. I picture little Jeremy in my head, trying to please his parents, trying to find acceptance, but still being ignored. I feel so sad for him. "I understand," I say, frowning.

"They never listened to me. Never believed anything I said. I almost think they didn't care if I had feelings about anything. I was like one of those little toy monkeys they could wind up and I would play music for them whenever it was convenient. So after my dad died, I turned my attention to rock. It's more me."

"Well, at least you have a happy ending. You're famous."

He laughs his careless laugh again, and I smile. "I don't really care about being famous. I just wanted to make enough money to have whatever I want. Whenever I want. Have power I didn't have when I was little."

He leans closer to me, his eyes smoldering. "And right now," he says, lifting his hand to trace my lips with his fingers. "I want you. So climb on me."

He grabs my hips and lifts me onto him. He enters me instantly and I gasp. I feel his direct skin against me, and it feels amazing. He makes me feel so full; so good. He uses my hips to help me move up and down. I whimper as I feel him move within me. This is completely new to me, and I feel the best I've ever felt. The things Jeremy can do to my body are almost surreal. He lets go of my hips and I keep moving as he reaches for my breasts. I wish I could stay in this room forever, and at that moment I know my life will never be the same without him in it. For the first time, I feel *need* for another human being.

When I finally wake up, I can tell it's morning by the light hitting the floor through Jeremy's windows. I lift my arms and stretch, sitting up as I do. I hold the sheet up to my chest and look down to the bed next to me. Jeremy is sleeping peacefully, breathing deeply with his long eyelashes hitting his cheeks. I want to reach out and stroke his face, but I don't want to disturb him. I climb out of bed and try to walk silently to the bathroom.

When I round the bed to his side, my foot hits something hard and cold. I hear a loud clang as it falls over to the floor. I look down, confused, and pause. There are at least fifteen bottles of beer on the floor beside the bed. On his nightstand, there are another six bottles, along with three shot glasses.

I take a step backwards. These were definitely not here last night. I remember that there was one bottle on his nightstand before I fell asleep. There's no way anyone was here last night; I would have woken. So then, did he drink all of these by himself?

I walk over to his dresser and open the second drawer. I find some basic T-shirts in there. I pull out a big black one and throw it on. It hangs down so that it's almost a miniskirt. I continue walking around the bottles and towards the bathroom. I go quickly and wash my hands, looking into the mirror, letting my hair out and smoothing it with my hands. My face is pale. My mind is racing. I feel like I'm forgetting something about the bottles, but for some reason I know I probably don't want to remember.

I walk out of the bathroom and back into Jeremy's room. I bend down and try to silently pick up all of the bottles. I walk the first couple down the hallway and into the kitchen across from the big living room. I put them down into the trash can and walk back down the hallway for the next batch. When I enter the room, Jeremy stirs and opens his eyes.

I smile, meekly. "Hi," I breathe.

"Hi," he says, rubbing his eyes. He's still groggy. "Ugh, man." He rubs his head.

I sit on the bed next to him. "Hung over?"

He looks up at me. His eyes are glassy and grey. "Excuse me," he says. Jeremy gets out of bed, moving me aside, and practically runs for the bathroom.

I sit on the bed, angry and hurt, until a few minutes later I hear him exiting the bathroom. He looks a bit better, but he's still walking funny.

I'm fuming, and I feel the familiar burning. "You want to explain to me just what the hell went on last night?" I snap.

He stops in the doorway and stares at me, confused. I open my arms to the remaining bottles on the floor.

He shrugs. "Just couldn't sleep I guess. Needed to relax after the show."

I scoff. "I think next time maybe three beers would suffice."

He laughs, almost giggling. "You look really cute in my shirt."

My scowl turns to a shy smile, and I blush. He looks good himself in his black pajama bottoms. His bare chest is hard and lean. I walk over to hug him, and he opens his arms to receive me. He holds me close to his warm chest. "Sweet Dylan," he whispers in my ear. I close my eyes and lean my head on his shoulder.

He lets go of me and holds me out from him so he can look in my eyes. As we're parting, I notice he has a small rash. Tiny red spots cover the inside of his arm and top of his hands. "What's that?" I say, pointing to it.

He looks down and laughs. "Heat rash. I get it often. Especially after a show-with the lights and sweating and stuff."

He looks back up into my face and grabs my chin, pulling my lips to his and kissing me sweetly.

Our lips break apart, and I look to the floor, almost sad. "What?" Jeremy asks me softly.

"You didn't drink because…because you were bored with me or anything, did you?" I cross my arms over my chest. Maybe last night wasn't as good for him as it was for me. I was extremely out of practice, and he was more experienced sexually…

He places his finger under my chin, lifting my face so I can see his blue eyes.

"Dylan, last night…" he begins, and pauses. I see him warring with himself in his eyes. I hold my breath, bracing for the harsh words I am worried are coming. "Last night was amazing. Don't do that to yourself, okay? I…God…" he stops himself again. He smiles at me, and I smile back at him.

After he cleans up the bottles on his floor, we grab some coffee in the kitchen. I tell him about the job Theresa and I managed to get, and he talks about his upcoming tour schedule. It sounds like a long tour, and he rarely has time off. I try to sound excited, but really I'm sad and scared at the thought of him leaving in just under two weeks.

When I look at the clock on the wall above his small kitchen table, I realize it's almost noon. "Wow," I say. "You better start getting ready for your last show tonight." I stand up from where I'm sitting and stretch. My body feels deliciously sore.

Jeremy smiles. "At least I'll have a few days off before I leave." I attempt a smile. He leans against the refrigerator, twirling his empty coffee cup. "I'll have Rich take you home," he says, almost sad.

I stare at him for a moment. His fingers are long and graceful. His neck curves up to his chin, his cheekbones sculpted. His hair is messy this morning, but it looks like it was done professionally that way. I notice his blue eyes meet mine. He stands uncomfortably. "What?" he asks, noticing my scrutiny.

"You're hot," I blurt out. I bite my lip and shake my head at myself. Now I feel really stupid. He probably thinks I'm a weirdo.

Luckily, he begins to laugh uncontrollably. I let out a shaky laugh, too, and hear a ding at the elevator door. He composes himself enough to walk out of the kitchen and step in front of the door before it opens and Rich walks out. I follow behind him. "Hey," Jeremy says, slapping Rich on the shoulder.

"Nice dress," Rich says, nodding at me. I suddenly remember I'm wearing a T-shirt, which is thankfully long, and run down the hallway into the bedroom. I hear Rich and Jeremy laugh together.

My cheeks burn as I take off the t-shirt and throw the gold dress back on. Stupid, stupid, stupid! I walk out and huff as I turn towards Jeremy, still laughing, so he can zip the dress. "I'm glad I amuse you," I say.

When Jeremy finishes zipping the dress, he grabs the tops of my shoulders and turns me around to look at him. Rich turns towards the elevator door and steps in, holding the button so the doors remain open.

"You'll be at the show tonight," Jeremy commands. I nod.

"I'll see you then," he says, kissing me sweetly on the lips. He puts his lips to my ear. "Last night was amazing, and I have more things I want to do to you."

My insides tighten. He releases me and I turn to walk into the elevator. Rich turns the key to go down, and the door shuts, leaving Jeremy standing in his living room.

Rich and I ride down in the elevator silently. I feel the elevator stop and the gold door dings as it opens. Rich steps out of the elevator and holds his hand in front of the door so I can safely step out. He turns and walks beside me. When we reach the main door across the lobby, I don't notice a doorman standing by it, which is strange. Rich opens the door and motions for me to walk out.

When I step onto the pavement, I'm suddenly surrounded by reporters pushing from all sides. They circle me and snap pictures. I quickly put my hands up to my face and freeze. My heart beat rises.

"Dylan, was this the first time you've spent the night with Jeremy?" a woman says, throwing a silver recorder towards my mouth. I smack at it and then move my hands back to my face.

"Dylan, how was he?" a man with a video camera taunts. I'm getting pushed and pulled. My heels almost make me fall over.

"Leave me alone!" I shriek. "No comment!"

I feel claustrophobic, trapped in this sea of people. They surround me; I feel them everywhere. I start to shake, and I'm terrified. Dear God, just get me out of this!

I feel big hands grab my arm and Rich say "Let's go!"

He starts pulling me ahead quickly. I hear the click of a car door opening and he throws me inside and shuts the door. I lock it immediately as Rich climbs in the driver's side. The photographers still click their cameras at me through the window.

Instead of shock or sadness, I'm angry. "Is this what I'm supposed to expect?!" I scream towards Rich as he begins to pull away. The photographers scramble to move out of the way. "This is fucking ridiculous. I'm so over this! Where were your guards?!"

We're passing the lake and getting onto the main street. I don't see anyone following us when I look out of the back window. "I'm sorry Miss Dylan," Rich says, flipping on his turn signal. "They really usually leave Jeremy alone at his apartment. I guess you're causing a lot of news."

"How did they even know I was there?"

I see Rich shrug. "I don't know. Probably paid someone off. I didn't see the doorman there."

I sigh. "Well you can tell Jeremy that I'm not going anywhere anymore unless those reporters can be handled. I'm not just going to take this goddamned harassment!" I'm so mad, I can't control myself. The burning in my stomach feels like a volcano erupted.

"I understand Miss Dylan. No problem." The car stops in front of my house which, luckily, has no reporters in sight. I step out onto the pavement and slam the door behind me without even saying goodbye. I kind of feel like a jerk but I'm so angry and embarrassed. I run up my steps and into my house.

I shut and lock the door behind me. I kick my heels off at the doorway and walk down the hall. Even though it's already 1:00, I put on a pot of coffee in the kitchen. I hear footsteps coming down the hallway.

Theresa is smiling at me, her brown curly hair pulled up into a messy updo. She has on casual jeans and a purple fitted tee. I smile at her and she walks over to me and gives me an excited hug. My anger at the reporters starts to fade.

"How was it?" she inquires.

I sigh. "Spectacular."

She giggles and pulls away from me. "Oh God, I hate you." I laugh.

She plops down on our couch and turns on the TV. I head over to the coffee pot and pour us two cups. "How was your date?" I inquire. I pick up the mugs and begin to walk into the living room.

"Great," she says, extending her hand to reach for her cup. I sit down on the other side of the couch. "I just got home not too long ago."

I laugh. "So is that it for him, then?"

She sighs. "No. I really like him actually. We're going out again tonight."

I inhale in shock. "I know," she says.

"When can I meet...er..." I'm embarrassed that I don't know his name.

"Sean," she says. "Soon I guess. Not tonight though. I know Jeremy is leaving town soon. You have to work in as much time as possible before he leaves you."

Her words make it feel like all the air has been sucked out of my chest. I feel the color run from my face.

"Wow, Dylan. What's wrong?" Theresa says, sitting up more on the couch. "I didn't really mean it that way, but honey, you have to accept it could be a possibility."

"I think I'm falling in love with him." I blurt out.

My mouth hangs open, astonished at my own words. Theresa freezes and her brown eyes get larger. The words hang in the eerie silence.

There. I said it. There it is. My ticket to heart break. How could I be so stupid? How could I let this happen?

Theresa tries to blow it off. "Girl, everyone falls in love with him."

Suddenly, I notice the TV in the background saying something about Jeremy. I turn my eyes towards the screen and see a news reporter, no older than me with pink hair, talking with a picture of Jeremy in the background. Theresa turns up the volume.

"…footage of new girl toy, Dylan, leaving his house in the same outfit she wore the night before." A video of me smacking the silver recorder outside of Jeremy's apartment is shown. The video lasts about twenty seconds, until Rich comes and grabs me and they show me getting into the car.

Fuck, fuck, FUCK!

Theresa turns the TV off. I stand up angrily and march into the kitchen. I put my coffee cup down on the counter and stand there, leaning against it, facing away from Theresa.

It's not like this is embarrassing enough for me, dating a rock star. It's not like I don't know I'm not anything special like he is. Why does the whole world have to know? Why does it have to be broadcast everywhere?

"You're in a heap load of shit, Dylan," Theresa finally whispers.

"Yeah, thanks," I snap.

"Keeping it real!" she says happily. I try not to smile.

Suddenly I hear the phone ring. I walk over to it and look at the caller ID. I recognize my Dad's phone number. I sigh, wondering if I should bother to pick up the phone. I click the answer button, and put it up to my ear.

"Hey, Dad."

"Hey, button," my Dad's warm voice answers. I smile. "How's the place?"

"It's great Dad. It's all set up."

"Uh, huh," he says. I know my Dad really isn't interested in stuff like that, but I appreciate the effort. "Are you preparing for school?"

"Uh, yeah," I lie. I haven't even thought about school the last couple of days. "I got a job at the bookstore."

My Dad sighs. "Dylan, I wish you would take me up on my offer and hold off working for a while. You know I think it's better for you to just concentrate on school."

I roll my eyes. "I know Dad. But I'm going to have a huge amount of loans to pay off from Harvard and you know I like being independent."

"Speaking of concentrating on school..." my Dad clears his throat.

Uh oh. Here it comes.

"I don't know..." he pauses and sighs. I cringe. "I don't know how much I like seeing my daughter on the news leaving a *man's* house." He sarcastically emphasizes the word *man*, to indicate he knows exactly who this man is, and his history.

Ew. Please not with my Dad. Please!

"Then don't watch the news," I snap. I'm so embarrassed now that I just want to crawl under a rock.

"Dylan, don't get defensive. I know you're an adult. I'm just worried about you and your schooling. You worked so hard to get to Harvard." Usually my Dad's warm, soft voice calms my anger, but not this time. I'm just over defending my relationship, especially since the relationship will probably end in less than two weeks.

"I'm *not* defensive. It's just, what do you want me to do? Every girl my age dates. Or is married. I happen to date Jeremy Mason. I have reporters following me. I don't *want* them to follow me, but I can't do anything about it. And I'm not going to lie to you and tell you I'm going to be virginal out here. I'm twenty-two years old for Christ's sake."

"Dylan," my Dad says, trying to stop me. But now I'm on a roll. Theresa stands across from me, eyes wide and hands held up with her palms facing towards me, as if telling me to stop.

"We all know how much *you* like sex. And don't even get me started on how much *mom* liked sex. And *I'm* not screwing the entire student body, or two different married men. Just *one* guy!" I scream

Theresa puts her hand to her mouth. My Dad is silent. For a split second I'm pleased with myself. That shut him up. But then, quickly, I feel like a jerk. He was only concerned for me, in the same ways I'm concerned for myself. I sigh.

"Dylan," he starts. Then he sighs. "Just prove me wrong when school starts. Get good grades. I'll talk to you later." His voice is sad.

"Dad..." I start, but I hear the phone click.

I hang up the phone. Theresa grabs it from me and places it on the receiver. "Wow," she says shocked, but with a hint of pride in her voice.

I walk over and plop down on the couch. I put my head in my hands. Theresa plops next to me. "Now what am I going to do?" I say.

"Well, I think you should have an amazing night with him. Don't pressure him too much. He's a loner, Dylan. He always has been. I've never heard of him with a steady girlfriend. I wish I could tell you better news, but just think of the time you have with him. It will give you better options in the future. Boys are kind of like stepping stones. At least you're finally dating. And you have feelings for someone."

She rubs my back. I know what she's saying is right, but it still hurts to think of him leaving so soon. "I'm going to take a shower," I say. I get up from the couch and walk into the bathroom, shutting the door.

After the shower Theresa does my hair again. This time I let it hang long and straight, the way I usually wear it, but Theresa uses a straightening iron. Tonight she lends me a green strapless dress that fits snug against my body and stops below my knees. The top has a silver strap right underneath my breasts wrapping around me. The green of the fabric really brings out my eyes. I don't put a lot of make-up on; I want to look more like myself than I did the night before. I don't want to feel like it's all a fantasy or dream.

At seven-thirty, the doorbell rings. That will be Rich. I put in my last teardrop silver earring and head to answer the door, sliding into my green high heels on the way. Theresa exits her room as I pass, wearing a little black mini-dress with spaghetti straps. I smile at her. She looks so pretty. I run to the door and open it.

Jeremy stands on my landing, wearing a black collared shirt, unbuttoned to the top of his chest, and dark blue jeans. His dirty blonde hair is in tousled spikes. He rests his right hand on my doorway and leans in. When our eyes meet, he smiles a bright smile, and his blue eyes sparkle.

I smile back at him and he stands straight, gliding towards me. He grabs my chin and pulls it to his face, kissing me hard. He runs his other hand from my hip slowly up to my shoulders. I shudder.

He pulls away and says, "Dylan." I motion for him to come in.

He steps into my house and I close the door behind him. "Dylan, you..." Jeremy says, looking me up and down. Jeremy turns his head as Theresa appears from the kitchen and freezes. She gives Jeremy a warm smile.

"Hi, Theresa," Jeremy says and walks forward gracefully. He puts his arms around her and kisses her cheek. Her eyes bulge open and a goofy smile appears on her face. I roll my eyes. Jeremy steps back from her. "You look lovely."

"Hi. I...date..." she says, pointing at herself. She smiles a ridiculous smile and walks towards the kitchen table where her clutch sits.

Jeremy smiles and walks towards me, extending his hand. I grab it as he opens the door and walks out with me. "Bye Therese!" I call as I shut the door behind me. Jeremy and I start to walk down the stairs.

"You do that to her on purpose," I say, smiling.

He shrugs. "I just want her to like me. I assume her opinion matters a lot to you."

We reach his black car and, surprisingly, he opens the front passenger door for me. I look confused as I get in and notice that there's no driver and no Rich. Jeremy opens the driver's side door, climbing in and reaching for his seat belt. "Where's Rich?" I say, looking in the back seat.

Jeremy starts the car and motions backwards with his thumb. I turn to look through the back windshield and see Rich in a red car behind us, with another big man sitting next to him. I turn around and sit back down as Jeremy pulls away from the curb.

"Why isn't he riding with us?" I inquire.

"Because I want this to feel, you know, as *normal* as possible."

I chuckle. He looks over at me, puzzled, and then back at the road. "What?" he says.

"I'm going to see you perform at your sold out concert on your sold out national tour."

He laughs and sighs. "Rich told me about the reporters this morning. I guess I just want you to feel…normal."

I blush and look at my lap. He's really making an effort with me. I admit I'm shocked and humbled by this discovery. He cares what Theresa thinks of him, because he cares what I think of him. He's going out of his way and ignoring his own safety, by putting distance between us and his body guards, so I can feel normal.

We pull up to the back door of the arena. Luckily, there are no reporters, just the usual few guards. The fans must be at another door again. Jeremy orders me to stay seated as he gets out of the car. I see him walk around the front of the car and over to my door. He opens it and extends his hand.

I laugh and take it as he helps me up. "What a gentleman," I say, sarcastically. He pulls me close to him, wrapping his arms dangerously low around my waist. "Oh, I'm no gentlemen," he croons, soft and low. My stomach tightens.

He lets me go and, grabbing my hand, leads me to the door. When we get inside, he's immediately surrounded by the same group of people. There are the men in business suits, a few groupies, and security guards. One of the guards hands him a beer, which he takes and chugs as we walk down the hall.

I quickly scan the group for the weasel-faced boy from the night before, but I don't see him. There are a few more groupies that I recognize. I'm relieved not to see the pixie or big breasted blonde from what seems like forever ago. He must have kept his word on not keeping them around.

We find his dressing room and the crowd begins to disperse, some shaking Jeremy's hand, some telling him "see you later." Jeremy opens the door for me and I walk in. I see a girl, with blue hair and a spiky collar, standing by the wall across from the door that hasn't left with the others. It looks like she hasn't slept in days. She has dark circles under her eyes, accented by her dark eye make-up. She looks young, maybe eighteen or nineteen, and despite her at first shocking appearance she's quite attractive. She's much skinnier than my size ten. She's probably a zero. Her black mini skirt and ripped up black tank top is made to show off her body.

As soon as Jeremy sees her, he can't take his eyes off of her. I stare at him, strangely, until I see her finally make eye contact back at him. Both of them smile at each other, she in a flirtatious way.

Jeremy turns and smiles at me in the doorway. "I'll be right back. I have some business to take care of, okay? Turn on some music."

I smile and nod, and glance again at the girl. Jeremy kisses my cheek and almost shuts the door, leaving just a crack open. I peer through the crack, watching him walk down the hallway with the girl standing close to him.

My mouth drops open in shock. I hope he knows I did get accepted to Harvard Law. I'm not going to buy that 'I have to take care of business' crap. I can only think of one business *that* chick could be in. And it's not a business I'd want *my* boyfriend to be messing with.

I stomp over and flop down on the red couch, trying not to be mad at him, or think about what he's doing. "Womanizer," my subconscious taunts me again. "Technically," I mentally respond, "he's NOT my boyfriend." I know that won't do anything to quell my anger. But it doesn't make sense that he would leave and go off with her, when I'm here and willing. Would he really go off with that woman while I was here? But if it isn't for something sexual, what possibly could it be for?

I run my hands through my hair. I'm kidding myself if I think I can keep a man like him. He can have anyone. I'm some awkward nerdy kid. I'm not skinny, and I'm not even particularly pretty. Let's face it- even my mom couldn't be bothered with me. The fact that he's paid me any attention at all, and that he's been sweet to me, is miracle enough. But I can't bear the thought of him never being in my life again.

I'm flipping through the music channels on the TV, trying to find something while I'm thinking. Ten or fifteen minutes later, I hear the door squeak open. I purposely don't turn towards him, to make it clear that I'm angry, when I hear a female voice say "Oh!"

I turn quickly around in surprise. Across from me is the big breasted blonde that I had seen the first night I met Jeremy. Only this time, she's clothed and sober…kind of. She has on a white peasant top that flows over her stomach, showing off a lot of cleavage, and light blue jeans. My mouth drops open in shock, and I stand.

"Hi there," she says, staring at me up and down. I furrow my brows at her.

"Hi?" I say as a question.

"Is Jeremy here? One of his guards left me a weird message on my phone saying not to come around anymore?"

"Is that so?" I say, curtly. *Then, why the hell are you here?*

She puts her white leather bag down on the floor and smiles at me. She tosses her blonde hair back with her finger. She laughs. "I assume that was due to you?" She looks me up and down again. "You have pretty eyes, baby," she says.

I freeze, my face hard. Is she flirting with me? "…Thanks?"

She begins to walk towards me. "Will Jeremy be back soon?"

I back up a step. "I don't know," I say, sadly. She stops inches from my face.

"You are very beautiful. I see why he likes you. Though you seem a little…fresh for him."

I stand very still. I'm not sure what she's after.

"Maybe we should give him a show. He loves that." She runs her fingers up and down my arm.

"He does?" I say. My heart sinks a little. That's something I know I'd never do for him. Is that why he keeps extra girls around? Maybe he's into things that he assumes, and probably correctly, I'd never do.

But, I want to keep him. Even if he'll never be completely mine, I know in this moment I'd do anything to have a part of him. To make him happy. I want to show him he doesn't have to go off with other size zero women; that I can do anything he needs me to do.

"Sure," she says, and raises a hand to my face. She really is very attractive, I think, annoyed. Her blue eyes stare into mine.

Hesitantly, she leans forward and kisses me softly on the lips. I'm motionless, disgusted, and unsure of what to do. She continues. I think of Jeremy off with the blue haired girl and my stomach knots.

I decide to kiss back, and she moans. She pulls away after a minute and walks back towards the door. I'm frozen in my place.

She looks both ways down the hallway and steps back inside the room, closing the door behind her. She undoes the strap of her white halter top, letting the top fall and exposing her breasts. She slides the top up over her head, and goes for the button on her jeans.

The woman walks over to me and begins kissing me again. I think immediately of Jeremy. I kiss her back, closing my eyes and thinking of his messy hair. When she grabs the zipper on my dress, I think of his rough hands undressing me. I moan as she kisses down my body, and I think of the scruff of his face against my skin.

Suddenly, as she's on her knees and attempting to get me to lay down on the floor, the door opens. My eyes open at the noise and I see him standing there, mouth open and eyes red.

He turns and slams the door. "Sabrina?!" he screams. "What the fuck?"

She stands and turns towards him. I see her smile from the corner of my eye. "Hey baby. I like this one. Come on over," she beckons to him.

He bends over and scoops up her clothes in one motion. He stands, his face full of glorious rage as he stares at her. Her smile fades when she takes in his expression. He throws the clothes at her, hitting her in the chest as her arms rise to catch them.

"Get. Out." He annunciates each word.

She begins to hastily throw on her underwear and jeans. "I don't understand," she says, breathlessly. "I thought you liked this?"

"Not with you. Not with her. Get out!" he screeches in his beautiful voice. She's tying the string on her shirt when he grabs her forcefully with one hand and opens the door with his other. I take a step backwards, finally moving, and cross my arms over my half-naked body.

He practically throws her out in the hallway as she pleads, "Jeremy!"

"Don't ever contact me again," he growls, and slams the door.

He leans against the door with both hands outstretched, head down. She pounds at the door furiously. "Whatever, you fucking pathetic drunk! You lonely womanizing asshole! Go ahead; tell her how you really are!"

My eyes widen. I can hear a man's deep voice telling her it's time to go, and then the pounding stops and footsteps trail away.

Jeremy doesn't turn, as if he can't even look at me. He's silent, deep in thought. His face looks disappointed somehow; depressed and guilty at the same time. Finally he says, almost in a whisper, "Baby, put your clothes back on."

I feel the urge to cry, but I suppress it somehow. I am horrendously embarrassed. I'm also a little appalled at how he treated someone he hypothetically used to care about. Or at least should have. I adjust my dress and pull up the zipper. The awkward silence between us is almost deafening.

Is he disgusted? Angry? What did I do wrong?

After I am back in my dress, he turns to me. His eyes are still red, as is the skin around his eyes. But his face is softer, almost sad. "Why, Dylan? I know you're not at all like that," he says.

I blink a few times in confusion. "I remember that first night...And then the girl you just left with...I just want to make you happy...I want to satisfy you..."

"You do," he cuts me off. He walks over to me and holds both of my hands. "I don't want you to succumb to my life in any way. To give in to who or what I am. I need to believe there is a girl like you out there who could care for me. The real me. You're my sweet, innocent, smart girl. I would never want you to change who you are for me."

"I *do* care for you," I say, with all the feeling I can put into my voice. His hand leaves mine and strokes my face.

"You don't know me yet. Not all of me. I'm charming, famous, attractive, rich…and I get that." He doesn't say it in a narcissistic way, just stating them as facts no one would refute. "But that's the surface. I am…completely fucked up. Completely."

I'm confused and hurt. Here I am, declaring my feelings for him, and he's not giving me anything in return. And the way he speaks about himself…

My eyes well up.

"Dylan, don't," he says. "I don't want anyone else to touch you. I don't want anyone else to feel you ever again. I want your lips, your body, everything all to myself. I want to be selfish with you. I want you to be mine, even when I'm gone. Don't you let anyone touch you, do you understand?" he says, grabbing my chin. His eyes are sky blue and sparkling like his guitar. I suppose I should be frightened, or disgusted, but instead I'm awestruck.

"Yes," I breathe. As if no was even an option.

He kisses me passionately. I grab him around his neck, holding him to me. I will the tears not to fall down my face. What if I never hold him again after he leaves?

He pulls away from me and looks at the clock. It is twenty minutes till showtime. "I need you now," he says, unbuttoning his pants. He pulls them down and sits on the couch as I remove my dress and underwear once again. I climb on top of him and lean against his chest, my cheek against his.

"Make love to me," he almost begs, in a low sweet voice. "No one makes me feel this way."

I place him inside me, and his bare skin feels good inside my body. It requires him to be very controlled and careful when the time comes, but it's worth it. I trust him.

I try to sit up, but he pulls me closer to his chest again and whispers, "Drown me in you."

I smile and begin to move.

Chapter 7- Official

We exit the dressing room, fully clothed and somehow put together, and are practically attacked by Jeremy's group. They surround us and lead us up to the stage, the same as the night before, and into the wings. I see a chair placed in the same spot I sat before, only this time it has a sign that says 'Miss Ackhart' placed across the back. I blush.

Jeremy is torn away from me by a stagehand. The stagehand hands Jeremy a beer, which he quickly downs, and crushes the can when he's through. I take my seat and watch him grab his silver guitar, throwing the strap over his neck. A woman is furiously playing with his hair again, while another is brushing his face with powder.

He breathes deeply, slow and steady. He turns to me and gives me a quick wink as the women back away. He raises his arm to the sky again and grabs the neck of the guitar with the other. He strums the instrument loudly, and the crowd again goes wild.

The show was the same as the one the night before, but I'm still transfixed by it. Every movement he makes is so graceful. I'll never get used to the way his body moves, or the way it makes me feel when I see him. The crowd screams, the girls wildly attack the stage, and he looks at home.

After he screams, "Goodnight everybody!" into the mic, he runs offstage towards me. I stand and he throws the silver guitar around his back. He gives me a kiss on the cheek before walking over to the men in suits, sitting where they did last night in the wings. They pat him on the back and congratulate him, going over the press schedule for later that night. My heart sinks. I forgot about the press meeting, and it's taking away from our night together.

I see the blue haired girl from earlier appear from the entrance of the stairway. Jeremy spots her, nods towards her, and she heads into the quick change room. Jeremy shakes hands with the men in business suits and walks into the room with her, shutting the door.

My mouth falls open. This can't be happening. My mind races. What should I do? We still really haven't established what our relationship is, but I feel like now this is just disrespectful. I straighten up and march towards the black door. I put my ear up to it, trying to hear what's happening inside. The crowd is still loud as they are exiting the arena, but I distinctly hear Jeremy sigh, "Oh God."

The fire in my stomach is the surface of the sun. I pound hard on the door. I hear scurrying.

"Open this door!" I scream.

"Dylan?" I hear Jeremy yell back in confusion.

"Don't bother putting your clothes back on. Do you think I'm stupid or something?"

I hear them continue to scurry. Finally, the light switches off and the door opens. Jeremy is there, adjusting the sleeve of his black shirt. He looks at me, confused. The girl appears from behind him, carrying a black bag. She scurries out from the room and starts to walk towards the stairs. "Whore!" I scream as she disappears from sight.

"Dylan!" Jeremy says in horror. "You think I'm sleeping with her? How dumb do you think I am?"

"What's she doing then? And who was the guy yesterday, while we're at it?" I cross my arms, full lawyer mode.

"They give me medical supplies for my heat rash. It acts up on stage because I sweat and it's so hot up there."

I laugh. "Please, Jeremy. I'm not one of your dumb groupies. That chick has no access to medical supplies. She's eighteen at the most. And weasel boy is skeevy looking."

He looks down for a moment and then back up at me, his eyes hard and serious.

"Drop it." His voice is firm and cold. It startles me out of my lawyer mode for a minute. He's never used that tone with me.

I pout my lip. "No."

He grabs me by the arm roughly and leads me down the stairs. I drag my feet, making it seem like I didn't want to go with him. Though of course, I kind of did.

I'm dragged through the hallway and out the gray metal door leading to the parking lot. Jeremy releases me and takes out a pack of cigarettes from his jeans pocket. He opens the pack, removing the lighter he has stored in there and a cigarette, and lights it. He takes a drag. He grabs his phone from his pocket and pushes a few buttons, putting it up to his ear,

"Rich!" he says, loud and angry. He takes a drag of his cigarette. "Miss Ackhart is ready." He takes the phone away from his ear and hangs up.

I stand still next to him, my arms crossed. After a few minutes in silence, he turns to look at me. He takes a drag from his cigarette and sighs. "Dylan…" he begins.

"No," I say. The burning in my stomach is probably giving me an ulcer. "Don't 'Dylan' me. I don't want you to see either one of them again. Neither one. Especially her."

"I can't do that, Dylan," he says, sadly. "I'm sorry."

I uncross my arms and look at him, hurt. "Why?"

He shakes his head. "Let's not fight about this. I'm not sleeping with her. There's no reason for this outrageous jealousy." He takes a drag of his cigarette and throws it to the ground. Watching the smoke escape from his lips makes me melt, and the fire dies down a little.

"I don't want to hurt you, Dylan," he begins. He grabs my hand. "But this is what I am. This is me. Sometimes I wonder if it wouldn't be better if I just never talked to you again."

The words cut me like a knife. "No!" I blurt out. What am I doing? I'm pushing him away. I panic. "No! Forget it. It's not a big deal. I'm sorry!"

What? Shut up Dylan, no you're not...

He shakes his head. "No. You have a right to know, but I just can't tell you. And..."

The panic almost drowns me. "Forget it! Please!"

Damn it! I'm not this girl! I'm not the girl that gives up on her ideals for a man. I never understood those girls. I never wanted to be those girls.

I hug him tightly around the neck and he grabs my waist. He chuckles. "Sweet, jealous Dylan."

I smile.

Damn it if I'm not one of those girls.

Jeremy asks before I get in the car if he could meet me after the press conference at my place. I don't ask him why, but I know it's because of the reporters. They would never expect Jeremy Mason to stay somewhere else, even at my house. I call Theresa and, after discovering that her date went well and she is planning to stay at Sean's, I agree excitedly to let him stay.

Jeremy opens the door to his black car and lets me slide into the back. I say 'hi' to Rich, who nods, and look back up at Jeremy.

"See you in a little while," he says, smiling.

I sigh. "Okay."

Jeremy closes the door and Rich puts the car in drive, speeding off towards my house. We pass the buildings that have become familiar to me on the way home. I wouldn't need a GPS to get to the arena anymore, and it's comforting that Boston is starting to feel a little more like home.

"Miss Dylan," Rich says from the front seat, stopping my daydreaming.

"Hmmm?" I say.

"When do you start school?" he says. I furrow my brow.

"In, like, two weeks. Why?"

"I'm just trying to see what my schedule's going to be like over the next few weeks." Rich flips on his turn signal and stops at an intersection. He makes a turn.

"What?" I say, even more confused.

"You know, when I take you to school and whatever."

"Take me to school?"

Rich stops in front of my house. Luckily, I note quickly, no reporters. I assume everyone is at the press conference. Rich turns and looks at me, just as confused as I must look.

"I'm staying behind in Boston, at least for a few weeks. Didn't you know?" He turns and exits the car on the driver's side and stalks around the front of the car. I sit in shock as he opens the door and holds a hand out for me.

"Wait, what? You're not leaving with Jeremy?" I grab his hand and exit the car. We walk side by side up the stairs.

"He thinks you need some extra security for a while after he leaves," Rich says. We reach the top of the stairs and pause outside of the door.

I turn and look at him, and he looks back at me. "But, he needs you…" I say.

Rich shrugs. "I guess he thinks you need me more."

I ponder that statement as we continue to stare at each other. "Is this," I begin, "something he normally does? For his other women?"

Rich laughs. "No, not even close."

He tries to open the door but notices it's locked. I pull the key from the top of my dress and unlock it. He allows me in first and I shut the door behind him when he enters.

Immediately, I kick my shoes off. My feet hurt so bad in heels. I guess I have to get used to them.

"Want something to drink?" I ask, walking towards the kitchen. I'm dying of thirst.

"Oh no, thanks," Rich says. "I'm just going to go wait at the arena for the conference to end."

I open the fridge and remove a bottle of wine. It's full, so I open it and pour myself a glass. I'm not much of a drinker, but I need to calm my nerves.

"No, Rich. Stay a while. I'm alone here." I walk back into the hallway and see him standing by the door.

He nods. "Okay. We can watch the press conference."

"Oh," I say in shock. "That's going to be on TV?"

Rich walks into my living room, passing me. "You bet."

He plops down on my couch and turns on the TV with the remote. He flips through the guide and finds a channel. I see Jeremy on TV, with gorgeous sweat running down his face, a cigarette hanging from his mouth. He's leaning back in his chair and listening to a question. The conference has already begun. I sit down on the other side of the couch from Rich, putting my legs up and curling them under me. I take a small sip of the light red wine, and listen intently.

"When is the next album due out?" I hear a woman ask from off camera.

A man in a suit, one that I've seen sitting in the wings, answers her. "Mr. Mason is currently working on new tracks for the album, which will be out hopefully next spring."

Jeremy takes a drag on his cigarette and blows smoke from his mouth. He looks bored. Painfully bored.

"Why isn't he answering anything?" I ask Rich, my eyes not leaving Jeremy's face.

"He don't like the press. Really, he's very shy."

I scoff. There is no way that man is shy. His cockiness alone is enough to disprove any shyness. But then I think back to Jeremy the boy. The boy who had to work all of his life for affection, and never received the approval he so badly needed. The boy who was too smart for his own good; who can't relate to people of normal intelligence…who understands all too well the character of people. And I begin to understand why Jeremy might be so shy.

The sound of my name brings my focus back to the conference. "…Dylan Ackhart on tour?" a man's voice from the crowd says.

"Miss Ackhart will not be accompanying Mr. Mason on tour. She will stay here in Boston. Any other questions not involving Miss Ackhart?" the man in the suit says.

The same male voice from the crowd presses on. "Will she stay here in Boston to start her classes at Harvard?"

I take a big gulp of wine. Rich looks at me from the corner of his eyes, and looks back at the screen. The man in the suit opens his mouth to speak, but Jeremy sits up and leans into his microphone that's placed on the table.

"I hope all of you understand that Miss Ackhart is to be left alone while I'm on tour. If she is bothered in any way, my lawyers and I will not hesitate to press charges, and I will never attend a press conference again. Not one."

The room is suddenly silent. The man in the suit's face turns red. "What Mr. Mason means to say is that Miss Ackhart will not be in contact with him after he leaves, and therefore, there is no reason to bother her. But we appreciate all of your support."

Jeremy gets up and begins to walk away from the table. "This is all a fucking waste of time," he scoffs. The camera shows the backside of him exiting through a doorway.

The footage cuts back to a news anchor, who looks caught off guard as she babbles on about the sudden exit. I take another huge gulp of wine and finish my glass.

Rich turns off the TV. "I better go get him, if you still want." He peers at me out of the corner of his eyes.

Of course I'm devastated, but I try to look bored. "Yeah, go and get him." I stand up and walk to the counter in the kitchen, pouring another glass of wine. I put the glass to my lips and tip the whole thing into my mouth.

Rich clears his throat and stands up. He strides down the hall. "Be back," he says, opening the door and shutting it behind him.

My cell phone vibrates from inside of my bra. I jump, then reach in and grab it, putting it to my ear without looking. "Hello?"

"Hey," Theresa's voice says, sadly.

"Yep," I say. I have a head rush from the wine. I'm such a lightweight.

"Don't let this get the best of you. Stepping stones."

I scoff again. "Right." How could you step off from Jeremy? Onto what?

Theresa sighs. "Have a great night together. Try not to be too mad."

"Okay, Therese. Bye."

"Bye."

I hang up the phone, putting it on my kitchen counter. I see lights flashing outside from my front windows, red and blue. I walk up and open my door a crack to look outside. I see four or so police officers removing people from the sidewalk across the street. Some were professional photographers, I could tell from the cameras, and some looked like regular fans. All came to see my reaction to the press conference I guess. I sigh and shut the door, amazed that I'm no longer surprised to see photographers around my house.

I walk down the hallway and sit on my couch in the living room. As soon as I sit, I hear the door open. I stand up again immediately, peering down the hallway. I see Jeremy's back as he closes and locks the doors, and hear a few shrieks and cries for him. I roll my eyes, although my stomach tightens at the sight of him. He turns and faces me, his black shirt fully unbuttoned now, jeans riding low. He leans against the door, and smiles wryly at me.

I smile back. I figure that Theresa is right. I try to be nice.

"Dylan," he says, low and sexy.

"Mr. Mason."

He struts down my hallway. "What am I going to do when I can't see you every day?"

he says, walking up to me. He stops and stands in front of me.

"Oh, I'm sure you'll get distracted easily enough. Especially since you won't be speaking with me anymore."

His eyes sparkle at me. "Don't you know not to believe everything you hear?" He puts his hand on my cheek.

My eyes expectantly well up with tears. He smiles. "Dylan, if you want to be in my life, you have to accept certain things about me. People are going to say nasty things. You have to harden up."

I look down and take his hand off my cheek. "I didn't ask to date someone famous. I don't benefit at all from it."

"Well, that's a statement I've never heard."

I look up at him. He still looks amused. I don't like it, and my stomach burns and my heartbeat picks up pace.

"Well, I don't! I wish you were just normal. I wish you didn't have to go on long tours. I wish you weren't followed."

"Please, Dylan," Jeremy says, collapsing gracefully on my couch. "Like you'd give a damn about me if I were 'normal'," he spits out the word.

I roll my eyes. The burning in my stomach makes words come out of my mouth before my brain can even comprehend what

I'm saying. "Jeremy, don't start that crap. I'm not your parents. I don't want to be famous. I'm a normal girl who just wants a normal boyfriend. I'm not some smut who's going to fuck you whenever you want and let you go off on tour and not speak to you for months. I don't want that part of your life. Maybe I *should* just go and get a normal boyfriend."

I look down at him as his eyes burn into me, like dark blue storm clouds. He stands, and grabs my arm roughly. "You won't leave. I want you. I want you here for *me*. And I don't want anyone else to touch you."

"So, what then? You just want me to sit around and wait here for you while you get to do whatever you want? You think you get to do that because you're a big hot-shot rock star? You need to learn that sometimes things won't go your way." I struggle to get away from his hand, but he tightens his grip even more.

"I can't bear the thought of you with anyone else!" he almost yells. His voice is low and rough. "I do what I do just for physical pleasure. I know you aren't like that. It would mean something more to you. I don't know how to be any other way. My whole life for the past ten years has been about making myself happy and doing what I want, and I don't have the energy to change now. I will fucking lose it. So what do you want?! Do you want me to lose it?!" he shakes me as he talks. We pause.

His words from earlier flash in my mind. *'I'm fucked up. Completely.'*

Suddenly, I feel a little afraid. His eyes are angry and glassy. I feel the fire in my stomach start to lessen. I put my hand up to his face, stroking his cheek. His hand loosens on my arms and he closes his eyes. "I want you," I begin, slowly. "And I don't want anyone else to touch you." I repeat his words, but in a sweeter way. His eyes open when my hand falls from his face, and they are calm again, bluer than the sky.

He sighs. After a few quiet minutes, he opens his mouth to speak. "Okay. Okay, Dylan. I'll try for you," he surrenders. "I don't know how to have a relationship. I don't know if I can handle a relationship. But I'll try. But Jesus, Dylan…" his voice cracks. "I'm so close to the edge here…"

I am taken aback by the emotion in his eyes. I don't understand why he's so unhappy and hurting. I realize that I am beginning to see Jeremy the person, not Jeremy Mason the legend. I know now there are a lot of things I haven't discovered about him yet. He's not a tough as nails playboy. He's a mentally ill, sad little boy, who can't connect to anyone. A thought crosses my mind suddenly. I'm trying to force him to be ready, but am *I* ready to take responsibility for someone like *him*?

I wrap my arms around his neck and pull myself near to him, feeling his body close to me. Do I even have a choice now on whether or not to continue this? I don't think I could breathe without knowing I could speak to him again or be with him again. I put my cheek against his. His breathing is hard and heavy; obviously he's trying not to cry. "I'll hold you together. I won't hurt you."

He sighs. I feel wetness on my neck. "Take me to bed, sweet Dylan," he says, and runs his fingers through my hair.

I stand back and look at him. His face still has a sheen of sweat, his eyes beautiful and glassy. cheeks look unbelievably chiseled in the light, aided by the dark black scruff on his face. His lips are pale pink, and I watch them turn up in a smile. The realization hits me that this brilliant, gorgeous man is somehow now officially mine.

I run my arms up his bare chest and push the shirt off from his shoulders. It falls to the floor. I lean over and kiss along his collar bone. He sighs, grabbing my hair. I trail my fingers down his chest, letting my fingernails dig into him.

"Careful," he says breathlessly. "We won't make it to the bed."

I stand up straight and look in his eyes, undoing my zipper and letting my dress fall to the floor. I step out of it. "Good," I say, low and deep.

He grabs my chin hard. "Oh, Miss Ackhart." He kisses me hard, biting my bottom lip. He pulls away. "You're in trouble," he says, his eyes burning with desire.

He releases my face and grabs the side of my bra, ripping it. I gasp. He grabs my arm and leads me into the kitchen, throwing me against the counter. I stumble and catch myself on the edge, holding myself up on my outstretched arms. He presses against the back of me and runs his hands down my back. I moan. I feel him unbutton his pants and hear them hit the ground. He grabs the side of my underwear and rips them open. I see them tossed into the dining room. I'm so excited, I could burst. He grabs my hips and enters me.

The next few days go on much the same way. We either sleep at his house or mine. Although we prefer to stay at my house, on the rare occasion Theresa is home, we stay at his place. The idea of her hearing us carrying on is deathly embarrassing to me. Although I'm sure she wouldn't mind it.

We really don't go out much, and I wonder if it's because Jeremy is trying to spare me from the reporters. They've been relentless lately. I'm constantly in the paper. They even went so far as to get my old high school photos. Ugh!

We would lie around pretty much all day. Cuddling, watching TV…it all seemed very normal. I would read as he would compose on the piano or play his guitar. We cooked dinner together. I was surprised he was a good cook. He constantly sang, and the home was filled with music all the time. My favorite would be when he would walk up to me, still singing, and pull me into his arms, dancing with me. It was all very romantic.

Sometimes, though, he felt distant from me. He would take long showers at least three times a day. He would wake up at night and leave the bed, thinking I was asleep, and not come back for a few hours. I wondered how he could be functioning on such little sleep, but when I questioned him on his insomnia, he simply told me that he had always been that way. I attributed it to him having bad dreams. I even caught him one night sweating and twitching in his sleep, and when I woke him up, he immediately left the bed and went into the bathroom to shower.

Eventually I think cabin fever caught up to us, and he suggested that we go out to dinner. I was honestly nervous, but it sounded so nice to get out in the world with him. As nice as our own private heaven was, I knew we'd eventually have to get back to the real world. It seemed like it would be easier to slowly adjust instead of it being thrown on me all at once.

Unfortunately, I have a feeling it might backfire in our faces.

Chapter 8- Reporter

We decided to go somewhere casual and dress inconspicuously. We even told his security that they wouldn't be needed tonight, much to Rich's dismay. When we leave his apartment, we are relieved to see no reporters outside of his building, and Jeremy takes me over to the parking lot, leading me to a silver Honda Civic.

I look at him, bewildered, as he reaches in his pocket for a set of keys and clicks the button to make the car unlock. He opens the passenger door for me. "A Honda?" I question him, surprised.

He smiles at me and shrugs. "Yeah?"

"Well, I just thought you'd have a Ferrari or something."

He chuckles as he helps me into the seat. He leans in the door and smiles a childlike smile. He almost does look normal tonight, young and happy. "On the rare occasions I do go out alone, I'd rather not draw attention to myself." He shuts the door and begins to walk to the other side of the car.

Well, I guess that does make sense.

He climbs into the driver's side. "Besides, they're good cars."

We drive not far from his building to a little corner eatery. We manage to find a parking spot on the street relatively easily, just around the corner. We have to walk just a little ways to the door of the restaurant and, as Jeremy opens the door for me, we enter.

The restaurant is small and mostly empty. It's decorated in maroon colors and has dim lights. The host, stationed just in front of the door behind a table, smiles at us. He is young, probably college-aged. I can feel Jeremy tense a bit, his hand squeezing mine. I tense too. Will he recognize us?

When we reach him, he simply introduces himself, welcomes us, and sits us at a table in the back. After he hands us the menus, he walks away. We sigh in relief. He didn't seem to recognize Jeremy.

It was a nice steakhouse type of menu. Jeremy and I discuss what looks good and what doesn't- a very normal type of conversation. I love that I just feel like a normal woman on a normal date with the man I am falling in love with.

The waitress is an older woman, and takes our order very casually. When she walks away, we figure it's going to be smooth sailing the rest of the night.

After a lot of laughter, snuggling, kisses, and a good meal, we rise from the table. Jeremy leaves a generous tip for our waitress, and we head out of the door to head to the car. Jeremy grabs my hand, rubbing his finger along the outside of it, both of us smiling like high school kids as we round the corner to the street where his car is parked.

Suddenly, we hear people yelling. Before we can even turn our heads or react, we're surrounded by photographers. The now familiar sight of flashing lights and microphones being pushed in my face starts again, but this time we have no security.

"No comment," Jeremy says, angrily.

"On a date? Are you two serious?" a reporter asks.

Jeremy ignores them and tries to make his way through the paparazzi. I keep my hand over my eyes, shielding my face. I'm panicked and claustrophobic again. My breathing increases and I begin to shake. Jeremy holds my hand tighter and tries to pull me harder through the crowd. We're barely making progress.

"She's not really your type, is she Jeremy?" one male reporter torments.

He turns immediately to glare at him. "Enough," he says, low and angry. The reporter just smiles at him.

From the other side of the crowd, a man with a video camera says, "Pretty girl- but definitely not the model type, eh, Jer? Kind of a cow, isn't she?"

I freeze, shocked. I turn and look at the man, confused. I'd never been called fat before.

Sure, I'm a size ten, but I have big hips and I'm tall. My feelings are immediately hurt. The man looks directly at me, pointing his camera at us and says provocatively, "More cushion for the pushin'."

Jeremy unexpectedly releases my hand. He runs at the man, grabbing his camera and smashing it. The crowd's cameras click furiously now, and the man provoking us looks suddenly afraid.

Jeremy doesn't stop moving towards him. The man backs into the brick wall of the restaurant, unable to escape. Jeremy, gloriously livid, brings his fist back and hits the man in the jaw.

The man grunts and falls to the ground. Jeremy jumps on top of him, flipping him around and punching him in the face again. The reporters do nothing to help the man or pull Jeremy off, they just continue clicking their cameras. Jeremy repeatedly punchs him. He screams, "Don't you *dare* talk about her that way. I'll fucking kill you. I swear to God."

When I snap out of my shock, I run over to Jeremy, pulling at his shoulders. "Jeremy, don't!" I yell, frantic. "He's not worth it. Please!"

Jeremy stands, putting his arm around me. The man lays on the ground, still conscious next to his broken camera. He looks a Jeremy through the blood on his face, terrified.

Jeremy gives him a kick in the ribs. The man curls up, moaning. "You piece of shit," he says, turning from him and leading me to his car. The reporters let us go now pretty easily. I assume it's because they got their story. Boy, did they.

Eventually, I notice as I'm in my seat waiting for Jeremy to come around to the driver's side, some of the reporters did help the man. Jeremy begins to drive away frantically.

"Someone at that fucking restaurant must have called them. Goddamnit. Anything for free press," Jeremy spits, beating his hand against the steering wheel.

We sit in the car in silence for a few moments, Jeremy fuming, me processing. "Jeremy," I say, quietly, breaking the silence. "You're going to get arrested. What's wrong with you?"

Jeremy looks at me and tries to smile. "I won't get arrested. He'll threaten me with charges and my legal team will settle it out of court. I'll unfortunately have to pay that fucker a shit ton of money, but it was worth it. I will never, ever, have someone talk to you or about you that way," he vows.

I relax a little about Jeremy getting arrested. I'm sure he's been in situations like this before. I remember from the few times I did pay attention to news stories of him before we started dating that he had gotten into fights quite often.

Not having to worry about him getting arrested allows me to feel the heartbreaking sadness and fear that I had pushed aside in my concern for him. The fear of those reporters in my face and the stress it causes me. My fragile self-esteem and their mean words. I sit silently, trying not to cry.

Jeremy sighs, looking over at me. "Baby, are you alright?" he says, quietly, emotion and worry filling his every syllable.

The sound of his voice sends me over the edge. I begin to cry. No, I begin to sob. I never sob. Well...never in front of anyone.

I'm sure I look like a mess. I should be stronger than this. I don't want him to think I can't handle being with him. *Shit, Dylan. Get yourself together. Stop! Stop!* But the tears continue, an ugly sound escaping my throat. Fat? Me? I look down at myself, grabbing at my stomach in surprise.

"Goddamnit!" I hear Jeremy scream, pulling the car over on the side of the road. I jump, and it makes my sobbing calm a little. He turns to me after he parks the car, his eyes both angry and sad.

"Dylan, I am so, so sorry," he says, putting his hand on my cheek. I turn my face into it. He leans his body over and embraces me. "Dylan, you're beautiful. You have no idea how spectacular I think you are."

I put my eyes on his shoulder and nod my head. It's strange to see him being so sweet after watching him beat someone until they were barely conscious. Actually, I think, in a way I guess that was sweet too. He said he would protect me. No one has ever protected me against anything. Maybe, just maybe, he does care for me more than I think he does.

I smile despite myself, and he notices my cheek rise. "See?" he says. "I think..." he stops for a moment. "I think you finally understand how I'm beginning to feel. I..." he stops again, and my heart stops. I don't look at him and he doesn't continue, he just smooths my hair.

"What a way to spend my last night here. I am so sorry," he apologizes.

My heart squeezes in sadness. "Just take me home," I say, trying my best to sound seductive. He backs away from me, smiling wryly, looking amazing. We drive to my house and, although early, we head straight to the bedroom.

I hear the alarm go off from my phone that's resting on my nightstand. I moan and rub my eyes, shutting the alarm off. It's nine in the morning. Strangely, I don't remember setting an alarm. I sit up in bed, and turn to look at Jeremy. He sleeps silently, breathing deeply. I smile and stretch. We haven't gotten more than two hours of sleep the whole night.

I get out of bed naked and walk into the kitchen. I start a pot of coffee and practically dance into the bathroom. I turn the shower on and allow it to get warm. After I go to the bathroom, I slide in.

A few minutes later, I hear the door crack open. I smile. "Hey, baby," I say.

"Dylan?" I hear Jeremy say. He sounds strange, like he's sick. Confused, I pull the curtain back. He stands with boxer shorts on, hands at his sides. He looks a little pale, but still stunning. His hands are shaking, even though by now the bathroom is filled with steam.

"God, Jeremy. Are you cold?" I nod towards his hands.

He looks down quickly and then looks back at me, smiling a little. "Excuse me," he says, leaving the bathroom. I close the curtain again and finish shaving and washing my hair. About twenty minutes later, I walk out of the bathroom in a white towel and in to my bedroom. Jeremy isn't in there, and his clothes aren't on the floor anymore.

I search in my drawers for underwear and a bra. I have to remind myself to buy more if he's going to keep destroying mine. I smile and throw on plain white underwear and a white bra. I find a suitable plain green tank top and a dark pair of blue jeans.

I walk out of my room, running the towel through my hair, and into the kitchen. Jeremy stands with his back to me and a bottle of wine held up in the air, pressed to his lips.

I laugh and he turns. "Wine at ten o'clock?" I say.

He takes the bottle from his lips and walks over to my trashcan, pushing the button for the lid to pop up and throwing it in. I hear it clang against another glass item inside.

"I don't like flying. Nervous." He shrugs.

I put the towel down on the table and give him a funny look. I don't remember seeing anything glass in my trashcan yesterday. His eyes are wide as I walk over to the trashcan to investigate, and push the button so that it opens. "Dylan..." Jeremy begins, then stops.

Inside the trash, I see three empty bottles of wine that I know were full when I came home last night. Two of them Theresa and I store in the back of a cabinet, just in case we have people stop by. The other was the bottle I had two glasses from a few nights ago. But there they are in the trash, now empty.

God, please tell me Theresa came home and entertained people and I somehow magically didn't wake up.

I look up at him, my eyes wide. "Did you drink all of these?"

He stands silently and his phone rings. He doesn't look away from me as he digs in his pocket and puts the phone up to his ear.

"Yeah? Okay," he says, and pushes a button to hang up.

I cross my arms.

"Yeah, I drank them. Nervous..."

I sigh, angrily. My mind goes back to the second time I was in the dressing room, when there were bottles everywhere. Then I remember when I woke up at his place and discovered all of the bottles scattered across the floor. Now that I think about it, during the days we spent together, I can't recall him not being near some kind of alcohol. And now here? My mouth drops open. How could I be so stupid?

"Jeremy, do you have a problem?" my voice is both sad and shocked.

He laughs. "No!" he says, pretending to be insulted by my question. I can tell he's lying. He's trying too hard to play it off. When he sees my expression isn't changing from shock and horror, he stops laughing and his face turns serious.

I walk over to him, and he crosses his arms and looks at the floor. I put my hand on his arm and try to get him to look at me. "Drop it," he says, trying to be forceful.

"Why don't you ever seem drunk?" I say, stunned at his basic validation of my accusation. An alcoholic? The things just keep piling up with him.

He looks up at me. "I'm not talking about it with you, okay? This is why I think maybe it's better if we just part. And you don't even know the half of it..." he starts, his eyes cold.

I feel the panic begin in my body. "No, no! Okay. Just promise me you'll try and get some help?" I say, stroking his cheek.

Dylan, you coward.

He scoffs. "Okay, Dylan. I'll get some help for my imaginary problem." He turns and almost shakes me off of him, grabbing two cups from my cabinet and pouring coffee into both. I see scratch marks down the side of his chest, and I blush. His stubble is dark against his cheek, I like the way it looks on him.

He hands me a cup of coffee, and I sip it and smile gratefully, trying to calm his mood. He sips his coffee and I see his pouty lips smile around the cup. He puts his free arm around me.

"I have to stop at the record store before I catch my plane. You want to come?" he kisses my forehead.

I smile. "Of course. What do you have to do there?"

He sips his coffee. "I have to pick up a check from the owner so I can send it to my mom."

I look at him, confused, over my coffee cup. Jeremy sighs. "Hal was my dad. You know, 'Hal's Records'."

My mouth drops open. He raises his eyebrows for a minute and takes a sip from his cup.

"Oh, and the owner is making payments?"

Jeremy nods. "The new owner is my uncle. My mom and my uncle don't really get along. My uncle thinks it's her fault my dad committed suicide and stuff like that. So I pick up the checks and deposit them for my mom. It's all really fucked up."

"Sounds like it," I say, taking the coffee from his hand and putting both of our cups in the sink.

I hear the doorbell ring before I turn back to him. I give him a confused look.

"That's probably Rich," Jeremy said sadly, grabbing my hand.

I stand up straight and my heart beats like a hummingbird. "Already? Why? When's your plane?"

He squeezes my hand. "Noon."

I take my phone out of my jeans pocket and look at the clock. Ten-thirty. I sigh.

Jeremy leads me to the front door, opening it a crack to let Rich in. Rich walks in and hands him a pair of black jeans and a blood red silk shirt. He releases my hand and bends down to put on his pants. Rich pats me on the shoulder.

I smile at him and sigh again. Jeremy throws his shirt on as I put on my wedge sandals. After Jeremy is fully dressed, he grabs me by the hand and leads me through the door. Rich follows behind us and shuts the door behind him. I lock the door and turn again, walking hand in hand with Jeremy down the stairs. I barely notice the reporters across the street, clicking their cameras, and the girls screaming for him. As long as they are at a comfortable distance from me, I can more or less ignore them.

Rich opens the back car door for us, and I slide in, allowing room for Jeremy to sit next to me. The three of us are very silent. Rich gets in the front seat and puts the car in drive, pulling away from the curb. Jeremy sits with his arm around me. I nestle into his body.

We stop what seems like only a short time later in the parking lot behind the record store. Jeremy kisses me quickly and opens the door. "Wait here," he says, climbing out of the car. He runs into the back door and I see it shut. Rich and I remain in the car in silence until Jeremy appears again, running back into the car. He slides in and shuts the door, putting his arm around me again.

"That was fast," I say, whispering. I like the silence in the car.

"He left the check in the back room for me."

I look up into Jeremy's eyes. They are grey today, not unlike the color of his guitar. His hair shines in the light from the window, almost looking white, but in the shade it turns dirty blonde again. He peers down at me with a smile. "You're beautiful, baby," he whispers.

I place my hand on his chest. I look out the window, not recognizing where we are. "Where are we going?" I ask.

"To a private air field. I have a plane waiting there," he says quietly. I turn my attention back to him, and he leans down and kisses me. We kiss for the next few minutes, and then the car stops. I break away from him and notice a large building out of my window.

Jeremy turns and looks out of the window, and then turns his head back to me. His face is pale. "This is me."

Rich puts the car in park and pops the trunk. He opens the door and exits, shutting it behind him as he walks to the trunk.

I take a shaky breath in. "Okay."

"We'll say goodbye here."

I feel panic in my chest. A lump forms in my throat. I thought I had at least a few minutes to prepare inside the airport. I try to compose myself.

"Goodbye," I say, my voice cracking.

He laughs. I furrow my eyebrows at him. "Is that all you got?" he says, amused. He smile is sparkling white.

"Aren't you upset?" I ask, a little hurt, even while blinded by his beauty.

He shakes his head. "I know I'll see you again soon. I know you're mine. I know Rich will keep you safe."

I sigh. "You really don't have to leave him with me."

He puts his finger to my lips. I shut up immediately. Rich knocks twice on the window, a signal to hurry it up. I clutch at his shirt. I know if he leaves, I'll probably never see him again. He'll forget me. Why wouldn't he?

I try to hold onto last night, and the way he protected me from the reporter. That's the real Jeremy. That's how much he cares for me.

He takes his arm from around me and grabs my hands. He lifts them up to his lips and kisses them. "Bye, baby. I'll call you tonight. I'm going to Cleveland first for two days. Okay?"

My breathing increases. "Okay."

I see him turn, and time passes in slow motion. He opens the door and gets out. He turns back towards me and hesitates a moment as men come up and grab his insane amount of luggage. He shuts the door and stares at me through the window. I scoot closer, trying not to look like a complete mess. Fans start to run at him, trying to claw at him as security holds them back. How do these girls even know where he'll be?

Rich gets back in the front seat and shuts his door. Jeremy and I don't lose eye contact until one of the guards grabs his arm and turns him, leading him inside the building as Rich speeds away.

I didn't realize I had begun sobbing until I hear Rich from the front seat. "Sorry, Miss Dylan."

Chapter 9- Tuition

I wake up the next morning around eleven. I got horrible sleep last night. When I got home, Theresa was there to greet me, and she held me most of the night as I sobbed. I actually didn't think it would hit me this hard. I clutched my phone in my hand all night, waiting for it to ring. But it never did.

I saw footage of him getting on the plane on the news. He looked fine. He was even smiling and waving to the fans. It hurt me so bad to see that he looks normal and I'm a mess. Then I saw a few people getting onto the plane after him: men in business suits, of course, and a few select crew members. But the real breaking point for me was noticing the blue haired girl and the weasel boy getting on the plane, only a few feet behind him on the stairway. The blue hair girl touched his back on the way into the plane.

I cried harder after that. For hours. And he never called.

I rub my eyes, trying to rub the memory out with it. I sit up and stretch and realize that I'm not alone in the bed. I hear a low moan and look quickly to my left, seeing Theresa stirring. She opens her brown eyes.

"Hey," I say quietly.

"Hey," she says, sitting up.

She lifts her hand and runs her fingers through my hair. I close my eyes tightly. "Don't. Please. I'll lose it."

She drops her hand and turns, putting her feet on the floor. "I'm going to make coffee. And then I'm going to check if our classes are posted online yet" she says excitedly, obviously trying to distract me. She walks out of the room happily.

Robotically, I check my phone, but there are no missed calls. I try to calm the disappointment in my heart. *You knew this could happen.*

I get out of bed and go into the bathroom, turning on the shower. I'm scared to look at what the crying fit last night has done to my face. I'm probably swollen and red. I peel my clothes off and climb into the bath. I let the warm water run down my body. I think about his warm smile. How he says my name.

A few minutes later, I hear the door to the bathroom open. "Dylan?" Theresa says. She sounds shocked.

I open the curtain a bit and stick my head out. "Huh?" I see Theresa holding the laptop in her hand.

"I went online to check for my first semester bill, but it shows it was paid already…"

"Really? It must be a mistake or something. Hold on," I say turning off the shower. "I'm getting out."

I hear Theresa leave the bathroom, and I step out onto the mat and wrap myself in a towel. I throw my wet hair up in another towel, crossing the hallway to my bedroom and going straight to my drawers. It's a sweatpants kind of day, I can tell already.

After I'm dressed in a light blue T-shirt and grey yoga pants, I walk out into the living room. I see Theresa sitting at our dining room table, still clicking around on the screen.

"Here," I say, pulling up a chair next to her. "Let me log in."

I log out of her account and into my own. I pull up the e-bill and stare at the account balance. My classes are listed and the price for my classes, but it also says my account balance is zero.

"See?" I say, looking at her. "Must be a problem with the site."

Theresa looks at the screen and then back at me. "Yea, but the bill is due in less than two weeks. Maybe we should call someone."

I roll my eyes at her. I stand up from the table and grab our portable phone. I have Theresa read me the number at the top of the bill for the Bursar's office. I give the cheerful woman who answers my call my name and student ID number.

"Uh huh, what can I do for you?"

"Well, I wanted to know the balance of my account."

"You don't owe us anything as of right now," the woman says, happily.

My brows furrow. That's impossible. Theresa raises her eyebrows at me.

"How is that possible? I didn't pay anything…"

"It looks like you recently changed your billing address online. To a law office here in Boston?" the woman asks.

"No, I didn't do that."

"Well, someone from that office paid your bill, sweetie. It looks like the check was written from some sort of trust."

My mouth hits the floor. After the woman asks me if I'm still there, I snap back to life. I give her Theresa's name and ID number, and put Theresa on the phone.

Theresa talks to her for a few minutes and discovers her account has also been paid from the same office. *Okay. That rules out my Dad.*

I sit down at the table as Theresa hangs up the phone. We stare at each other for a minute. Theresa is the first to speak. "There's only one person I know who could afford this," she says, and shoots me a huge grin. "We owed over ten thousand."

I smile at her.

"But why? He didn't call like he said he would. And how? Did he hack into our accounts to change the billing address? I don't understand..." Well, I guess he could have had someone do it for him. When you have enough money, I suppose nothing is impossible.

I turn back to the computer and click around some more, trying to find the address of the law office. After searching around to no avail, I decide to try to search for high-end law firms here in Boston through a search engine. I figure if the lawyers are Jeremy's it should be a well-known firm. Theresa pulls out her cell and says she'll search as well.

When I type in the web address for a search engine, it loads a colorful page with streaming news articles under the search bar. Immediately, I notice Jeremy's face in a picture. He's wearing a blue shirt and light black jacket. Initially, I'm overtaken by how beautiful he is. I smile.

Although, now that I look more closely, I notice he's barely standing. He's being basically carried out of some kind of restaurant by two members of his security that I recognize. Behind him follows a group of beautiful women, including the blue-haired girl that followed him onto the plane. The heading underneath the picture says, "Jeremy Mason Parties in Cleveland."

I freeze, my mind shutting down as a defense mechanism. Slowly, I move the pointer and click on the story. A page pops up, showing the picture again with a story underneath. According to the story, Jeremy and his group of 'young men and stunning women' arrived at the bar after his show and drank for over four hours. A witness in the bar said Jeremy drank so much that he had to be carried out of the bar. They mention that he looked like he had been intimate 'with at least one or two of the beautiful women.'

I feel my hand slam down on the table next to me. I stand up from my chair, still staring at the screen. Theresa looks up from her phone in shock. "What?!" she exclaims.

I'm scared to open my mouth. I'm not sure if I want to scream or cry. "Excuse me," I manage to mumble. I see her look strangely at me and grab at the computer before I turn and walk towards my front door.

I take my phone out of my bra and find Jeremy's number in my contacts. I push his name and put the phone to my ear. I swore last night I'd wait for him to call, but I'm done playing games. He can't keep sending me mixed signals like this.

The phone rings four or five times, and then his machine picks up. It's a female pre-recorded message with just his phone number repeated. I assume he doesn't want anyone to know when they accidentally stumble upon his number.

I hang up and call back. I hear someone pick up after the second ring. "Hello?" Jeremy grumbles. My stomach tightens and my body tingles.

"Hi," I say, trying to remember how upset I am.

"Dylan?" he grunts, confused. "What time is it?"

"Twelve-thirty. In the AFTERNOON," I emphasize.

"Honey," he says, more clearly, "what's wrong?"

I feel a lump forming in my throat. I never ever cry, and now I've cried in the last few days more than I've cried in my entire life. Is this what love is? "Why didn't you call last night?"

He sighs. "You know, with the show and everything…"

"The show?" I say shortly. I feel the burning in my stomach. The lump in my throat almost chokes me as I try to speak. "I saw you on the news barely able to walk." I will not lose it.

He's silent. "Okay. So what do you want me to say?" He's defensive.

"I thought you weren't going to drink like that."

"I'm sorry you found out about it," he growls.

"I didn't say 'don't drink like that around me.' I said, 'I don't want you to drink like that anymore.' You promised." The burning rises in my stomach.

"You never said that, actually," he says curtly. "You told me to get some help. And since it's an imaginary problem, I got some imaginary help."

I growl, "Okay, boy genius. The fact that I didn't want you to drink like that was more than implied."

He sighs. "Last night was a bad night. Being without you."

His sweetness catches me off guard. I absorb that for a minute. "Jeremy, I don't want to be an excuse for your drinking. And that doesn't explain the women."

He laughs lightly. "I'm always followed by beautiful women. But not one of them has affected me like you. Dylan, I was trying to explain to you that this is my life."

'Well, now you're *my* life' I want to say, but I hold back. We've only known each other for a couple weeks. It sounds ridiculous. I try to lighten up on him. "I know about Harvard. And I can't possibly accept your help."

He laughs. "I was wondering when you'd realize. When you claimed you didn't benefit from my fame, I thought I'd stick it to you."

I snort. "You are such a child. But I still can't accept this. And neither can Theresa."

I see Theresa peek her head around the corner and make a slashing motion across her throat. I wave her away and she disappears back around the corner.

"Dylan, I have nothing to do with my money. Let me invest in the assholes of the future." I hear him intake a sharp breath, like he's stretching.

"Gee, thanks," I laugh.

"Anytime you need books or anything, rent money or whatever, send the bill to Steinbrook and Barr. Just address it to Steinbrook. He knows who you are. He'll reimburse you. There's more than enough money to see you through, baby. And it will be there no matter what. It's a trust, I can't touch it now. So it will just sit there untouched if you try to give it back, anyway."

My anger melts away, and I'm touched. "Thank you," I say, gratefully.

I wanted to bring up the girl with the blue hair, but I remember how his mood shifted last time I brought her up, and decide to save those questions for another time. This is the first time we've talked since he left, and I should be happy. I try to talk more about his day and his plans for the tour. He tells me

217

endlessly that he misses me, and promises to try harder. We talk for about an hour while I sit on the floor beside my front door.

Time passes quickly the last week and a half before school. August turns into an almost chilly Boston September. Jeremy makes good on his promise and calls me religiously every night. Sometimes we talk only for a few minutes, sometimes for a few hours. I don't see news reports about his wild escapades anymore, and he never seems intoxicated when he calls. Maybe he was right, and he really just likes to drink and doesn't have a problem.

The reporters are still on me endlessly, and Rich has faithfully taken me to and from wherever I have to go. Thankfully, with Rich by my side, the reporters tend to keep their distance. I'm not front page news anymore now that Jeremy isn't around me, so my news exposure has at least dwindled. I'm hoping no one notices who I am on my first day of school.

My Dad has been in contact with me over the past few weeks, and tries his hardest not to sound happy about Jeremy's long and extensive tour. My Dad still thinks I shouldn't work and still offers to help me with the mortgage and books, but I obviously decline, especially with the fund that I now have. The truth is, I'm not ready to tell him about the account. Sometimes the fact I even accepted it makes me feel gross. I've done nothing really to earn it. Besides, I think working will be fun and will help me take my mind off Jeremy. I've set a personal goal to do something other than think about him or talk about him for at least thirty minutes a day, and I seem to be able to do it.

It shocks me how much he's changed me in the last month. My entire life was surrounded by nothing but school and thoughts of my own success for a very long time. When I finally realized how quickly classes were approaching, I was surprised they hadn't crossed my mind almost at all.

The night before our first day of classes, Theresa and I pack our very professional-looking black bags, including my brand new laptop. I'm very excited to have Theresa in most of my classes. It will really make studying easier. After we finish packing the bags at the kitchen table, we walk them over and sit them by the front door. Our classes begin early at eight-fifteen and they last until two o'clock, but luckily we only have classes Monday through Thursday, giving us long weekends.

"Is Sean going to show you around campus tomorrow?" I ask Theresa, walking back into the living room. Sean is a second year and top of his class. I met him last week when he finally came over for dinner. He has perfect dark skin and bright white teeth. He towers at 6'3". He graduated from UCLA, where he attended thanks to a basketball scholarship. Theresa is so happy with him, she's almost a different person.

"Yeah, we're meeting after our first class. You want to come?" she asks. I shake my head, deciding against being a third wheel.

Theresa's smile fades. "I wanted to talk to you about something."

I sit down on the couch in the living room. She sits across from me and crosses her legs. "What?"

"Well, I just wanted to let you know that I'll probably be staying with Sean pretty regularly on the weekend. You know, to see how we get along when I stay there so often..."

She trails off. My eyes widen. "Are you thinking you might move in with him?"

She shrugs. "We've been dating only about a month so I'm not rushing into it or anything. But, you can afford the mortgage here now that you aren't paying tuition and you have that fund. So I'm considering it."

"Oh," I say, sadly. What will I do with my weekends? I'm not much of a party goer, and I don't make friends easily. My heart drops.

"Don't worry, I'm sure once the tour is over, Jeremy will fill your weekends."

I smile, trying to appear happy. But the tour isn't over for months, almost a year from now.

Later, I do get some good news when Jeremy calls. He tells me he's doing a show in Orlando, and he'll have a day or two after he lands there before he has to perform, so he's sending a plane for me. It's not for another few weeks, but at least it's something to look forward to. "Dylan," he says, in a low husky voice, "I can't wait until I can be with you."

His sweetness still takes me by surprise. "I miss you," I say, shyly. He makes me feel so wonderful when I talk to him, like nothing else matters in the world to him but me.

I'm still not sure if I'm in love with him. I've never been around love and I've never felt anything close to the love that I've read about in books or poems. All I know is that when I talk to him, I'm happy and content. When I'm not talking to him or around him, I feel incomplete and depressed. Does that mean something?

These thoughts, plus the normal stress of starting school and work tomorrow, make me toss and turn all night. When the alarm finally goes off at 6:00, I've barely slept at all. I get up slowly and walk into the bathroom. I start the shower and wave to Theresa, who walks by and says, "Hey," in an equally tired voice. After showering, brushing my teeth, and doing my hair, I walk to my bedroom, smelling the sweet smell of coffee. I dress in something sensible- a black pair of pants, pink shell, and a black blazer. I pull my hair back into a low ponytail and secure it with a barrette. I put some make-up on for good measure.

When I make it to the kitchen, Theresa is standing by the counter, waiting to hand me a thermos of coffee. She's wearing a blue business dress than touches her knees with sandals. "Chic," I complement, grabbing the thermos from her. We head towards the door.

Rich is outside at the door, and I give him a smile and quick hug before we walk down the stairs. My poor little red car hasn't been driven in over a month, and I stare at it longingly. There are only one or two photographers outside anymore, so Rich is hardly necessary. But I've gotten such little sleep, I'm thankful I can rest on the short drive to campus.

I was worried it might draw attention to us if we were dropped off at the college by a driver, but thankfully we aren't the only ones with a chauffeur. In fact, many students show up with drivers. The cars that actually are driven by students and parked around the school are expensive: Porsches and BMWs. The people walking into the school are tapping away at iPads or carrying Louis Vuitton brief cases.

I turn my attention to the building. The main building, large with many windows, looks airy and light instead of intimidating as I had feared.

"Harvard," I breathe, under my breath. I worked so hard to get here my whole life, and now here I am.

Chapter 10- Scott

I can't seem to stop smiling and looking towards the school. Theresa laughs at my gawking. "So excited!" she squeals, opening the door and getting out onto the sidewalk. I scoot over to the door and say goodbye to Rich, telling him I'll call when I'm done my last class.

The hallways are large and shiny, crowded with people. Theresa and I are able to find our first class easily, Criminal Law, and sit in the middle of the room at a long, shiny brown table. Theresa sits at the very end of the table to my left. The classroom isn't huge, not like my old college, and it will be nice to have a smaller class size for a change.

Theresa grumpily pulls out her laptop and sits it on the table. Theresa wants to go into corporate law, and she's convinced she'll find this class useless and boring. I take my time pulling out my laptop. We're early, and there is hardly anyone in the classroom yet.

After I pull my laptop free of my bag, I start daydreaming about my trip to Orlando. I turn and set my laptop on the table. Out of the corner of my eye, I see someone sitting to the right of me. Instinctually, I turn and see a man looking at me.

His hair is unusually blonde, slicked back with every strand in perfect place. His face is tan and smooth. His eyes are a dark blue and his lips a light pink. Without even looking at his body, you can tell that he's built like a brick wall. He looks like an All-American football player...like Captain America or something. I thought I was sure men like him didn't really exist outside of Abercrombie ads. He shoots me a bright white smile. "Hello," he says in a deep voice.

The sudden attraction I feel towards him catches me off guard, but I assume that any woman would be attracted to someone like him. "Hi," I say in a meek voice.

I feel Theresa look over at the interaction between us. The man extends an extremely muscular arm towards me, his huge hand open. "I'm Scott Hillman," he says, as I put my hand in his. His hand is warm and soft, without the roughness I'm used to.

Of course he is. Handsome *and* rich.

"Scott Hillman, of the Hillman Company?" I ask. The Hillman Company, as I understand, deals in steel and iron. The family who founded the company is worth billions.

He smiles, embarrassed. His smile is kind, and it shows in his eyes. "Yes. And you are..."

"Dylan Ackhart," I breathe. Our hands are still touching. He finally pulls his hand away and leans over to Theresa. They introduce themselves and Theresa immediately goes back to her computer, apparently not as interested in him as I'm trying not to be.

I turn to start up my laptop, but he opens his body more towards me. I strain to ignore the huge chest muscles I see almost breaking through his blue collared shirt. "I'm sorry, your eyes…are they contacts?"

I turn my head reluctantly at him. I don't like looking at him, or the way he makes me feel. I feel…guilty.

"No."

"Extraordinary," he says, under his breath. I stare into his eyes as he continues to examine mine. More students file in.

"Thank you," I say, looking down to break our gaze while blushing.

I feel a rush of relief as the professor walks in, a little man in dark green pants and a white and green plaid shirt with a bowtie. I turn fully towards my computer and pretend to prepare for class.

Class goes by pretty quickly, and I am happy to understand a lot of what he talked about. I was often the only one who could answer some of his questions. Theresa could barely stay awake the entire time. I actively avoided looking to my right, but every now and then I'd glance over, and he'd be looking at me.

After class is through, I put my computer away in my bag quickly, purposely rushing. Standing up, I feel him bump into the back of me. He puts his arms on my shoulders to steady me so I don't fall over.

"Dylan, I'm so sorry. I thought I could squeeze by." I look behind him at the rest of the table. No one was there, and it would be a more direct path to the door.

I sigh. I look back into his gorgeous face. "No, it's okay, really."

He smiles. "Let me buy you a drink tonight. I'll make it up to you and we can celebrate our first day."

I look back at Theresa, who is still on my left but standing now and smiling at me with raised eyebrows. I turn back to him.

"Actually, I work at the bookstore here on campus, and I start tonight."

He smiles. "Maybe next time."

I nod and turn as he lets go of my shoulders. The three of us walk out of the room and on to our next class.

After our classes end for the day, Theresa and I walk towards the grassy area to the right of the school, where she planned to meet Sean. Tired and overwhelmed from our first day, we walk silently for a while. Finally,

Theresa turns to me. "You want to talk about that delicious man that asked you out?"

"No." I say, curtly.

"You're right. Anyway, Jeremy is still hotter... and badder... and so sexy. Uh, I hate you!" Theresa says.

I stop when we see Sean waiting on the grass. Theresa waves to him. He's wearing a white shirt and black pants, and his dark skin almost shines in the sun. "Sean's pretty handsome."

Theresa gets a dumb smile on her face. I roll my eyes. "Yeah," she breathes.

Why can't I be as blissfully happy as her? I feel like someone punched a big hole in my heart all the time.

I say goodbye to Theresa and take my phone out of my pocket to call Rich. Rich picks me up a few minutes later and takes me home.

"This is how you type in a book title someone is looking for," Sean explains to me later that night at my new job. It's nice because there isn't a dress code, so I can wear a T-shirt and jeans. Better yet, I'm allowed to study when it's slow. Making money while studying; it's a definite win-win.

He pushes a few simple commands on the computer that I commit to memory. I ring out a few people and do well. I feel like I'm getting the hang of everything. Sean sends me out with a cart of books that need to be put away, by section and then alphabetically by author.

I push the cart up and down, slowly working through the books. It's almost therapeutic meditation. It's very quiet and peaceful and I find myself alone with my thoughts. I think of Jeremy strumming his guitar, his wet hair sparkling in the stage lights. The way his eyes sparkle when he gets excited. I hear him laugh, low and sexy in my ears. My stomach tightens.

I'm thinking about the way he says my name when he greets me. "Dylan," I hear in my head.

Yes. Just like that, but not as deep.

"Dylan," I hear again, still deep.

I feel something touch my arm. I jump about ten feet in the air, and look around, dazed. I look up into the face of Scott Hillman, wearing a gray T-shirt and some jeans. He jumps too.

"Woah, sorry. Didn't mean to scare you." He gives me a million dollar smile. I stand in shock.

"Scott?" I say in shock.

"Yeah, you know I came to buy books, and I thought I'd say hi." I look at his hands. He's carrying two coffees.

"Uh," he says, holding out one of the cups towards me. "I thought you could use this. We were in class early."

I stare at the cups for a moment and then look back up to his face. After a minute of processing, and Scott looking at me like I might be crazy, I take the cup. "Thank you."

I take a sip, and then push the cart further away from him, sticking a book on the shelf. I don't know how to handle this situation. Do I tell him I'm taken? What if he asks me about my boyfriend? Do I lie? What if he's just being nice and I'm only assuming he's trying to pick me up?

He walks behind me, obviously unaware of my polite attempts to get away from him.

"How's your first day going?" He asks, nodding to the cart.

"Great," I say, turning to him to smile and then turning back to the cart.

"So, did you want to get that drink tomorrow night?" he asks as he follows me.

I sigh. How can I word this right? "Scott," I begin. I pause as I look at his face, taking in his handsome body. "I'm...I...I just started dating someone. And it's new, so..."

He smiles and puts his free hand up. "Oh, I'm sorry. I understand. I didn't realize that was still going on."

I furrow my eyebrows. "What was?"

He blushes. "You know, you and Jeremy Ma…"

"Shhh!" I say, hurriedly. He stops as I look around frantically. He laughs under his breath.

"Dylan, *most* people here wouldn't care *who* you're dating. You have to realize, you're at Harvard. Some of the most powerful people in the world have their kids here." He grabs my arm and leads me to the end of the bookshelf, pointing with one finger. I look at a boy sitting in a chair a few feet from us, reading a textbook. "That guy dated Paris Hilton last year. And there's a guy in our class who dated Chelsea Clinton not long ago."

I look up at his face, which is much closer to me. He looks down at me, and his face turns serious. I back away. "Oh," I say.

He drops his hand from my arm. We both sip our coffee. "Everyone knows who you are."

I absorb that. He's right, nobody bothered me today. I guess they really don't care.

"Well, I'd really like to not advertise that we're still together all the same. I just want to be private."

Scott smiles at me. "No, I understand. We can still be friends, right?"

"Friends," I agree.

231

Scott stayed with me for a while, keeping me company while I worked. I found that we had a lot in common. He was determined to try to make his own name for himself, and didn't want to take his parent's money any more than necessary. He had gotten into Harvard because of his own hard work and excellent grades. Although popular due to his success in high school sports, he rarely went to parties. We never ran out of things to talk about, and while that was nice, I didn't get any studying done at work as I'd hoped.

The next night I have another shift at the bookstore, and I am surprised to see Scott waiting by the counter for me, coffee in hand.

"Hello," I say, smiling at him. He smiles back at me and hands me a coffee.

"Hey, Dylan. What did you think of class today?" He watches me enter behind the counter and pull my hair up in a ponytail.

"Good, but it is really hard. A lot of work, you know? I'm surprised to find myself so overwhelmed, to be honest. Usually school is pretty easy for me."

We discuss school, the professors we have, and the few exams we have coming up. By the end of the night, Scott and I agree to study together, since Theresa isn't around as much as I would hope. Plus, she's not as crazy about school as Scott and I are.

We set up a schedule. He will come to my house three nights a week after I get off of work. I relax a little, hoping that together we can get through our classes. I guess it is nice to have friends sometimes after all.

Life continues pretty much as expected. Jeremy and I still talk every night. He's staying out of the news, and I have no reason to suspect anything. Every three days or so, flowers are delivered to my door, and my house is covered in beautiful roses all the time. He seems so light and happy when he talks to me, and when I talk to him, nothing else exists. When I'm not talking to him, I miss him terribly, but school keeps me distracted.

My Criminal Law class is going really well thanks to my study buddy, and Scott and I have become great friends. He comes over three nights as planned. That weekend, however, is the first that Theresa is gone. At first, I actually welcome the solitude, and I'm able to get a lot done. But the quiet in the house is almost unsettling, especially since I had become accustomed to always being with someone, whether it was Theresa or Jeremy. So Saturday night, Scott comes over and we order a pizza.

Being with Scott is a lot of fun. He's so different from Jeremy. He's laid back and calm, not intense, unless it's about school. Sometimes it's hard to remember he's a zillionaire. His attractiveness is getting easier and easier to handle, especially as Jeremy and I grow closer.

After a while, Scott's weekend visits become a regular thing. We watch movies, play games, and study. My grades continue to do well and I attribute most of that to Scott. With the weekend visits and weekday studying, he's over my house more often than not. I feel myself growing closer to him than I am to Theresa, which surprises me. I'm so happy I could find a kindred spirit in Scott. Although, he often makes it known that he doesn't like the idea of me with Jeremy because of his sketchy past. I let him lecture me to be polite, but I don't really believe the things he tells me he's seen on the news.

One night, during one of our debates, he turns to me with a mouth full of pizza. "Dylan," he says. "You've seen the news. They guy is a partier. A drinker, a cokehead. A lot of the women he's been with say he beat them. Trust me, it's good he's not around."

I roll my eyes. "You can't believe everything you see on the news. They've said some crazy things about me."

He grabs another slice of pizza. I swear, the guy eats like it's his last supper. And yet he's super fit. Damn him. "Yeah, but a lot of people are saying these things. There's got to be truth in it somewhere."

Most of the conversations with him about Jeremy go like this. Sometimes I smirk at him, knowing he's saying these things out of jealousy. But, I never say that to him. It's actually kind of cute and sweet. Someone jealous over me?

My Dad is happy with my grades and is content with the fact that I'm doing so well in school. He has even gotten off of my back about my job, since he learned that I'm able to study there. He is not, however, particularly happy to hear about my trip to Orlando. I try not to talk to him much because the more he attempts to convince me not to go, the more nervous and excited I get to go there.

The night before I'm finally supposed to leave for Orlando for my three day weekend, Jeremy and I talk on the phone. It's only a short conversation as the plane will be at the airport for me at six in the morning, and I want to make sure I'm well rested.

"You better be well rested," Jeremy croons. "You won't be getting much sleep. I've been unattended to for over three weeks now. That's longer than I've ever gone since I was twelve."

I smile. "It'll be worth it. I know I'm not one of your usual fly-by-night girls, but I'm worth the wait."

He sighs. "You are, baby. And it means everything. You mean everything. You are everything."

I pause, waiting to hear the words. I mentally will him to say he loves me.

"Goodnight, baby," he says, yawning.

I sigh and hang up.

In the morning, I wakeup to my alarm blaring annoyingly in my ear. I go through my normal morning routine- shower, coffee, brushing my teeth. Theresa isn't here to do my hair or help me with my outfit since she's staying with Sean, so I'm left on my own. I put my hair up into a high ponytail. I choose a plain black tank top that fits snuggly. It pushes my breasts up high and exposes some cleavage. I put on high jean shorts and black wedges. It might be a chilly September here, but it will still be summer in Orlando.

When Rich arrives, he gives me a hug and grabs my suitcase for me. After we get into the car, we take a short ride to the same airport that Jeremy had been weeks before. I remember how sad I was last time I was here, and it's in direct contrast to the way I feel right now.

The flight takes about three hours, so I'm thankful to be on a private plane. I've never been on a private plane, but I assume that Jeremy's is larger than other private ones.

Rich and I are the only passengers in the entire plane, plus the stewardess, so the space is wonderful. The interior is brown with a white couch along the side where the door is located. There is a shorter white couch opposite the door and a white table with white seating surrounding it. The bathroom is much larger than on a normal plane, too. The door at the back of the cabin leads to a similar brown room with a large, light brown bed and two night stands. I stare, annoyed at the bed, and try not to wonder who he's had in it.

I try to entertain myself on the plane to no avail. Towards the middle of the flight, I start to fidget. I move and adjust every few seconds. The latter half of the flight, my stomach begins to hurt. I go to the bathroom three times to fix my hair and try not to hyperventilate.

When the plane lands, I feel like I'm going to pass out. I've never been so nervous in my entire life. Most of our relationship at this point has been through phone calls and text messages. What if he's built me up in his head and I'm not what he remembers?

I see the door to the plane open and stairs being placed next to the doorway. The engines cut off, and Rich tells me it's time to go. I tremble as he helps me up. Rich laughs at me and puts his hand on my back. "It's okay Miss Dylan. Don't be nervous. He loves you."

I stare at him, surprised.

Rich nods. "Trust me."

I adjust my shirt and walk towards the door. Immediately, the bright sun and sprawling heat hits me. I shield my eyes as I see the long steps in front of me. *Damn me for wearing wedges.* Rich walks in front of me and I clutch to the railing, concentrating as I walk down the stairs.

Suddenly, I hear "Dylan," over the wind. I stop and look up, and see Jeremy at the bottom of the stairs. His face is so beautiful, chiseled and defined. He hasn't shaved recently, and he practically has a full beard. Short dark hair almost covers the top of his lip and haphazardly grows around his chin and up towards his hair. It's the sexiest thing I've ever seen.

His hair is being tossed in the wind, along with the skinny black tie he wears around the collar of his white shirt. Despite the heat, he wears a black short sleeved blazer and long black jeans.

I see him smile and his bright blue eyes sparkle. Surprisingly, I find myself choked up. I'm no longer scared of the steps, and I almost run down them, wedges be damned.

He opens his arms when I get close, and I fall into them. The spicy sent of him hits me instantly. I bury my head in his neck and he puts one of his hands around my head and one around my waist.

"Miss me?" he whispers in my ear.

Tears fall down my cheeks. "Oh, Jeremy."

I press against him, and feel him growing hard against me. He pulls away. "Sorry about that," he says, as I giggle. He wipes the tears away from my face. "You look amazing, as usual, and it's been a while…" he trails off. He grabs my chin and brings my lips to his. The kiss is sweet and soft.

He pulls away and smiles. He grabs my hand and says, "Let's go."

He walks me a short distance across the asphalt to a long, black limousine. The driver, a tall, lanky white man dressed in a blue driver's uniform, opens the door for us. I slide across the black bench in the back of the long car, and Jeremy gets in after me. The driver shuts the door and walks towards the front.

"What about Rich?" I ask as we start to pull away. Jeremy puts his arm around me, fiddling with his pockets.

"He's catching his own ride," Jeremy pulls out a cigarette box. He takes his hand away from around me, flicking the lighter from the box and lighting the cigarette hanging from his mouth. I watch him blow the smoke out of his lips.

He turns to stare at me. I stare back. "I missed your eyes," he says, stroking my cheek with his free hand. I smile. I don't know what to say.

He takes another drag on his cigarette and blows smoke, slow and steady, out of his mouth. I bite my bottom lip.

He laughs. "What?"

"How long before we get to the hotel?"

His smile fades and his eyes smolder, picking up on my sensual undertone.

"Twenty minutes or so," he says, low and deep. He flicks his cigarette out of the open window and shuts it. He hits a button on the ceiling of the car, and a black window separating us from the driver closes.

Suddenly, I find myself climbing on top of him. He gasps. I grab at his tie and move my fingers through his beard. I pull his face towards me and kiss him, hard.

He grabs my waist. "Dylan, wait," he says, but I kiss him harder.

"Shut up," I tell him between kisses. His eyes look amused. I undo his black tie and he pulls my shirt up and over my head, exposing my new lacy blue bra.

"Wow," he says, admiring. I kiss him passionately.

"I hope you're not too fond of this shirt, Mr. Mason," I quote him, putting my hands in between the button openings in the front. I pull hard and watch the buttons pop off, exposing his tattooed chest. I run my hand over the dream catcher.

"Holy shit," he says, breathing heavily. He looks astonished. I'm not sure what's come over me either. Excitement to have him here, relief to be with him again, the memory of the way he makes my body feel, there are so many emotions I can't handle when I'm around him.

Jeremy and I fully enjoy our ride to the hotel, which luckily takes more like 30 minutes instead of 20. When the driver opens the door to let us out in front of the huge glass doors, I think I see him smirk at the sight of Jeremy, who carries his tie in his hand and exits the car with his shirt wide open. My clothes, luckily, seem to have survived intact.

After we step onto the sidewalk, the madness begins again. I hear clicking and see lights flashing wildly around us. Girls scream at Jeremy, desperately trying to get to him. Fortunately, I see as I look side to side, the police have already been informed that we were coming, and block off the girls and photographers.

I look up at the huge doors, lined in gold. Jeremy grabs my hand and squeezes it quickly. "Go ahead, I'll be there in a minute," he says, smiling. I smile and walk towards the doors as Jeremy walks over to some girls and begins to sign a CD cover.

The doorman opens the door for me, welcoming me to the Waldorf Astoria, and I walk into a huge lobby. I gasp at the elegant interior. The floor is a white and brown pattern, swirling around a statue of an antique looking clock. Above the clock is a dome ceiling with a twinkling chandelier hanging from the middle. The walls are all white except for directly behind the clock statue where the wall turns a deep shade of blue, offset by five huge different color paintings.

It's so quiet in the lobby that when I step slowly towards the front desk, my footsteps echo. The screaming girls suddenly get louder, and I turn around towards the door and see Jeremy enter. The sound of the girls die down as the door shuts behind him. His shirt is still open, and he struts into the lobby, smiling widely.

He reaches me and puts his hand lightly on my back. "I think I'm a little under dressed," he whispers in my ear as he leads me up to the front desk. I snort, stifling a laugh.

The front desk is a long, dark brown monster that lines the entire back wall. There are a few women standing behind it, wearing black vests and smiling happily at everyone. "Mr. Mason," an older brunette woman says. "How can we help you?"

"I'd like an extra key to the suite for my *girlfriend*," he purrs. My stomach flip-flops excitedly at the title. The woman happily reaches in a drawer under the counter and produces an extra key. She wishes us a good stay and Jeremy leads us to the elevator.

"Suite?" I say, turning my head and raising an eyebrow at him as we enter the silver elevator doors.

"You have no idea," he chuckles lightly, leaning nonchalantly against the wall.

The elevator reaches the top floor and we step out into a room with a large decorated carpet. Across from the elevator are three door openings, through which I can see a large, ornate sitting room. "Oh," I say, walking towards a doorway. It's like walking into the past.

I enter the first room, a large living area with Victorian-style décor. The walls are light green with gold rectangular accents scattered throughout. There are two large windows to my left that are decorated with large gold curtains. A plush gold couch and two green chairs sit underneath the windows with a dark brown coffee table in front of them. There are two more green and gold couches facing each other in the center of the room. Towards the back of the room in the corner, a black baby grand piano sits. Dangling from the ceiling is an elegant crystal chandelier.

I run my hand across the antique gold and brown desk to the left of the doorway. "Do you like it?" I hear Jeremy say, low and quiet.

I turn towards him. He leans in the doorway, his feet crossed. "Yes," I breathe passionately. "Though, it's not really your style."

"I got it for you. It's called the 'Royal Sweet.' It's new here in Orlando. They have one in New York," he babbles nervously. His eyes trail my body. I blush.

"You didn't have to do this, Jeremy." He's given me so much already, and I know I can't keep encouraging his lavish spending on me.

"Sure I did," he says, walking gracefully past me and smiling wryly. "Especially since you've been hanging around with what's-his-name." He approaches the piano and turns to sit at the bench.

I roll my eyes as he lifts the drawer covering the keys. "*Scott*," I correct. Jeremy has made it quite clear that he does not approve of the friendship between Scott and I. And that's without my mentioning the way we met. Or the fact that he comes over when Theresa isn't home.

"Well, I thought it was important to show you that I may not be a billionaire, but I can show you a good time," he stretches his fingers for a moment, and closes his eyes, escaping into deep concentration. He runs his fingers across the keys. A beautiful chord plays.

I smile lovingly at him, though he doesn't see it. "I don't want money from either of you. Besides, Scott isn't a billionaire yet."

"Oh that's right," Jeremy plays a few more chords. "Because *I*, unlike *him*, made *myself* rich and wasn't born with the good fortune of having a wealthy Mumsy and Dadsy." His voice is dripping with sarcasm.

I laugh, but I still feel a pang of guilt whenever he talks about Scott. "Oh, stop."

I walk over to the piano and lean on the glossy, black top. Jeremy looks down at his fingers. The music slows and he begins to play a soft, sweet classical tune.

With his eyes closed again, he begins to rock slowly to the music. I watch his fingers flow over the keys, amazed. They move gracefully, almost dancing to the waltz he plays. His right leg tenses and relaxes as he presses his foot on the pedals beneath him. His chest muscles harden and soften through his shirt as he pounds the keys.

I don't recognize the piece. "Who is this?"

Jeremy opens his eyes. They are a pale blue. He looks up at me, almost bashfully. "Me."

My mouth drops open. "You?"

Jeremy nods slightly, the light moving through his hair. "I wrote it when I was three. I performed it at five for the Queen. This room reminds me of it." He continues to play the intricate melody.

I'm feeling extremely stupid and inconsequential. I shake my head. "What?" Jeremy asks me, finishing his song with a last, haunting note.

"You're just amazing." And brilliant. And beautiful. And kind. And completely too good for me.

He stands from the bench and walks around the piano towards me. He reaches out grabs my hand, softly rubbing the back of my palm with his thumb. "Can I show you the bedroom?"

I smile timidly at him. The light from the windows hits his face, accenting his beautiful skin and glowing eyes. It's quiet except for the loud beating of my heart in my ears. Immersed in my ogling, I forget to answer.

He laughs under his breath. "I'll take that as a yes." He picks me up into his arms and I giggle.

He walks me into a massive bedroom, also with a beautiful crystal and gold chandelier hanging in the middle. I briefly notice a writing desk to the left side of me. The far wall has a fireplace with two ornate blue chairs in front of it, a coffee table in between them. Jeremy throws me down on the huge king sized bed. I grab onto the white, flowered printed sheets to steady myself.

He throws off his white shirt and stands in front of the bed. Slowly, he leans over me and undoes the button of my shorts. He pulls them down over my legs, taking my underwear with them. He pulls my wedges off my feet as the shorts reach my ankles and throws everything onto the floor. I peel my shirt and bra off from over my head as he undresses me and lie completely naked in front of him.

Jeremy kneels on the bed in front of me between my legs, naked except for his black pants. He leans over me and my body tenses. But instead of touching me, he reaches for a beer can already placed on the nightstand beside the bed. He straightens back up again, and I look at him like he's just lost his mind.

He laughs as he pulls the can away. "I've come up with an idea that will allow me to drink around you without getting you upset."

"Oh?" I say, breathlessly. I doubt it.

He extends his arm out over my chest and tilts the beer can slightly over me. The cold beer hits the skin between my breasts and rolls down along my body. I don't expect the liquid to be so cold, and I gasp in shock. He leans over me and runs his tongue along the liquid. I moan.

He pours more cold liquid on my lower body. It falls over my lower abdomen and drips down between my legs. Jeremy slowly trails his tongue down, following the beer until he reaches my core and continues.

I tense. *Okay. This* is *acceptable drinking.*

Chapter 11- Problem

I begin to wake up sometime later, feeling groggy and still tired from the latest Jeremy whole body experience, and roll over to stroke his perfect skin. I can tell by the light hitting my face through the windows that the sun is low in the sky, indicating it's probably late in the afternoon. I feel around with my eyes closed for his warm body, but after searching and not finding him, I open my eyes to discover he's not in the bed.

I sit up and look around the room but don't see him. I look at the floor, noticing his pants are no longer thrown beside the bed. I pull on my shorts and shirt and walk barefoot out to the sitting area.

After entering the silent room, my eyes shoot around, looking for him. It takes me a moment, but I eventually find Jeremy sitting at the black piano, his head on the keys. He looks almost as if he's fallen asleep there, but from the way his hands are dangling from his side and the way his face is placed on the keys, it looks much too uncomfortable of a position for anyone to be able to sleep. Panic hits me immediately, and I run over to him. When I reach him, I'm slightly relieved to see him breathing. It's slow and too shallow, but still breathing all the same. I shake him. He doesn't immediately respond, so I shake harder. "Jeremy?!" I yell, my voice trembling with alarm. His head lolls to the side and makes the piano play lightly.

"Mmmmm?" he mumbles. He doesn't open his eyes.

I back away from him. I'm shocked at the sight of him. His face is a gray color, his lips chapped and dry. His beautiful features appear almost a bit swollen.

Realization of what must be going on comes over me. Still in a daze, I turn towards the kitchen and walk slowly into it. I see a trash can sitting on the cold tile and peer over the side to look at the contents, seeing it almost full with empty beer cans and a few empty bottles of other spirits. He only arrived yesterday, a little over twenty-four hours ago.

I stand in the kitchen for a moment, absorbing this. All hope of him not having a problem is now officially obliterated. What do I do now? I have no idea how to handle this. Should I call someone? I fear that would cause a media frenzy. Is it normal for him to pass out like this? What if he stops breathing? How would I know what to do?

I have a flashback to my mother, lying cold on the kitchen floor. Feeling helpless, useless, and unable to help her.

I cross my arms over my chest, trying to stop the panic from consuming me. I'm terrified, and my heavy breathing is a sign I'm going into a panic attack.

Before I have the chance to fully lose it, I hear loud and uneven footsteps coming towards me, and I turn to the doorway in time to see Jeremy. He slams his body hard against the doorway to the kitchen, steadying himself.

"Hey," he says, rubbing his eyes. I don't answer him, but seeing him up and talking calms my breathing instantly.

He opens his eyes and looks at me. They are bloodshot and glassy. I don't know this person. My eyes well up with tears against my permission.

"Dylan," he says, stretching out a limp hand towards my face. I see the heat rash on his arm and the snake tattoo up by his shoulder. I let him touch my face softly.

Suddenly, his body tilts backwards and he almost falls, barely regaining his footing. He leans back against the doorway. When I gasp and reach out to him, he laughs.

"What in the name of God is funny about that?" I say, curtly.

His smile fades. "Just relax, will you?" he slurs.

My eyes well up again. "You are disgustingly intoxicated."

He shrugs. "I've got to do what I've got to do. You act like I'm…like I'm…the only musician…or *person* for that matter…who drinks." He wobbles back and forth.

I will my tears to not spill over my cheeks. I won't blubber like a teenager. I'll fight like a woman. "This isn't normal. And I don't care what other musicians are like. You have a problem."

"I have LOTS of problems," he says, waving his hand across his face. He stumbles away from the doorway for a moment, catching himself again and leaning back on it.

I sigh angrily while I walk over and grab him around the waist. He leans on me, and I feel his erection grow on my hip. "Mmmm, that's more like it," he says, kissing my ear as we exit the kitchen.

I jerk my head away, "You can just forget that."

We walk slowly to the bedroom and I help him onto the bed. He lies down, moaning and stretching. I sit next to him, pulling the covers up and over him. His head lies on its side facing the opposite wall. I can see his eyes change slowly, from his unfocused, faraway look to disgust. I reach out and stroke his cheek, calming him.

He turns his head towards me, and I put my hand in my lap. His eyes are wide, filled with self-hatred and repulsion. "Dylan, I'm sorry I upset you," he slurs.

I close my eyes, stroking his cheek again. I open my eyes and try to sound sincere. "It's okay."

He closes his eyes angrily. "I can't stop."

My breath catches. "Jeremy, let's not talk about this now." I don't know how to handle this…

He opens his eyes and grabs my hand on his face. "Just please don't leave me."

I sigh. "I'm not going to leave you, Jeremy. But you need help."

He nods. Looking up at me, he quietly says, "I love you, Dylan."

I stop breathing. My mouth drops open and my mind goes blank. That came way out of left field. Of all the times he could have chosen to tell me, why do it now? When I'm mad and afraid and confused?

I feel anger form in my stomach, a slight burning. He stole this beautiful moment from me. *Alcohol* stole this moment from me.

He looks at me in anticipation. I finally speak, maybe a little more harshly than intended. "Let's *definitely* not talk about *that* right now."

He removes his hand from mine, and I stand. I throw my shoes on and walk towards the door. "I'll be back in a little while. When you regain your senses," I spit.

Outside of the sitting room in the foyer, I spot my luggage. I silently praise God that I

253

have a clean pair of clothes and roll one of my suitcases to the bathroom. I decide maybe I should just hit up the pool for lack of anywhere else to go, so I throw on my light pink bikini and grab a beach towel, some sunglasses, and some sunblock. I grab my wallet from the suitcase and, leaving the luggage open on the bathroom floor, walk out of the hotel room and towards the elevator.

When I reach the large, rectangular pool it's extremely crowded, even though it's almost evening. I pull my sunglasses down and look around for a place to sit. I find an empty blue lounge chair under a cabana and walk towards it. I throw my towel over the chair and lay on it, kicking my wedges off. I lay for a couple of minutes in the sun and spray sunblock on myself. I'm not much of a sunbather and am bored in minutes, so I dig around in my oversized wallet and pull out my phone.

I have two text messages, one from Theresa and one from Scott, asking me how my flight was. I decide to call Theresa instead of texting her. Of course, she was at Sean's house, getting ready to go to her shift at the bookstore. Sean had just gotten a great grade on an important exam, and they were going out later to celebrate. I lied and told her things were going well and that both Jeremy and I were at the pool. I know she suspects something is wrong, but she doesn't press me about it. I'm scared I'll start to cry if I talk about it, and I'd rather continue being mad instead of sad. Mad is easier to handle.

I text Scott back that the flight went well. For some reason, I don't feel like it's appropriate to call him on a trip to see my boyfriend. I know we're just friends, but sometimes that boundary line can be a little shaky. Even though I'm mad and hurt, I don't want to disrespect Jeremy like that.

I get a text back from Scott almost immediately.

Scott: Glad to hear you're safe. How's the warm weather?

I smile quickly. I remember how desperate he is to get back to somewhere warm. Being warm is a novelty when you live somewhere that's always freezing. I'm not really in the mood to exchange pleasantries.

Me: Fine.

My phone dings again immediately.

Scott: You ok?
Me: Sure.
Scott: What's wrong?
Me: Nothing.
Scott: Did I do something?

Me: No, Scott. It's fine.
Scott: You're not fighting, are you?

How is it he can pick up that something is wrong so easily? Why am I so connected to him? I roll my eyes, annoyed. Am I that obvious? I guess I'm not being my usual chatty self with him, so that probably isn't helping.

Me: God, no. I'm ok.
Scott: Do you want me to send a plane for you? Do you want me to come and get you?

I pause for a moment. For a split second, I think that I do want to come home. I think I do want Scott to come and get me. Things would be so simple and easy. I could have study dates with Scott, do well in school, and not have to miss anyone or anything. I could even go places without being chased or harassed.

Me: No, no. I'm having a great time. I'll call you on the way back to Boston. Bye.

I turn my phone off and set it beside me on the ground.

I drift in and out of sleep and take a few dips in the pool to cool off. I'm not used to such warm weather, and the pool is just cool enough. I turn my phone on but put it on airplane mode and read a book I downloaded earlier in the year. I get about 100 pages into it until I decide the main character, dark and sexy and damaged, reminds me too much of Jeremy. When I check the time, six o'clock, I realize that three hours have passed.

I turn airplane mode off on my phone. Three messages pop up, the first from Scott.

Scott: I miss you, Dylan.

I delete the message immediately. The next two are from Jeremy.

Jeremy: Dylan, I'm so sorry. I'm awake, and I want to make it up to you. Come back up, okay?

It was written only thirty minutes ago. The second was written just a few minutes ago.

Jeremy: Don't leave. I really meant what I said.

I sigh, trying to fight off the feeling of bliss at reading his last message. I stand and collect my things. I head back into the hotel and to the elevator, curious as to where we go from here.

When I step off the elevator and into the foyer, I walk into the waiting room and see Jeremy sitting on the green couch in the middle of the room, strumming his silver guitar with a cigarette hanging from his mouth. His face has a little hint of his normal, pale pink color returning and his lips have changed once again to pouty pink. He's shaved his facial hair, and I'm both disappointed and happy. At least he looks like he did when I first met him.

He looks up at me when I walk in but continues to play. His muscles look amazing as he strums. I throw my wallet and towel down in the foyer and put my glasses up on my head. I walk in and sit on the couch across from him, staring into his blue eyes.

The song is slow and hard, the cords rough.

"What are you playing?" I ask, quietly.

"A new song," he mumbles around his cigarette. "Do you like it?"

I nod. He stops playing and takes a final puff of his cigarette, putting it out in the ashtray on the table.

He looks up at me again and smiles. "Sexy," he says, nodding towards my bikini. I roll my eyes as he begins playing again.

"So that's just it? You just think everything's back to normal again?" I say, exasperated.

"Where were you? You didn't bother to answer my text messages." he asks nonchalantly, ignoring me. I know the curiosity is killing him.

"At the pool, obviously," I indicate my bathing suit.

"Did you call him?" He stares hard into my eyes. The strumming gets harder.

I shake my head. "No, I didn't call Scott."

Technically that's the truth, right?

His face flushes.

"You're lying," he growls.

I huff. "Just stop, okay? Let's just enjoy ourselves. I'm here, with you, and no one else can have me."

He ponders that for a minute. His face softens and he stops playing. "You still want to be here?" His voice is unsure.

I smile and rise from the couch. I walk over towards him and sit next to him. He takes his guitar off of his chest and sets it beside him on the floor.

"Will you get help?" I ask after he looks back up at me, looking into his eyes.

He nods. "Right after the tour. I promise."

I furrow my brows. "That's not for months."

He puts his arm around me. "Dylan, I've been drinking for a long time. The detox isn't going to be pretty or easy."

I nod reluctantly. I know absolutely nothing about alcohol or detoxing. At least he's decided to get help. Isn't admitting you have a problem the first step?

He grabs his guitar and stands, extending a hand towards me. "We're going out. I'm showing you off."

I put my hand in his and he pulls me up. The idea makes me uncomfortable. Show *what* off? I'd be embarrassed to be seen with me. "Mr. Private is going to show me off?"

He laughs. He walks over to the piano, his normal swagger almost back, and grabs a purple velvet box off the top of it. He sways his body as he walks back to me.

He holds out the box. I give him a strange look as I take it into my hands. "Open it," he says excitedly, eyes sparkling and smile beaming.

I push the lid open and gasp, almost dropping the box to the floor. "Oh my God," I sigh.

Inside the box is a necklace. A monstrously big, beautiful necklace. The entire necklace is made of diamonds, looping all the way around to the back where the clasp sits. The diamonds form a single loop until at the front of it they break off into two rows. Seven teardrop shaped emeralds, also surrounded by diamonds, hang from the diamond chain in a semi-circle. They start small on the outside, and increase in size until they reach the large middle one that hangs the lowest. In the middle of the necklace, attached to the box, hang two teardrop shaped emerald earrings surrounded by diamonds, the same size as the middle emerald on the necklace.

I'm speechless. "Do you like it?" Jeremy asks, quietly.

"Jeremy, I…" *I love them! I want to wear them everywhere!* "I can't accept these. They must have cost a fortune." Literally. Emeralds have always been my favorite stone since I was a kid, probably because I liked my eyes so much back then. I know that the necklace is well over a hundred and fifty carats alone. This set must have cost a half million dollars at the very least.

Jeremy shushes me and grabs the box from my hand. He removes the necklace and places it around my neck, managing to fasten it without looking. Setting the box on the couch, he pushes me towards a mirror on the wall. He stands behind me and looks at me in it.

I look at the necklace lying delicately on my neck. "How did you know emeralds are my favorite?"

He shrugs, looking secretly pleased with himself. "I didn't. I just thought these would bring out your eyes. I was right."

My eyes dance like the light hitting the necklace.

"When did you buy these?" He runs his hands down my bare shoulders. He kisses my right shoulder lightly and tenderly.

"A few weeks ago," he whispers. I tremble, feeling his warm breath in my ear. "I think about you, always. Even when you're away. You're the most important thing in my life."

I sigh and close my eyes as he kisses my shoulders. It's the sweetest, most endearing thing he's said to me. I know in my heart that he wishes it were true, but we both know there is something more important in his life than me, and it will continue to be that way until he detoxes.

He turns me towards him and smiles, handing me the jewelry box that still contains the earrings. "Get dressed, we're going out."

Standing in the bathroom, where my suitcase is still lying open from this morning, I stare blankly at myself in the mirror. I barely recognize myself. My cheeks are rosy red, my skin is glowing. My eyes are sparkling like the emeralds placed around my neck. The dress I chose is jet black and super short, and it makes my eyes and the necklace stand out more. I put my hair up into a messy up-do so my earrings can hang freely from my ears. I did pretty well without Theresa for advice, if I do say so myself.

I exit the bathroom, turning off the light as I shut the door behind me. I walk into the sitting room and see Jeremy standing in front of me, dressed in a gorgeous black tuxedo. I gasp as I look at his breathtaking physique.

He stops playing with the sleeve of his jacket as he looks up at me. His eyes shine and he smiles widely, saying nothing. I look down towards my feet uncomfortably.

"Hey," he says, walking towards me. He grabs my chin with his hand and lifts my face towards him. I stare into his aqua eyes. "You are beautiful, Dylan."

I feel my cheeks burn as he kisses me passionately. I get distracted for a moment, but finally pull away from him, my curiosity getting the best of me.

I giggle. He still holds my chin. "Where are we going?" I say, a little mumbled.

"The opera," he says, releasing my face and turning from me, walking to a table where his wallet sits. He picks it up and places it inside his jacket. I stand, confused, and try to process that. "You? At the opera?"

Jeremy turns towards me with a crooked smile. "I'm not completely uncultured. I started as a classical composer."

His face is beautiful when he's spunky. I smile back at him excitedly. He laughs under his breath. "I've never been. It sounds interesting," I say.

"You'll love it," he says, extending his arm out for me to grab. My eyebrows raise at his gentlemanly gesture. I grab his arm and he leads me towards the door, strutting and smiling.

When we exit the elevator into the lobby, I try to ignore the people that stop and stare at us. A young girl runs up to Jeremy and asks him for an autograph. I release his arm and he signs it quickly. He makes general conversation with her, and she smiles brightly at him. Before he stands, he gives her a big hug and long kiss on the cheek. She's ecstatic, her year clearly made, and my heart warms.

Unexpectedly, she hands the autograph book to me and asks me to sign it as well. I sign the book and hand it back to her, blushing scarlet. I look at Jeremy and he looks terribly amused, but says nothing about it.

From the lobby, we exit the hotel and head down the steps towards the black limo that's already waiting at the bottom of the stairway. We luckily leave with only grabbing the attention of a few photographers. We're able to duck into the car and drive off relatively unnoticed.

"So, where is the Opera?" I ask, adjusting my dress as Jeremy brushes off his blazer.

"In a center in Miami," he mumbles back nonchalantly.

I look at him, baffled. "That's hours from here."

Jeremy looks dead into my eyes, cocking a crooked grin. "I have a plane, my dear. We'll get there within an hour."

When the limo stops outside of the now familiar airport, we are able to quickly get onto the ramp and into the plane. It's nice having a private plane, I must admit. Not having to go through endless checkpoints and baggage claims and all of that saves massive amounts of time.

Jeremy and I settle onto the couch as the stewardess hands us a glass of champagne. I smile at her and turn to Jeremy, take a small sip. It's good, and I can tell very expensive.

Jeremy puts the glass up to his lips and, in one gulp, swallows the entire thing. The stewardess hasn't even had time to turn around to go back to her seat. Jeremy hands the glass back to her and asks for another.

Before he is able to look at me, I focus my eyes away from his face and towards the cabin that contains the white bed. I don't want to fight or make him feel badly, and I figure if I'm not staring at him, he can't tell how upset I am.

The stewardess walks over to where the serving closet is kept, and I hear the tinker of glass and pop of a cork. Jeremy looks in the direction I am.

"Looking at the bedroom already?" he says, amused. Obviously, my diversion tactic had worked.

I look at him, rolling my eyes, as the stewardess hands him another glass. His eyes sparkle at me before he tilts his head back, letting the liquid drain into his mouth. He hands the stewardess the empty glass again. She looks at him, surprised, and turns to walk to her seat.

"Another, please," he says as she walks away.

This time I can't hide my worry and disappointment. I sigh and Jeremy turns towards me on the couch. He gives me an apologetic look and lightly places his hand on my face.

The stewardess must have already seen where this was going, so she put the bottle in an ice bucket on top of a serving cart. She places two glasses on the cart and rolls it in front of us. Jeremy thanks her as she goes to sit and begins to pour himself another glass. "You can put some stronger drinks on the cart as well," he says to the exasperated stewardess.

I look again appreciatively towards the bedroom. I was hoping that on the way home but at this point I'm praying he'll still be conscious.

When the plane lands, Jeremy has had a bottle of champagne and two glasses of whiskey, but doesn't seem inebriated in the least. He puts his hands gently on my back as I walk down the stairway and towards another black limousine. The driver opens the door, and we slide into the back with grace. I'm getting the hang of getting in and out of a limousine in a dress. It's not as easy as you would think.

A short drive later, we pull up to a magnificent building. It's huge and lit up so that it can be seen from far away. The roof of the building isn't flat, rather it's spiked up haphazardly. I have never been to an opera house, but it looks very different from what I would've imagined.

The driver doesn't pull up to the main entrance, but goes around to the back of the building where there is a green steel door. To my surprise, Jeremy doesn't wait for the driver to get out and open his door, but opens the door himself and jumps out of the car almost before it has come to a stop. He runs around the back of the car and opens my door, offering me a hand to help me out.

I smile bashfully and grab his hand, rising out of the car. He leads me towards the green door after shutting the car door behind me, the limo speeding off.

"What is this?" I ask, curiously.

"I arranged to have us dropped at the stage door. I was hoping we wouldn't get bothered. So far, so good," Jeremy says, flashing me a sparkling smile. He looks so devastating handsome in his tux, I try not to look at him too often for fear my heart will explode.

Reaching the green door, Jeremy knocks hard on it and steps back to wait. The door opens and an older man peaks his head out from behind the door. He nods his grey head when he recognizes Jeremy and opens the door wider to allow us inside.

It's a short walk down a dark hallway and some stairs until we're out into the main hall. When I step through the door, I gasp at the lavish auditorium. The hall is full of rows of seats, which appear golden in the brilliant lights that hang above them. The stage has a unique circular chandelier that hangs above it, and there are square balconies surrounding the hall.

"Do you like it?" Jeremy asks, still walking and squeezing my hand.

"It's beautiful," I say, maneuvering past people walking down the aisle. Most of the couples are older and obviously from money, dressed much like we are tonight- the men in expensive tuxes and the women dripping in expensive jewels. Jeremy and I finally come to a doorway with carpeted steps leading upstairs. "We have a balcony?" I ask, excitedly.

"Indeed," he says, smiling. "A private one."

Maybe I should eat my earlier words about his fame not doing anything for me. Every experience with him is more amazing and fantastic then the next.

Pushing by a golden curtain, we take our seats at the front of our balcony. I look towards the other side of the hall, watching other couples as they take their seats. Jeremy has not let go of my hand, and the warmth of his skin feels so nice against mine.

We sit in silence as we both take in all of the commotion around us. The hall is almost completely full now. I look towards the balcony to the right of us and see more couples sitting down. As the lights finally begin to dim and the overture plays, I notice there is no one to the left of us. I smirk, wondering if Jeremy has rented that one out, too, to give us more privacy.

I see a woman appear on stage, wearing a black Spanish-inspired gown with red flowers in her hair. She's not fat like I imagined or wearing a Viking hat. When I mentioned my amazement of this fact to Jeremy, his body is wracked with silent uncontrollable laughter. "Not very cultured on the arts, are we?" he asks in a teased whisper. I smack his chest playfully.

Her voice is beautiful, singing in Italian. I don't understand the words, but her emotions are clear. I look over at Jeremy who has his eyes closed. He almost looks as if he could be sleeping, but his face gives away that he is overwhelmed with the emotions of the song. Obviously, he can understand the words.

I'm surprised to see him this way, looking so emotional and tender. It's nothing like the bad boy rock persona he tries so desperately to uphold. Every day that I'm with him, another one of his walls seems to come down, giving me glimpses of the real Jeremy.

Looking at him, seeing this different side of him, makes my heart swell with my own feelings. This is the man I'm falling in love with; the sensitive, genius man that has these amazing passions. I see in this moment a future with Jeremy. I see us traveling the world together, marrying on a private beach, and making love in different hotels every night. I see the face of a beautiful baby boy, with the same bright blue eyes as my brilliant and loving husband. I see us in a house in Boston, with ivy and brick and a big yard. We hold hands just as we're doing now, and his face is overwhelmed with emotion just as it is now, as we watch our children play in the back yard.

He opens his eyes slowly and looks at me, smiling when he sees me staring so intently at him. He smiles at me as if he knows what I'm thinking, and I return an amazed smiled back. From the corner of my eye, I see three people enter into the balcony to our left.

I instinctively looked towards them, noting with surprise that even in the dim lights, I can tell they are younger. The two men are dressed in more modern tuxedos, one with bushy hair and the other's spiky. It's obvious the girl is very attractive, wearing a long purple gown and short blue hair.

Immediately, my blood runs cold. I look over at Jeremy, noticing he once again has his eyes closed and is moving his lips quietly to the music. I turn back towards the people on the balcony and squint my eyes. My heart stops when I confirm my suspicion. One of the men is the weasel boy and the girl is the blue haired hooker that has been touring with Jeremy.

I can't hold in my anger. I turned towards Jeremy and, in an angry voice I don't bother to lower, I ask him loudly, "What are they doing here?"

Jeremy's eyes shoot open as the couples on the balcony to the right of us look towards the noise. Jeremy looks over at the balcony to the left, instantly knowing what I'm talking about, and looks back towards me. His eyes turn cold, but his voice is lower than mine. "I thought we agreed to drop it."

"No," I say, not backing down even though the look in his eyes scared me. "YOU agreed to drop it. I don't like them and you know it and yet you keep them around. Even on a date with me!"

"Because I'm not doing anything with them that affects you. Or us. So it's therefore none of your business," he snaps.

"When you're in an actual *relationship* Jeremy, everything you do affects the other person," I say smugly.

"And you have so much experience with that." His eyes are still cold. Is he trying to hurt my feelings?

I hear a few shushes directed our way. When Jeremy sees the hurt in my eyes at his last comment, he sighs and grabs my hand. He pulls us out of the balcony through the curtain and into the hallway.

He spins around to me as soon as we're in the hallway. "Why do you make me hurt you?"

I stare at him, aghast. "I *make* you hurt me?"

He doesn't look angry anymore; instead he looks desperate and afraid. He puts his hands out open palmed towards me. "Why can't you just drop it? Why?"

I am lost for words. What about these people would make him so desperate that he would fight tooth and nail to keep them around? Why won't he introduce us, if they truly are his friends or employees and he has nothing to hide?

Jeremy stands frozen, his eyes still wild with desperation, palms still towards me. He looks so vulnerable, and it's so distractingly beautiful.

I try to stay calm when asking him, "Are you sleeping with her? Is she, like, your mistress?"

Jeremy makes a disgusted sound and turns away from me, grasping his hair with both hands. "What do you take me for, Dylan? You're so naïve sometimes it's unbelievable."

The fiery anger rapidly bubbles over, through my stomach and into my mouth. "You're goddamned lucky I am naïve, Mr. Mason. If I had known what a fall down drunk you are when I first met you, I wouldn't have come near you with a ten-foot pole!"

His back instantly straightens and the room falls silent. I clasp my hand over my mouth. I can't believe what I just said, and I know I took it too far.

He slowly turns towards me and looks into my eyes. His eyes are flat, the color of rain puddles on asphalt. It surprises me to see them glisten with tears. It shocks the anger right out of me.

"I didn't mean that," I said, although I'm not sure it isn't true. I shouldn't have said it, regardless. The growing guilt begins to build an increasing pressure on my chest.

"Yes, you did," he whispers. His eyes never leave mine. "Dylan, I know I have problems. I have so many more than you know. I know I'm hiding things from you. But I do it to protect you. Protect you from my problems; protect you from me. I'm being selfish keeping you with me, and I know that."

I open my mouth to refute that, but he holds up his hand. "Let me finish. I am being selfish because you deserve better than me. Someone who can give you a normal life. Someone you could be proud to bring home. Give you children. Make you a better person. Someone…someone like Scott."

I wasn't expecting our conversation to turn like this. I wonder if he's breaking up with me. The pressure from the guilt has turned unbearable in my chest. It makes it difficult to speak. "Jeremy," I whisper.

"No," he interjects. "It's true. But goddamnit Dylan, I love you. I've never loved anything before in my whole life, except my brother, and that was different. No one makes me feel the way you do. I need you. I need you like the alcohol. I need you like the music. Do you blame me for being selfish? Because if I tell you all of the things you want to know, Dylan, you'll leave. And that's a fact."

I find the air in my lungs again. "I will never leave you." And at this moment I truly mean it. Seeing him declaring himself- I know in this moment that he truly loves me. And that doesn't come around often, a love like this.

"No matter what?" he challenges.

I'm nervous but my voice is clear, "No matter what."

He raises an eyebrow at me. "Are you ready to marry me, then? Would you walk down the aisle with me, an hour from now?" He stares intently into my eyes, searching for my response to his surprising questions.

I hear myself exhale as his words punch me full force in the chest. He smirks, thinking he's won his little challenge. He's about to say something else when I cut him off before he can begin. "Yes."

He looks confused. "Yes?"

I stand straighter now, more confident. "Yes, I would marry you tonight. Right now."

Chapter 12- Mystery Solved

"Dylan," Jeremy starts, looking horror-struck. "Are you nuts? You don't even know what I'm hiding from you."

I realize this, and yes, I may be a little nuts. But I love him, and I want to know all of him. If marriage is the way for him to let me in, to prove to him I won't leave, then I'll do it. "I don't care what it is you're hiding. It won't change my feelings for you."

He suddenly appears very intense, almost as if he's angry again. He walks closer to me, his eyes flaming with rage. He points his finger in my face, as if I'm a child. "You obviously have a lot of growing up to do if you would marry someone based solely on the unpredictable feeling of love. You'd do well to remember that in the future. This isn't a fairy tale, Ms. Ackhart, and I'm no prince."

He moves quickly past me before I can respond, fading into the distance down the hallway before I can even process what I'd want to say.

I stand like an idiot in the hallway, still staring in the direction he has gone for a number of minutes after he's left. I am completely heartbroken and confused, but unable to cry. Well, unwilling to cry in such a public place. And here I thought for a minute he was actually asking me to marry him. I don't understand. He wanted me to say no? Or was it a question that didn't have a right answer, no matter which one I picked?

I notice the lights grow brighter in the main hall through the curtain of our balcony. Everyone begins to file out of their balconies, so I decide to go into mine. I look down at the people on the floor below me: some still sitting, others stretching, and some filing towards the bathroom. I assume it's intermission. I sit in my seat, deflated.

After a few minutes of being numb, I wonder if I should be worried that Jeremy hasn't returned. Would he have just left me here? Should I leave and grab a cab, or stay and wait to see if he comes back? I scan the crowd below me, looking through the people making their way back to their seats to see if he has gone down there. I look to my left, noticing that Weasel boy and the other man are still sitting in their seats, but the blue haired girl is missing.

Something doesn't sit right with me about the fact she's absent. I notice the lights begin to dim. I decide to go looking for Jeremy.

I walk out into the hallway again, and continue slowly in the direction I had seen Jeremy wander after our fight. As I walk up the hallway, I pass a few windows before I reach the doorway to the stairs. Before I enter onto the stairway, I look out of the window at the cars and notice movement below. I instinctively step closer and look down. There are two people talking below me.

I recognize Jeremy immediately from his dirty blonde hair and cigarette dangling from his mouth. I note he's talking to the blue haired girl in the purple dress. The conversation seems relaxed, and as I watch in horror, they even begin to laugh. I'm up here brokenhearted, and he's down there laughing with her?

I see her take him by the arm as he flicks his cigarette to the ground and lead him towards the black limousine we arrived in, parked by the stage door where we had entered. Jeremy opens the door and extends a hand, letting her slide in first. He enters after her and closes the door.

My mouth gapes open. Is he serious? Is this happening?

I debate with myself on what to do for a moment, but the rage I feel is almost too much to bear. I find myself moving towards the stairs before I realize what I'm doing. Hot, angry tears stream down my face as I find the exit door and throw it open. I step outside and try to get my bearings as to how to find the limo. I make a right and run as fast as I can in my heels.

I round a corner and spot the limo. I stop for a moment and catch my breath, staring at it. I don't see any movement, but the windows are tinted.

Walking towards it, my nervous anticipation grows. I am about to find out what exactly is going on. I'm terrified I might catch him fucking that young girl. Then what? He won't be able to charm his way out of that one, or tell me to just drop it.

I reach the limo and quietly place my hand on the handle of the side door. My arm tenses as I throw the door open, thanking God it's unlocked, and throw myself into the car.

The next few seconds happen in a blur. I see the two of them turn to me with shocked expressions on their faces. They're not sitting together and they are fully clothed. Relief passes over me and I begin to feel like an idiot. Maybe they are just friends, after all?

But the relief fades as I look down to their lap. I see a spoon and lighter lying between Blue and Jeremy. Jeremy's right shirt sleeve is rolled up and his arm is tied with a rubber tourniquet, almost at his elbow. Dangling from the crook of his arm is a needle that he steadies with his left hand.

The emotions that flash over me are dizzying. Terror, panic, anger, sadness, pity, disgust. "Oh my God," I choke out.

Jeremy rips the needle out of his arm and blood begins to drip from the wound. He throws the needle on the seat and unties the rubber from his arm. He falls to his knees in the car, putting his hands on my knees. "Dylan, I…" he begins, then stops.

Blue stays still, not moving as if that could keep her unnoticed. I look up from Jeremy, his head resting on his hands on my knees, and towards her. I feel my stare intensify and, to my delight, she visibly shrinks.

"Go. Away." I pronounce each word slowly.

The girl turns towards the door opposite the one I came in and, after fumbling nervously with the handle, gets out and begins to run, slamming the door behind her.

My anger returns to Jeremy. Out of all the emotions, I pick anger because, let's face it, anger is so much easier to feel than anything else.

"So, she's your drug dealer, then?" I spit, stiffening my body. I suddenly don't want him to touch me.

He feels me stiffen and must hear my disgust. He drops his hands from my knees but doesn't raise his head or get up from kneeling.

"Not exactly…" he begins. I scoff.

"You're really going to sit there and bullshit me now?"

He gets up and sits on the bench to the right of me. He brings himself to look at me, but only barely, and doesn't meet my eyes. "No, she's a mule."

"Mule?" I ask incredulously.

"Her father is a big time drug dealer. Seth, the guy with curly hair? That's her brother. They both work for me. They carry the drugs on them that I buy from their father. I'm on probation, as you probably know, and the label said if I'm caught one more time for drugs they'll drop me. Not to mention I'd go to jail."

I stare silently at him, waiting for him to continue. I'm still not understanding. Jeremy looks up and makes fleeting eye contact, seeing that I want him to continue.

"So they are always around because they carry my drugs on them. That way if we're ever searched, the drugs will be on them and not me. I won't get arrested or in trouble. Seth also takes all my urine tests for me so that they'll come up clean."

I snort. "You've really thought of everything, haven't you? That is, except how to get clean. Dear God, Jeremy. I've had unprotected sex with you, and you're taking drugs, using needles?" I look around the car again, seeing the paraphernalia scattered around, and I feel sick to my stomach with disgust. I'm disgusted with this situation: with her, with him, with me for letting me believe he could care about anyone other than himself.

"How can you do this to me?" I say, hyperventilating. He looks up at me, his blue eyes shining. "My mother. You know. You know what happened. And you let me continue this relationship."

A tear slides down his cheek. "Oh, Dylan," he starts, unable to say anything else.

I look towards him once more and see all of the dreams I had just an hour ago drifting away from me. No wedding. No children. No happy life together.

"I can't do this," I say, grabbing the handle and opening the door. Jeremy's arm catches mine before I can step out.

"Dylan, you said you wouldn't leave. I need the drugs, but I need you too."

I don't even bother to turn and look at him. I can't take the sight of him like this. The man that I love, that I thought I loved, is gone. Or maybe never existed. "You've been getting worse and worse the whole time I've known you. Or at least I've been picking up on it more and more. I love you, Jeremy. But you are going to turn out just like my mother. Dead. And obviously I'm not worth enough to you for you to stop." His arm tenses around mine. I turn my head back and look into his pleading, sky blue eyes that are teary and red from the drugs.

"I'm not going to stay and watch you waste your genius. I'm not going to stay and watch you kill yourself."

With that, he drops his arm from mine. I take the opportunity to exit the car. "Don't bother contacting me unless you're ready to stop," I say, slamming the door behind me. I walk away from the car, rummaging in my clutch for my phone. I dial 411 and ask, barely hanging on to sanity, for a cab company.

While sitting in the back of the cab, he enormity of the situation finally hits me. I hold my chest tightly and try not to hyperventilate. Before him I didn't think I was capable of love. And now I find out he was lying to me the whole time? Did he ever really love me? If my own mother didn't love me enough to stop how on earth can I expect Jeremy to?

How could I be so stupid? I should have known. I should have seen the signs. Heat rash? I roll my eyes at myself. The shaking, the sweating at odd times, the way his eyes would turn red and watery... For as smart as I may be, I feel so stupid right now.

I try to push the thoughts out of my mind so I don't break down in the cab. The driver can tell something's wrong, but thankfully doesn't ask. He just keeps looking in the rearview mirror at me like I'm crazy.

I told the driver to take me to the airport, but what am I supposed to do once I get there? I don't think going back to the hotel in Orlando is a good idea. If I know Jeremy, he'll probably use his connections to make it back to the room before I get there. But what if there aren't any planes leaving to Boston tonight?

I need help. I can barely hold myself together, so coming up with a plan on my own seems impossible. I don't want to call Theresa. I know she's with Sean right now and I don't want to ruin. Besides, I couldn't take her happiness right now. My Dad definitely isn't an option. It would send him over the edge, hearing what Jeremy did to me even though he knows about my mother.

I take my phone out of my clutch and open my contacts. I find his name and hit the call button. The phone rings a few times before I hear his deep, groggy voice answer, "Hello?"

"Scott?" I choke out, as hot tears fall down my face.

His voice changes immediately to panic. "Dylan? What's wrong? Where are you?"

I inhale deeply, my breath shaky. "I need help," I say, not ready to explain. "I want to come home."

"Are you in Orlando?"

"No," I take a shaky breath. "I'm in Miami. I'm going to the airport."

His voice is red hot with anger. "Dylan, you listen, okay? I'm going to go make some calls and get you on a plane back to Boston tonight, alright? Just get to the airport, I'll take care of the rest."

I cry harder. Speaking the words out loud, especially to Scott, is almost making it real that Jeremy and I are over. And after everything, this is how it's going to end. I see the driver glance in the rearview mirror again. He's probably going to be glad to be rid of me. "I don't have any of my things."

"Dylan, don't worry baby. I'll make sure you get your things back. Calm down. It's going to be alright. I won't let anything happen to you, okay? You'll be home soon."

I nod, even though I know he can't see me. I do feel a little better. I know Scott is more than happy to get me away from Jeremy, and that I would be okay. Before we hang up, he tells me he'll call me back as soon as the arrangements are made. The cab stops in front of the airport. I search my clutch for the little money I have and manage to scrape together enough to pay the cabbie. I notice as I get out that he looks relieved. He almost runs me over pulling away.

I enter the airport and try to hide my face the best I can from the few other people walking around. It's a smaller airport and it's late, so thankfully not many people are travelling. Although, it's hard to look discrete in a ball gown wearing five hundred grand worth of jewelry around your neck, I look around trying to find somewhere with a bit of privacy to sit. I clutch my phone in my hand. I see people turning to stare.

I find a seating area and sit down in one of the blue cushioned chairs. A man and a woman are also sitting on the other side of the room, reading magazines. I feel my phone vibrate in my hand and sigh with relief.

My body freezes when I check the caller ID.

I want to pick up and talk to him. I want him to tell me he loves me and that he'll stop. I want him to tell me he's sorry. But even if he were to say those things, I know it would be a lie. Even if he didn't mean it to be. I've been through it before. If he didn't want to change for me before, he's not going to do it now.

I hit the deny button. I put the phone down in my lap and look at the people coming and going down the hallways of the airport.

A few minutes later, my phone dings to alert me I have a voicemail. I sigh, knowing it will be from Jeremy. I know I shouldn't listen to it, but I need to.

I put the phone to my ear and hear his sweet voice. The sound of it makes my heart constrict and eyes water, but even with the pain, I can't bear to stop listening.

"Dylan," he begins, his voice shaking. He starts sobbing. Strange, I had never heard him truly cry before. It's silent for a few seconds, then I hear him take a sharp breath. "I don't know what to say. I always knew I was a loser. That you were too good for me. That I could never deserve someone like you. I wish you could have heard what I was thinking when I first saw your beautiful face in the crowd." He stops. My eyes clench closed, the pain overwhelming.

"I'm a bad person, Dylan… a selfish person. But the love I feel for you is so beautiful. You made me feel like I was worth something. You made me feel like a better man. The music, the fame, the girls throwing themselves at me… that never mattered. It never made me feel anything."

I'm shaking. Even through all of this, I still love him. I fight with myself not to hang up and call him. I hate hearing him talk about himself this way.

He takes a few breaths; I can hear he's still crying. Then he continued. "So thank you, Dylan, for making me want to be better; for believing that I'm more than this. If even for a little bit. It meant more to me than you know. I'm sorry I disappointed you," his voice cracks on the last sentence. Tears pour down my cheeks.

He clears his throat. "My plane is waiting for you at the airport. Please use it so I know that you're safe."

After then, the message ends.

I put the phone down in my lap and wipe my cheeks quickly. I wonder if I should just take Jeremy's plane home. It's here already and I wouldn't have to bother Scott.

My phone begins to vibrate again. I nervously check the caller ID, and answer it when I realize its Scott. I'm a bit calmer now, but my voice is still shaking. "Hi," I breathe.

"Dylan," Scott's low voice is still full of worry. "I have a plane ready to go in thirty minutes, okay? Go to terminal 34A, there'll be someone waiting to take you to the plane."

"Scott, I appreciate it. But Jeremy left me a message letting me know his plane is already here to take me home."

"No," Scott interrupts. "No way. I don't know what he did, Dylan. And right now it's probably best because I'd want to kill him. But I know it has to be pretty bad for you to be so shaken up. I don't want you anywhere near him or his plane or tied to him in any way."

I sigh. "Okay, Scott." He's probably right, anyway.

"Dylan," Scott begins hesitantly. "Just tell me… shit…" he pauses. "Just tell me he didn't lay his hands on you."

"God no!" I say. "He wouldn't do that."
Even after all he's put me through, I find
myself still defending him.

Scott seems to pick up on that. "Right,"
he says, almost sarcastically. "34A, okay?" he
says, more gently.

"Okay. Thank you so much, Scott." I
really tried to sound grateful. I had no one else
to call.

"Anytime. Thank you for letting me
help. I'll be at the airport to meet you when
you get off the plane. And I'll take you home,
stay as long as you need, do whatever you
need me to do."

After I get on the plane, I'm amused to
find Scott's plane is much bigger than Jeremy's.
Somehow, Scott always seems to one-up him
on everything. The flight home is long and
grueling. Alone with no distractions, my
thoughts have nowhere to turn but the events
of tonight. I cry long and hard, hoping for
sleep to save from this ache, but it never
comes.

When the plane finally lands in Boston, I
wait as the door to the plane is opened and the
stairs are pushed to the door. The sun is rising
now over the horizon, making it hard to see the
stairs below me. I place my foot on the first
step and grab the railing tightly. I get to the last
step and feel two big, strong arms wrap

around me. For a moment I forget myself, thinking it's Jeremy.

"Are you alright?" Scott's deep voice speaks softly in my ear.

"No," I said, flatly. I'm too tired to lie. Scott puts his hand on my back and leads me to his car, making sure I'm situated comfortably in back before sliding in next to me. He tells his driver my address and puts his arm around me. It feels so nice to be in his arms. I feel protected and safe. I nestle into his chest.

We stay that way, silently, for the rest of the ride home. I can tell Scott is anxious for me to tell him what happened by the way he fidgets from time to time, but he doesn't push me. That's not Scott's style. He'll wait for me to tell him when I'm ready.

But I know I'll only be able to talk about what happen when the pain stops. And as of right now, I don't think that will ever happen.

Chapter 13- Fight

I vaguely remember walking up to the door and into my home, but I don't remember how I got into my bed. I wake up later that morning, with Scott asleep on a chair next to the side of the bed. I am still in my black dress, but the necklace and earrings are laying on the night stand next to me.

I stir and stretch, relishing in my post-sleep daze, until the heart crushing ache returned with the memory of what happened. I pull my knees up to my chest and look at the time. Eleven in the morning.

Scott begins to stir in the chair. I watch him as his long eyelashes flutter open. He looks surprised to see me awake and begins to stretch his long arms.

"You could have slept on the couch..." I say, lightly. I feel bad knowing he slept in that uncomfortable chair.

"I was alright. I wanted to be in here with you." He rubs his handsome face for a moment. He stands up and sits at the end of my bed, tapping my knee. "You okay?"

I make an effort to give him a smile. It probably looks as ugly as it feels. "Trying."

His hand still rests on my knee, and he begins to move his finger lightly, stroking it. His big, tan hand covers my knee almost completely. Honestly, it did feel good having Scott touch me.

"Do you want to tell me what happened?" he asks, not making eye contact. I sigh, and figure he deserves at least that much, so I tell him the story. I go back to the beginning, describing his strange behaviors, the alcohol, the brother and sister…everything. His face grows more and more horrified as the story goes on.

"Jesus, Dylan. I thought the man was supposed to be clean now? And I never heard about him using heroin. That's a whole different league than marijuana or cocaine."

"I know," I say in a small voice.

"That selfish prick. Did he even know the kind of danger he put you in? What if you had been around him when they found the drugs on the people in his party? You could have been arrested and expelled from Harvard. Even if they just brought you in for questioning on something like that, no DA office would want to touch you."

I guess I had never thought about it that way. Although the way Jeremy would make comments about not being good for me makes me wonder if it was something he thought about. Did he know how much he could jeopardize my career? My sadness turns to anger. I guess he really didn't care too much about what would have happened to me.

I stand up, conveniently knocking Scott's hand from my knee, and grab the necklace and earrings. I find a shoe box in my closet and throw them inside of it.

I turn and hand the box to Scott. "Can you overnight these back to him?"

Scott stands up and puts the box under his arm. "With pleasure." I see him take a phone out of his pocket and text someone. He walks out of the room a few seconds later, and I hear him open the front door and talk to someone. The door closes and he walks back into my room without the box.

"My driver is taking it to my office now to be securely overnighted. It will be there tomorrow morning at the latest."

Suddenly, there is another knock at the door. Scott looks confused, but walks out of my room to answer it. I take this opportunity to quickly fling my dress off and throw on a pair of jeans and a T-shirt from the floor. I vow to try and take a shower later.

I hear Scott's voice getting louder and louder, as if he's arguing with someone. I walk out of the room and down the hallway, peering around the corner of the kitchen towards Scott at the door.

"She's being well protected. By me. We don't need or want any of your help. We haven't been bothered here by anyone yet so why don't you get lost so you don't cause a frenzy?"

Hearing his words makes my throat close and terror rise in my chest. *Oh my God, Jeremy is here.* But the voice I hear responding on the other side of the door is too deep to be Jeremy, I realize. And anyway, Scott would probably have different things to say if Jeremy showed up here.

"I was sent here to help Miss Dylan and that's what I'm going to do. It's my job."

"Well, then, I'm officially releasing you from the job. Goodbye," Scott says, attempting to close the door. I see a massive, dark hand come around the doorframe.

"Rich?" I say loudly. Scott turns towards me and allows the door to open. I see Rich standing at the door, looking worried.

I walk down the hall towards him. He opens his arms and I give him a hug. "I'm sorry, Miss Dylan. But he told me to come and check on you. And to still stay with you awhile."

"Why didn't you tell me?" I ask, still in his embrace.

Rich sighs. He knows I'm asking about the drugs. "It wasn't my story to tell." I guess I can't blame him, even though I wanted to be angry at anyone and everyone. He's been with Jeremy for years, he only met me a few short weeks ago. I probably wouldn't have told, either, if I were him.

I can feel Scott's glare on my back, so I release Rich and lean against the doorway. I sigh, looking at Rich. Just seeing him reminds me of Jeremy, and that just isn't going to work. "Rich, listen. I really appreciate you being here. But I don't want any connection to him anymore. I don't want his help. I just…" my voice shakes for a moment. "I just want to forget he even exists. Forget that I ever met him."

Rich nods. "Okay. I'll tell him."

I nod sympathetically, knowing that Jeremy will probably unfairly ream him out for not doing his job. But I think Rich secretly agrees with me and knows where I'm coming from.

I step back away from the doorway as Rich turns to leave. "Bye, now," Scott says sarcastically and slams the door.

I turned to him, annoyed. "You don't have to be mean."

"Sorry," he says, shrugging his shoulders and trying to look guilty. "Just wanted to get the message across."

We walk into the living room and I flop down on the couch. Scott stands, studying me. "I talked to Theresa this morning before I fell asleep. I told her the little bit I knew. She wanted to come home but I told her to stay with Sean and give you space."

I sigh. "Thank you." It's not that I don't want to see my best friend. I just don't want to have to talk about it. I don't need another person looking at me as if I'm going to lose it.

Scott runs his hands through his hair. "I had my driver drop some clothes off for me. So I can stay as long as you'd like."

I look down, embarrassed, and nod. I'm beginning to think he might be worried I'm going to try to kill myself. But after what my mother did to herself I would never do that. No matter what, I will never do that.

"You need to eat. What can I get for you?"

I am hungry, but thinking of eating makes me want to vomit. "I can't right now," I say.

I hear him start to protest, but I stop him. "I will," I say. "I promise. Just not right now."

He sits on the edge of the couch by my feet and puts his hand on my leg. "Dylan, I know you love him. It kills me, but I know you do. I just want you to know that it will get better. Someone as special as you deserves better. Deserves someone who can give you better," he says, with implied meaning. I stare back and him blankly, not knowing how to respond. I know I shouldn't lead him on. I should tell him no now. But I'm selfish and I don't want him to go.

He stands up when he realizes I'm not going to answer. "I'm going to take a shower. Then your turn. Okay?"

I nod and watch him walk down the hallway. After he disappears into the bathroom, I pick up the remote and turn on the TV. I flip through channels, not paying attention to what's flashing in front of me. My home phone rings, but I decide to let it go. No one calls me but telemarketers and my Dad on that phone, and I don't want to talk to either one right now.

The phone stops ringing after the fifth ring, but almost immediately starts again. I furrow my brows and look over at it, getting up from the couch and walking towards it. The caller ID says it's an unknown caller. It's obviously a telemarketer. Are they seriously calling twice in a row? Jeez, pushy.

I am about to turn and sit back down once the phone stops ringing, but as soon as it stops it starts again. I pick up the phone and mumble an angry, "Hello?" ready to give them a piece of my mind.

"Are you trying to hurt me?" I hear a silky, angry, lovely voice speak into my ear and directly to my heart.

My heart beat quickens to an unbelievable pace. I can tell he's waiting for an answer. Should I hang up? I think that's the best idea but I can't seem to make my muscles move to take the phone from my ear. "Huh?" I say, confused.

"I asked, Dylan," he purrs, sending another shock through me, "if you are trying to hurt me purposely? Because, bravo baby, you're doing a damn fine job."

I know he's speaking words but I have to focus to process them. The adrenaline is making my mind race. "Why would I be trying to hurt you?" I say, softly.

"I don't know," he continues, his voice irate. "But the fact that you didn't take my plane last night and had me and all of my employees driving around the city to find you, only to see a picture of you online this morning landing in Boston in someone else's plane is a good way to start. And not just any other plane, Dylan, but *his* plane. The pictures really are lovely, real fucking romantic. Him catching you at the end of the stairs. Holding you in his arms. His arm at your back as you climb into his fucking limo."

I hold my breath. Did he have me followed? But then why would the pictures be online?

"How? Pictures?" I stammer.

"Oh Dylan come on, those reporters were expecting a plane to come in soon that had you and I on it. They didn't know when it would come so I'm sure they had people stationed there every minute. But what a surprise to all of us when you decided to take off with one boyfriend and land with ANOTHER," he screams. I feel as though he's slapped me, but before I can speak he continues.

"And then, Rich hears your little boyfriend, who I can only assume has been at your house all night, talking to his driver about overnighting jewelry to our hotel room. And then you refuse Rich's help because you want to 'forget I exist,'" he quotes. I cringe. "So I stand by my initial question. Are you trying to hurt me this badly? Are you trying to get me to fucking kill myself?"

My anger washes over me. "Don't put that shit on me Jeremy Mason," I scream. "You were killing yourself long before you met me, weren't you? You put me in danger. You knew I wouldn't like it but you made no attempt to stop!"

"I CAN'T STOP DYLAN!" he screams. "You think I want to be a fucking junkie?"

"Yes!" I scream back. "Because you think it takes your pain away. You think it's easier to not feel anything. You think you need drugs because it's the only way you know how to cope with all the bad shit you've had to deal with. You haven't bothered to try and get help."

299

"It's not that simple. You don't understand. It's not just that easy. I don't do this because I'm a rich boy with too much money and nothing to spend it on or because I want to feed into the fucking rock star stereotype. I need them to survive."

"Then you don't love me, Jeremy," I say, choking up. "Because you can't have both of us in your life. And you're choosing heroin over me. Just like she did. You honestly expect me to practice law and go home to a junkie? You expect me to marry you or have your children while you're shooting up? So they can walk in and find you dead, too?"

He's silent. I'm silent. My question hangs there for a moment before I hear footsteps behind me. I have been so focused on Jeremy that Scott must have gotten out of the shower without me noticing. He crosses the floor and rips the phone out of my hand before I can stop him.

"Hey!" I scream. Scott holds his hand up.

"You need to stop calling here," he says sternly. I can't hear what Jeremy says on the other end of the line.

Scott laughs. "I don't care what you think I am, you pathetic junkie. She doesn't want you. She doesn't want to speak to you. And you know what? If you really loved her, or gave any kind of a shit about her, you would want that and respect that. Because you know what a pathetic man you are and you know she deserves better. Don't ever call here or come near here again, or you'll have to talk to me, and it won't be pretty, Mason." Scott slams the phone down on the receiver.

I find myself furious with Scott for a moment. He didn't have the right to do that. Even though I know it's for the best. Nothing good can come from talking to Jeremy, it only makes me more hurt and angry.

Scott puts his arm around my shoulder and hugs me to him. I sigh, saying nothing. He pushes me away after a moment and looks down into my eyes. "Shower?" he offers. I nod. "And, uh," he continues, "I should probably get dressed."

I look down at him and notice he's only in a towel. My eyes bulge and I giggle a bit. He laughs too. "Awkward," he says, walking towards my room. "I mean, unless you want me to just change here…" he loosens his grip on the towel and it falls down a bit in the back as he walks away.

I clasp my hand over my eyes and laugh louder. "You idiot," I say. It feels nice to smile.

After he's safely in my bedroom, I continue into the bathroom and turn the warm water on. I undress myself and sit at the bottom of the shower, leaning back against the tub. I let the water fall over my body, trying to relax.

Thinking back to the phone conversation, I find myself panicking over his words. He wouldn't really kill himself, would he? I think maybe he was manipulating me but I can't know for sure. Am I over reacting? Should I have tried to stay with him and help him? Convince him to get help? I know somehow that wouldn't work. I've heard enough about drugs to know that you can only quite when YOU decided you don't want to use anymore. No one else can make you. And I guess he is slowly killing himself, in a way. The drugs will eventually kill him. The thought of Jeremy dying, whether or not it was due to me, made my panic level raise uncontrollably. I am borderline hyperventilating. How long will it be until I hear from some disgusting news story that he was found dead? How long before he became just another rock star stereotype? The world would never have the chance to see how special he truly is. No one would know but me. And I'd be left having that guilt on me forever. As if I needed that.

"Oh my God," I say out loud. "He's going to die," I say, bursting into hysterical tears. Scott starts pounding on the door, waiting only a second before flinging it open. "Dylan, what's wrong?"

I'm crying so hard I can't answer.

"Um," he says, reaching behind the shower curtain with only his hand, fumbling to turn the water off. He succeeds and reaches over to grab a towel from the door. He hands it to me.

I'm able to grab it and wrap it around me. After I stop moving, I guess he assumes I'm decent and opens the curtain. I'm still crying hysterically on the floor of the bathtub.

Scott picks me up into his arms. "God damn him. God damn him for making you feel responsible for his problems."

He exits the bathroom and lays me down on the bed covering me with my blanket. I'm exhausted. As soon as my head hits the pillow I begin to fall asleep.

The last thing I remember is Scott's hands stroking my hair.

I wake up to the sound of two men screaming at each other. At first, I think it's another dream. I slowly open my eyes and look around in the darkness, realizing it's early evening and the sun has just set.

I still hear the screaming and my blood pressure rises as I realize it isn't a dream. I pull the towel that I'm still wearing tighter around me and run out into the hallway. I round the corner of the kitchen into the hall by the door and stop.

I see Jeremy, dressed in black, long and beautiful, inches from the face of an infuriated Scott. My heart leaps and flutters at the sight of him. His face is even glorious when he's angry. He's here. He's come for me. He loves me...

"I'll be God damned if you see her, Mason!" Scott booms. I see Jeremy's eyes flicker over towards me. I stare at him.

I see sadness flicker past his eyes, but it fades back into rage. He looks up and down my body. I understand how this must look, with Scott being here since yesterday and me being in nothing but a towel.

I look down at myself and back up at him. "No," I say softly, shaking my head.

Scott looks over to me and back at Jeremy, knowing what I'm implying. "It's none of his goddamned business anyway, Dylan."

"The hell it isn't!" Jeremy yells, pushing Scott hard. Scott, surprised, falls backward into my wall roughly, making a dent.

My mouth drops open as Jeremy runs over to the wall where Scott has fallen, fists up. "No, Jeremy!" I scream in horror.

I see Scott stand before Jeremy reaches him. He grabs Jeremy by the throat, throwing him against the opposite wall and holding him there. "Are you fucking crazy, bro? Are you?!" Scott screams in his face.

I run over to Scott and grab the arm holding Jeremy's neck. "Scott, please, no!

Please!" I scream. Jeremy looks over at me, unafraid, a cocky smile on his face. "He won't hurt me," Jeremy chokes out.

I hear Jeremy gag as Scott squeezes his throat harder. "The hell I won't," he says, darkly.

I don't understand why Jeremy isn't fighting back. For as tall and lanky as he looks, I would bet money he could beat Scott in a fight any day. But he's doing nothing. I stare at Jeremy, and realize with horror how bad he looks. His skin looks grey and the whites of his eyes are almost yellow. His lips are pale and chapped. I claw harder at Scott.

"Dylan, go call the police," Scott instructs.

"Okay!" I scream in desperation. "Just let him go and I'll call!" I purposely scratch Scott's hand in an attempt to surprise him into letting go. He winces, but he doesn't loosen his grip.

"Why are you shaking, Mason? Scared?" Scott taunts.

Looking down at Jeremy's hands, I see that they are noticeably trembling. I stop clawing at Scott's hand and take a step back, examining Jeremy's face again. His eyes look far away, and I see the cocky smile has left his face.

"Scott," I say, terrified. "Scott, I think something's really wrong."

Scott's anger fades a bit as he takes in Jeremy's changing expression. He releases his grip on Jeremy's neck apprehensively. Jeremy leans against the wall as Scott backs away. He doesn't attempt to move or speak, but his trembling continues.

"Jeremy?" I ask, stepping towards him.

Suddenly, Jeremy collapses on the floor. His body makes a sickening thud. He starts shaking uncontrollably, like he has no control of his muscles. I scream and fling myself on him, trying to hold him still.

Scott stands back in shock. "I didn't choke him that hard, I swear, it wasn't that hard..."

Jeremy continues to shake. "Oh my God!" I scream. Oh God no, this is my worst fear coming true. Please not here, not now!

Scott kneels down beside me. He hands me his cell phone. "Call 911."

Jeremy continues to shake. "We can't do that. The press...I'll call Rich and have him bring a doctor." Jeremy's shaking subsides, but he lays unconscious on the floor. Scott holds his finger against his throat. "He's alive," he says.

I dial the phone with one hand, keeping one of my hands on Jeremy's face. I stroke his hair, "It's okay baby," I whisper to him.

The phone rings twice before Rich picks up. "Hello?" he says, confused by the unfamiliar number.

"Rich!" I almost scream. "Please come to my house! Bring a doctor!" I beg.

He starts to ask me what's wrong, but I feel Jeremy start to tremble again. I can sense it slowly building. "Rich!" I scream. "Just get here! Now!" I toss the phone on the floor.

I feel like I'm going to lose my mind when he starts to seize again, shaking so hard his body almost lifts off the ground. I cry hysterically.

"Scott! Scott what's happening?!"

Scott holds his legs down, trying to control his shaking. "I don't know. He's seizing. I don't know why. I don't know how to stop it. Jesus!" he says as Jeremy's lower body bucks harder.

After a few more seconds his shaking subsides again and he lays still. I sob and put his head in my lap, using the bottom of the towel to wipe the bubbling saliva from his mouth.

"We have to make sure he doesn't hit anything," Scott says. He stands up and moves everything out of the way, all the furniture and shoes, and then returns to the floor at his feet.

"I think we have to time them to see if they're getting longer. The last one was about twenty seconds."

I look up at him in terror. "You mean there's going to be more?"

He shakes his head. "I don't know. I hope not."

I tremble and stare desperately at Scott. "Did he overdose? Is he dying?!" I scream.

Scott shakes his head again. "I don't know. I don't think so," he says, quickly.

I look down at his lifeless body, his head lulling on my lap. "Jeremy," I cry out. "Jeremy? Wake up! Jeremy, please!" He doesn't respond.

After several quiet minutes, I feel his body start to move, but it's trembling again. "No, no, no!" I say over and over. But it doesn't stop the shaking from growing, traveling down his body, until his whole body is again bucking. His head flies back and forth on my lap.

I put my hand on his cheek and steady his head. I whisper in his ear. I tell him how much I love him and how special he is. I tell him that he can't leave me, and that I need him. I tell him I'll never love anyone the way I love him, over and over, until the shaking subsides once again.

His breathing is hard and uneven. I look up at Scott, who is staring at me, disappointed. Whether or not it's at the state that Jeremy is in, or if at the words I said, I can't tell. Surely he wouldn't deny a dying man some comfort?

My stomach rolls at the thought that Jeremy could die here in front of me.

"Thirty seconds," he whispers to me as I sob. It's getting worse.

A few more minutes go by until I hear my door knob turn and the door burst open. I see Rich run in the doorway and stop when he spots Jeremy's body on the floor. The doctor, the same doctor I saw when I was rescued from the crowd, comes around Rich and drops immediately to the floor.

"What happened?" he demands, rummaging in his bag. I open my mouth to speak, but an ugly crying sound is the only thing that escapes.

"He's seizing," Scott volunteers. "He started shaking and fell to the ground. He's had three seizures. They keep getting longer."

The doctor removes a long needle from his bag and a vial of liquid. He sticks the needle in the vial and draws up the medication, spraying some out of the top before sticking it into Jeremy's upper arm. He pushes the medicine into his arm and withdraws the needle.

"Ativan," he says to me. "To stop the seizing."

I nod and try to calm myself. The doctor suggests that we get him into a bed. I stand so Rich can grab his upper body while Scott carries his legs.

I grab jeans and a t-shirt from my drawer while they move him and run into the bathroom. I make record time throwing my clothes on and run into my room just as the men are placing him on the bed and backing away. I walk over and kneel by the side of the bed. I grab his limp hand, running my fingers over the rough tips of his. Silent tears fall from my eyes.

We all stay like that for a few moments, relieved that Jeremy hasn't seized. He still trembles a bit, but his face seems serene. He almost looks like he could be sleeping peacefully. After the doctor takes Jeremy's vital signs and determines they're stable, he excuses himself to make a few calls. Rich sits in the chair that Scott slept in the night before, rubbing his face from strain and worry.

"Rich," I whisper. "You know him better than anyone. What's going on?"

Rich shrugs. "I don't know Miss Dylan. I've seen him get the shakes sometimes, sure, but never seen him like this."

I look up at Scott who is standing by the foot of the bed, looking intently at my hand clasped in Jeremy's. He makes eye contact with me for a brief second and then looks away. He clears his throat. "Excuse me," he whispers, exiting the room.

I feel incredibly guilty, but I can't bring myself to leave Jeremy's side. This may be the last time I'm with him. Scott would forgive me, but I'd never forgive myself if I wasn't there to comfort Jeremy at the end.

The doctor comes back into the room and stands at the edge of the bed. I see Scott standing by the doorway. I hold my breath as the doctor begins to speak.

"I'm relatively sure he's going through alcohol withdrawal. The shakes and seizures he's having fit. I'd say he hasn't had a drink in a day or two, and for a major alcoholic, that's a long time."

"Since I left," I mutter in surprise.

The doctor continues, "I also happened to notice he has track marks on his arms and hands. I think Mr. Mason is in serious jeopardy if he doesn't get some help."

My breath catches, "What kind of help?" I ask desperately.

"Rehab. I can get him into a facility quickly."

"But what about his label? They said they'd drop him if they found out he was using drugs again. And he'd be violating probation." I say, dazed.

"Miss Ackhart, he will recover from this incident, but without rehab I believe Mr. Mason will eventually die."

I stare at the doctor as that sinks in. I know what he says is true. I've thought it many times myself. But no one knows Jeremy like I do- the problems he has now and has faced his whole life. Because he's a genius, he sees the world differently. He sees people and situations differently. No one is truly on his level; he feels no one could ever understand him. How are these counselors and nurses at the rehab supposed to make him better, if they don't understand him? If he can't communicate effectively with them?

The doctor sees that I'm conflicted. He sighs. "I suppose there is another option, but it's risky."

My eyes shoot to him. "What?"

"We could try to get him to detox at home." The doctor waits for my reaction.

I think for a moment. "Why would that be risky?"

"Because it's not as secure as a rehab center. The center has resources wouldn't be available to him at him. Not to mention the lack of security, he could find a way to get drugs or alcohol. Does he live alone?"

I bite my lip. "Yes."

The doctor nods. "We can have a nurse stationed with him at all times. That would help."

I consider the idea. It seems like it could work. Except Jeremy would basically be all alone with a stranger. What if he gets lonely or bored and wants to use again? "What if…" I say, quietly. "What if he stays here?"

I hear Scott choke. "You can't be serious?" he almost pleads.

"Why not?" I ask. "He wouldn't be cared for by only a perfect stranger. I could be here and help the nurse. Help him. Wouldn't it be helpful to have someone he knows?"

Scott stares at me, open mouthed.

The doctor considers the idea. "Actually, it could work. He doesn't have drugs that he's hidden here. But it isn't a decision you should make lightly. Detox can be nasty. It can change people, make them say and do terrible things. Not to mention the physical suffering, no matter how much we try to control it."

I look over at Rich, who is looking at me. He shrugs.

Scott moves from the door, pushing past the doctor. He grabs me by the shoulders and stands me up, forcing me to let go of Jeremy's hand.

"Dylan," he begins. "What makes you responsible for him? What makes this your problem? You're in your first year at Harvard! In your first goddamn semester! You don't need this bullshit. You're going to ruin your life over this. There's no way you can handle school, a job, and all of this shit."

I look down towards my feet. I can't bear looking at his face- so full of concern and caring for me. Honestly, deep down I'm worried that he's right.

"He has people that take care of him," Scott continues. "I know you love him. But you don't have to throw away your life for the stupid choices he's made."

I look back up at him. "You're right. I don't have to." Scott looks relieved.

"No, I'm not done," I continue. He tenses. "I don't have to, but I want to. Because I love him. And when you love someone, their problems become your problems, and their pain becomes your pain."

He whispers to me, "So how do you think watching you throw your life away… watching your pain…will affect me?" He stares into my eyes intensely. His blue eyes search mine for a reaction.

Did he just tell me he loves me?

When I don't respond, Scott lets go of my arms and turns quickly, walking for the door. I want to call to him, to stop him, but I know whatever I say isn't going to be what he wants to hear. Visions of what Scott and I could have flash through my mind: sweet kisses not tinged with booze or cigarettes, Thanksgivings at home with my Dad and Scott at my side, graduating from Harvard top of my class and earning my dream job with an engagement ring on my finger, a nice home with a blonde haired baby and a dog. But when I hear my front door open, those dreams follow Scott out the door.

The doctor nods at me when I focus my eyes again on him. "I'll make the arrangements, then. I'll have a nurse here within an hour. I'll stay until she gets here." He walks out of the room, digging his cell phone out of his pocket on the way.

I look at Rich, who's staring at Jeremy, still by the bed. "What are they going to do about the tour?" I ask.

"His publicist will take care of all that. We'll say he's sick with something and needs time to recover." Rich looks exhausted.

"Go home, Rich. We'll be okay. No one knows he's here."

Rich nods. "I'll have a police car stationed across the street anyway. But I'm going to get some sleep."

I scoot against the wall to allow Rich to pass between me and the bed. I watch him quietly walk out the door before turning back to Jeremy. His breathing is now light and even; his body still. His skin is disturbingly grey, but even so his beauty is breathtaking. His hair is haphazardly lying on the pillow, and I find myself pulled toward him to fix it. I run my hand through his hair, smoothing it, caressing him.

I realize how tired I am, looking at him sleep. I debate whether or not to sleep in

Theresa's room. I know since it's Saturday she won't be home until at least tomorrow night. I remind myself that it would probably be wise to call her in the morning to warn her about what she's walking into. I'm hoping Sean offers her a place to stay while Jeremy's here. I wouldn't want Theresa burdened with this mess, too.

I let my hand run through his hair and onto his face, the stubble tickling my fingers. I think about him in his prime, on stage, sweat dripping from his head. I see him strum his silver guitar, raising his hand above his head and arching his back: his sparking eyes, his white smile, his infectious laugh. How far he's fallen…how broken he looks…

I don't bother to change out of my t-shirt and jeans. Instead I round the bed to the empty side, gently climbing on and pulling the covers over my legs. I slide carefully over to Jeremy and rest my head on his chest. I mold my body against his and drape my arm around his waist. I hope he can feel me, know I'm here. I hope my body feels as wonderful and familiar to him as his does to me.

When I saw him standing in the foyer of my house and we made eye contact, I knew he was there because he loved me. He was coming to tell me he wanted to change, that much is clear because he stopped drinking the moment I left. Knowing that he loved me, I know I would do anything and give up anything to see him better. I was no longer a single person; I was drowning in him again. Except this time, it wasn't just physically, but mentally and emotionally, and every other way imaginable. My person was consumed by him. At this very moment, feeling the man I love against me, knowing I'm comforting him in his hour of need- it makes me happy. That should be enough, right?

Chapter 14- Uphill Battle

The night flew by in a blur. I vaguely remember meeting the nurse, an older lady with graying hair. I drifted in and out of sleep as she hooked Jeremy up to different machines: an IV in his left arm, a heart monitor, and every hour or so a blood pressure machine.

I begin to stir late the next morning, when I feel a hand running through my hair. My eyes flutter open, adjusting to the light. I don't feel well rested at all, due to waking up multiple times during the night. I lift my eyes up towards the hand that's caressing me and see a pair of ice blue eyes staring down at me.

I lift my head up off of Jeremy's chest and smile at him. He smiles back. His eyes are bright and sparkling again aside from their slight yellow color, but his skin is still grey, and a sheen of sweat is on his forehead.

"You're awake," I say, relieved.

"You're here," he breathes, his voice still smooth and exquisite. "You let me stay?" he questions, surprised.

"Of course I did," I place my hand on his face, running my fingers along his cheekbones and stubble, down to his chin. His smile widens.

"I'm sorry I scared you. As soon as you left and I couldn't find you, I knew that I never wanted to touch that stuff again. The way I felt when you left me…no substance on Earth could make me forget that feeling…" Jeremy trails off.

"I know you love me, Jeremy. And I love you. We're going to do this together," I comfort him. I look at his forehead that continues to sweat. I take part of the blanket and wipe his head. "How are you feeling?" I ask him, worried.

He shrugs. "I've been worse. I'll be okay. The nurse has me on some medications; a benzodiazepine to get me off of the alcohol and some stuff for seizures. I'm on an antidepressant, too, and they're going to have a psychiatrist see me weekly," he says.

"That's wonderful!" I say, excitedly. "I'm so proud of you for doing this. For really trying."

He smiles for a moment, but then his face turns serious. He pushes a strand of my blonde hair back behind my ear. My heart beats faster with the intensity of his gaze.

"When all of this shit is over, when I can finally be the man you need me to be, I'm going to marry you."

My cheeks flush. "Jeremy," I say, softly. "There are a lot of things to think about. When you go back to your music, your tour, . . . And Harvard, I can't just leave."

"No," he cuts me off. "I don't care about anything else. Everything will work itself out. I need you. I love you."

I avert my eyes, embarrassed, and push off of him to get myself out of bed. I feel gross being in the clothes from yesterday, so I make my way over to my dresser. I pull out new underwear and a bra from the top drawer and a long sleeve shirt and jeans from the bottom.

I hear Jeremy adjusting in bed, sitting himself up. With my back facing him, I take my shirt off and throw it to the floor, and then my bra.

"Getting dressed so soon? Why not come back to bed for a while? It's Sunday, no class for you," he says. I can hear the smile in his voice.

I turn my head over my shoulder and smile at him. "It's almost noon."

I drop my jeans and step out of them.

"Dylan," Jeremy says, more seriously. I stop and turn my head over my shoulder again. His eyes are hungry. My heart beats faster as he looks the back of my body up and down. I stand there frozen in just my underwear.

"Come back to bed," he says, again. This time, it's an order.

I give him a disapproving look. "I don't think it's a good idea. I'm nervous it's too much for you. You were really bad yesterday."

He nods in agreement, but smiles. "I don't have to do any work, technically." He looks up at me from under his long beautiful lashes. He takes his shirt off and throws it to the floor.

I try to look annoyed with him but I know I'm failing. He's so beautiful, his long muscles pronounced. Okay, two can play at this game.

I wait until he's looking at me again, and then I turn around to face him, the front of my body bare. His eyes widen. "Dylan, please baby, come to me. I'm not above begging for you."

I lower my underwear to the floor and step out of them. I walk over to Jeremy, naked, and climb on top of his lap so that I'm straddling him. I expected him to start putting his hands all over me and kissing me passionately, but instead he hugs me to him, so that our bare chests push together.

"I honestly thought I'd never hold you like this again," Jeremy says, mumbling into my hair.

"Me either," I confide.

"I'll never disappoint you again. Nothing is worth being without you."

I pull away from him and look into his ocean blue eyes. He smiles tenderly at me, brushing my hair back. I climb off of him for a moment to take his pants off and throw them off the bed. I climb back onto him, stopping as I remember, "Where's the nurse?"

He kisses my neck softly, "In the living room. She gave me a bell to ring if I need her. She checks on me every half hour or so. She'll knock." He continues to kiss my neck.

That's good enough for me. I lean over to my bedside table and grab a condom from the drawer, part of the stash I kept there during the weeks I spent with Jeremy before he left for the tour. After sliding it on him, I lift myself up a bit and then down onto him. He gasps softly, grabbing my back. I feel him fill me, and close my eyes.

I move slowly on him, running my hands through his soft hair, watching his pleasure dance across his face. For a second, it almost looks as if he's grimacing. After I see it again, I ask, "What's wrong?"

He shakes his head without opening his eyes. "Nothing," he chokes out.

I slow slightly, worrying that I'm hurting him, but he places his hands on my hips to will me to move faster. Jeremy, what's wrong?" I ask again.

"It's just...my body, it hurts everywhere. But don't stop," he says as I freeze. I hesitantly start moving again. "You make me feel so good. I want to feel good again."

I move faster and our breathing increases. Jeremy reaches his hands behind me, grabbing my ass. "God, yes," he says. I continue to pick up my speed.

Jeremy hangs his head back, leaning it against the wall. His face is clenched, his jaw tight. I know he's close, so I drive myself down on him, hard.

"Fuck," he moans, as he topples over the edge. I slow my movements and collapse on top of him.

We sleep for a while off and on, staying in bed all day. He sleeps more than I do, and I'm glad to see he's catching up on rest. I read or watch movies. Sometimes I just sit and watch him sleep. He mumbles and sweats in his sleep from time to time, stirring as if he's having a bad dream. I rub my hands on his arm or face, which seems to settle him a bit, and he's able to eventually fall back into peaceful slumber.

I notice the sun beginning to set, causing the sky to become a bright orange. I hear a knock at the door, and the nurse enters a few moments later, holding a tray of food for us. She sets it on the table next to me. I smile and thank her in a whispered voice, and she nods at me and quietly leaves the room.

I rub Jeremy's arm. "Jeremy?" I say, softly. "Wake up and eat. You haven't eaten all day."

He moans towards me, sweat appearing on his forehead. I bite my lip, unsure of what to do. Should I just let him sleep? Somehow I think that he should eat something, especially since he hasn't eaten at all since he's arrived. "Wake up. You have to eat something," I press.

He rubs his eyes and sits up in the bed. He looks over at me and tries to smile, but I can tell he's in pain. He's shivering as if he's freezing, but he has multiple blankets on. Sweat is pouring down his face.

"Oh, honey," he says, his voice tight. "My stomach is killing me. I'm just not up to it."

I give him a concerned look. "I don't understand. Why are you so sick if you're on medication?"

He looks away from me for a moment, and then meets my eyes again, as if he's warring with himself. "Tell me," I beg.

"This isn't from the alcohol withdrawal. It's from the heroin." A deep shiver ripples over his body.

"Okay," I say, still confused. "What can they give you for that? Don't they have methadone clinics for that?" I know just the general basics about the subject, especially because I've avoided hearing anything about that drug after my mother.

He shakes his head. "I don't want to get on that stuff. It's just another addiction to feed an addiction. Besides," he hangs his head. "I deserve to suffer."

I furrow my eyebrows disapprovingly. "Come on, Jeremy. You don't have to suffer." I grab his hand, squeezing it. His palms are drenched and his hand trembles. "You're doing the right thing right now by getting clean."

He wraps his free hand over his stomach. "God, it hurts so bad." His shaking gets worse.

I'm suddenly afraid. "Please, Jeremy, take something. I don't want to see you in pain," I said, my voice breaking on the last word.

He snickers a bit. "Babe, I'm going to be in pain for a while. There's not much to do about that."

I give him a smug look. I reach over him to grab the bell on the bedside table near him, ringing it before he can get to it himself.

The nurse enters the room almost instantly, and I plop down in my spot on the bed. Jeremy looks at me, annoyed.

"Mr. Mason?" the nurse questions.

Jeremy opens his mouth, but I cut him off. "Actually, it was me."

"Miss Ackhart?" she says, turning her attention to me.

"Jeremy is in pain. Can you help?"

Jeremy looks at me, still angry, and then back at her. His shaking is still obvious. "It's fine, really."

She walks over to him, grabbing the blood pressure machine from the corner of the room and takes his vital signs. She says his blood pressure is high.

"Mr. Mason, I'm going to give you Clonidine, which will help with the chills and sweats. It'll bring down your blood pressure, too. Also, I'm going to give you Bentyl for the stomach cramps, and Motrin and a muscle relaxer for the muscle aches. Okay?"

He sighs heavily. "Yeah, okay."

"Hold out your hands, please," she instructs him. He raises his arms in front of him, palms down towards her. They are extremely tremulous. I look at the nurse in concern. She, also, looks concerned.

"Maybe I should give you more Librium?"

"No," Jeremy cuts her off, crossing his arms over his chest again. "No, no narcotics. Not more than I have to."

"Jeremy," I say, my annoyance increasing. My stomach churns. "Alcohol withdrawal is no joke."

"I know that," he snaps at me. "Unlike you."

I look at him in surprise. He can be so mean when he's talking about drugs. It's like he's a whole different person.

His face relaxes after he says the words. "I'm sorry, Dylan. I'm sorry. Okay," he looks towards the nurse. "I'll take the rest of the stuff, but no Librium yet."

The nurse nods and exits the room, returning a few moments later with a cup full of pills. Jeremy takes it with water and, grabbing his stomach, lies back down on the bed. Within minutes, he's asleep again.

I sigh. I guess I'm eating alone.

The next morning comes and my alarm goes off at six as it does every weekday morning. I jump at the sound and quickly hit the snooze button, rolling over to see if it has wakened Jeremy. He doesn't seem to move.

I lay there for a minute, trying to decide whether or not I should go to class today. Jeremy looked terrible yesterday; he was moaning and crying in his sleep. I decide to shower and then see how Jeremy is doing when I come back.

In the shower, I wonder how weird it's going to be to see Scott in class. I don't want it to be weird, but I have a feeling it will be. That alone makes me want to skip class. I have a hard time in awkward situations and dealing with confrontations.

After showering, I enter the room with a towel on, and sneak over to my dresser to find some clothes. I choose simple black pants and a light pink blouse. I try to get dressed as quietly as possible because Jeremy's still sleeping.

When I'm dressed, I walk over to the bed, and pause when I see his eyes are open. He's staring off into space, and doesn't even look up at me when I approach. His skin and eyes are extremely yellow. His face is a bit puffy and swollen. If it weren't for his regular breathing, I would think he was dead.

"Jeremy?" I say, running my fingers through his gorgeous hair. He shuts his eyes tightly, and a tear runs down his face.

I kneel by the side of the bed. "Honey," I said, my voice breaking. "What can I do? Should I stay?"

His eyes still closed, he shakes his head no.

I sigh. I have a feeling I'm not going to class today.

"I'm just in pain," he whispers. I feel his body trembling. Another tear runs down his face.

"I know," I whisper back. "I wish I could take the pain away from you."

He looks up at me; his blue eyes are red from crying. "No, it's my job to take your pain away. And I swear I'll do that for the rest of my life. You'll never see me like this again. The only thing controlling me will be you."

I smile, touched and amused. "As if I could ever control you."

He attempts a smile back at me. "Go to class," he orders.

I sit there, still hesitant. He narrows his eyes at me. "Go."

I stand up and pull the blanket up his bare back so that it's touching underneath his neck. I turn and walk out the bedroom door, shutting it lightly. I give the nurse detailed instructions about calling me if something happens just as Rich knocks at the front door. I grab my bag, throw my shoes on, and open the door to see him standing at the top of my steps.

We share a smile and I grab onto his arm. There are a few reporters outside, but not many.

"Dylan, do you know the whereabouts of Jeremy Mason?" a woman says, sticking a microphone in my face. I squeeze Rich's arm, and he gives me a reassuring smile in return. "Why has he postponed the tour? Do you know what hospital he's in?"

Rich opens the door to the black car for me and I slide into it, shutting the door in the reporter's face. I'm relieved to hear that they don't seem to know what's going on. I thank God Jeremy has a good team to handle this situation.

When Rich enters the car, we drive away to campus in comfortable silence.

Somehow, I'm the first one to arrive in my Criminal Law class. The silence in the room is almost eerie. I walk up a few steps and sit in my unofficially assigned seat. As I'm taking my laptop from my bag, I notice Theresa entering the door. She stops when she sees me and shoots me a huge smile, running up the stairs and wrapping me in a big embrace. I try hard to hold it together.

"Hi," she says, her voice full of concern. "How are you? How is he?"

"Both good and bad," I sigh.

"Listen, I don't mind coming home and helping you. Sean said I can stay with him as long as I need, but if you want me to come home, I will."

"No, no. I'm okay for now. It gets-messy. Overwhelming," I try to explain without scaring her. More people are entering the class now, so she just gives me a nod, and we take our seats.

As more people enter the classroom my heart beats a bit faster. I'm nervous to see Scott. When the class is nearly full and the professor walks in, I think that maybe Scott isn't coming. I feel both relieved and concerned.

Class begins with still no sign of him. Just as the professor begins his presentation, Scott enters quickly through the door.

"Mr. Hillman, nice of you to join us," the professor scolds.

Scott nods and finds his seat next to me. I look at him, but he doesn't turn to me. He doesn't even make eye contact with me. Throughout the class that seems to drag on longer than normal, I continue to look over at him from time to time. He never returns my gaze.

When the professor excuses us from class, I turn to Scott. I plan to ask him what his problem is, but instead I'm met with his back as he walks out our aisle and down the stairs. He's through the door before I can think of anything to say.

I turn to Theresa, a frown on my face. She shrugs her shoulders, grabbing my hand and squeezing tightly. We pack up our things and leave the now empty classroom for our next class.

After a long day at school, I am anxious to get home to check up on Jeremy. The nurse hasn't called me all day, which I hope is a good sign. I'm praying that he has improved since this morning.

When I enter my front door, turning to shut it tightly and lock it, I kick off my shoes and hurry down the hall. I stop in my living room, expecting to find the nurse there. I furrow my brows when I don't see her.

I enter the bedroom quietly in case Jeremy might be asleep. My chest tightens when I see an empty bed. Did they go to the hospital, and not have time to call me? My breathing increases. I knew I shouldn't have gone to school. What if something had happened and I wasn't here for him?

Shit, shit, shit!

I hear a small noise coming from the bathroom across the hall. I turn and immediately enter into the hallway, opening the bathroom door slowly. I see the nurse on her knees in front of a shirtless Jeremy, covered only by a towel, with blood covering his forehead.

He looks up at me and smiles like he's seen the sun for the first time. "Dylan," he breathes. He's still yellow and swollen.

"What happened?" I ask, panicked.

"Jeremy had a seizure when he was in the shower," the nurse explains, dabbing his head with a cloth. "He took a little spill."

"I'm alright, Dylan," Jeremy reassures me in a small voice.

"Does he need to go to the hospital? Does he need stitches?" I ask the nurse. I know Jeremy would tell me he was fine even if his leg was falling off, so I don't trust him to answer truthfully.

"No, no. Head wounds bleed a lot. It looks worse than it is."

I give him a suspicious look, narrowing my eyes. "Did you coach her to say that?"

"Dylan, little such faith you have in me," he says, grinning.

The nurse helps him up from the floor, and I walk over to grab his other arm. He holds the towel around himself as we walk into the bedroom and lay him on the bed. I help him under the covers and the nurse finishes cleaning the wound on his head and leaves us alone.

I sit on the bed beside him and place my hand on his leg. "How was school?" he asks me, running his hand through my hair.

I shrug my shoulders. "Okay. Except Scott isn't talking to me. And I probably shouldn't have gone. I think I should be here with you."

"Okay, first of all, you need to go to school," Jeremy begins. "You're not going to fail out of Harvard because you were taking care of me all day. It isn't necessary. Secondly, let me tell you how extremely devastated I am that Scott isn't talking to you." He smiles, trying to make me laugh. I just look at him, still hurt.

He sighs. "Dylan, he'll come around. He's just jealous and needs to get over the fact that we're together. He got his hopes up when you came home, and it didn't work out the way he wanted it to. He's not used to handling disappointment. Once he learns to deal with that you'll be okay." I sigh and think that maybe he's right. One day, maybe my life will go back to semi-normal.

Jeremy crosses his arms over his stomach. I tell him to rest, rubbing his shoulders until he's asleep.

I'm in the living room a few hours later watching TV when I hear a loud crash in the bedroom. I jump and turn to look at the nurse who is sitting and reading at the kitchen table. We make eye contact for a moment and stand up, preparing to run to the bedroom.

Suddenly, Jeremy throws my bedroom door open and enters into the hallway. He's only wearing a pair of jeans, and his face is magnificent and angry. His eyes are wild, furious. He glares at us.

"I have to go. I have to get out of here."

I'm frozen. "Why?" I stammer out.

"Don't ask me why, Dylan. You don't want to fucking know the answer to that."

I try to stay calm. He starts wringing his hands, bouncing a little as if his legs won't stay still. "I do want to know the answer, Jeremy," I say, quietly.

He turns, slamming his fist through the wall in my hallway. The nurse and I jump, and she takes her cell phone out of her pocket, as if she's going to make a call for help. I hold my hand up to her, telling her to wait.

"You don't want to fucking know the answer! You're hurting me, you bitch! You're making me suffer. Fuck you, Dylan! You fucking bitch!" he turns and punches the wall again.

His words sting, but I know I need to stay calm. He begins pacing up and down the floor of the hallway, screaming obscenities. "I'm not a goddamned caged animal! If I want to go, I'm going to go! I have the power. You can't control me! No one controls me anymore. NO ONE!" He punches a hole in the other wall. I jump again. The nurse gives me a wary look, obviously thinking it's time to call someone. I shake my head at her.

"No?!" he asks, appalled.

"Not 'no' to you," I clarify, in a calm voice. "You can go, Jeremy, if you really want to."

"Oh, I fucking know that, and I'm going," he says. We stand still for a moment, staring at each other. I see him warring with his decision as he stares at me. His breathing starts to calm, and the anger drains from his face. "Dylan," he says. "I *have* to go," he pleads.

A tear spills over my cheek. This is it, then. He's leaving. He's made his choice. I should have known I wasn't enough.

His eyes become angry again, and I realize I said the last sentence out loud.

"Goddamnit!" he screams, marching back into my room, slamming the door shut. I hear him scream more obscenities and the sound of things smashing. The nurse immediately makes a phone call.

My front door opens suddenly and I look over in time to see a man running towards me. I scream before I notice it's Scott. He grabs the tops of my arms as he reaches me. "Dylan, are you alright?!" he asks me frantically.

"I'm okay," I say unconvincingly.

"Should I go in there?" he asks, as Jeremy continues to scream and we hear the breaking of glass.

I push my head into his chest and let him put his big arms around me. The nurse is speaking quickly on the phone but I can't hear anything. "No, just stay with me," I beg Scott.

He puts his hand on the back of my head, smoothing my hair. I start to cry, hurt from Jeremy's unkind words and scared because of his actions.

I cry into Scott's chest until the sounds in the bedroom finally die down. I turn my head to the nurse, while still holding Scott around the waist. "Beverly, who did you call?"

"The doctor," she says. "To see if there was anything I could give him. Just in case he'd actually take it."

I sigh in relief. I was afraid she called the police.

I look up at Scott, who is staring down at me, his handsome face concerned. Our faces are inches apart, but it doesn't occur to me to be uncomfortable. In this moment, it just feels good to have someone to hold me. "What are you doing here, anyway?" I ask, smiling at him through my tears.

He looks confused. "It's Monday. A study night."

I laugh a little. He chuckles. "I'm sorry about the way I acted," he says, in a serious tone. He smooths my hair with his hand again. "I'm going to be here for you. To help you. Because, I…" he pauses and I hold my breath.

Oh please, no. Not now. I can't handle it.

I hear footsteps in the hallway, and we turn to see Jeremy standing there, watching us. His hands are dripping blood onto the hallway floor. I watch the emotions flash across his face: anger, shock, sadness, hurt, and then pain. Heart wrenching pain.

I look up towards Scott, who's looking at Jeremy in disgust, and then back at Jeremy. I immediately release Scott's waist and step away. "Jeremy," I say, my voice breaking.

Jeremy turns slowly, walking back into the bedroom. It's silent for a moment before we hear a horrific heart breaking scream, and then sobbing.

I put my hand over my mouth. I begin to sob harder, shaking and unsure of what to do. I'm scared to go in, but I'm scared not to.

Jeremy's loud, painful sobs continue. The nurse sighs, her shoulders heavy with stress. Scott doesn't move from my side. Another scream comes from the bedroom.

I can't stand being away from him anymore, and I walk forward slowly towards the bedroom. "Dylan," Scott says, as if he's begging me not to go. I ignore him.

Looking in the doorway, I have to repress the gasp from escaping my lips at the state of my room. There is glass all over the floor. My dresser is tipped over, clothes spilling out. The windows are smashed open and the curtains are ripped down from above them. All of the clothes in my closet lay on the floor. There is blood on some of the broken pieces of glass.

I see Jeremy, sitting on the edge of the bed, his back towards me. I quietly enter the room, thankful I have sandals on, as I hear the crunching of the glass beneath them. Jeremy doesn't turn, just continues his heart wrenching sobs. His shoulders shake up and down with the force of them.

I reach him, as he sobs into his hands, and sit next to him on the bed. Slowly and carefully, I put my hand on his shoulder. He turns to me quickly, and I freeze, afraid. But he wraps me tightly in an embrace and cries on my shoulder.

I sob with him. We hold each other for a long time, rocking back and forth. His hands twist in my hair, my hand grabs the back of his lovely blonde locks.

Finally, he says in a broken voice, "I'm so sorry. I'm sorry Dylan. I can't believe I said those things to you."

"Shhh. I know you didn't mean them." But they still hurt.

"I never want anyone to say those things to you. I…I don't deserve you. But I don't want to live without you. Please don't leave me. Give me another chance. Don't let me push you away." He sounds frantic.

I shake my head on his shoulder. "You haven't. You haven't pushed me away. I'm here, and I love you."

"You don't ever have to be afraid of me. I would never hurt you."

Would he? "I know," I whisper, running my hand down his back.

"I'm going to get better, and we'll be together. Forever."

Will he?

"Forever," I promise.

Chapter 15- Turning a Corner

Surprisingly, Scott, Jeremy, and I were able to get the room back in order. I lost my mirror and had to replace the dresser, but other than that, the damage wasn't as bad as it seemed. Nurse Beverly bandaged Jeremy's hands, and I moved him and his things into Theresa's room while we had the window repaired.

A week went by, and Jeremy improved dramatically. His shakes were less noticeable and he was doing well on his Librium taper. I was told by the doctor the day after the incident that Jeremy's anxiety and aggression weren't uncommon in people detoxing. But thankfully, he has had no violent outbursts since. He has been getting shots for his yellowing skin, and the puffiness around his face is almost gone.

Scott has been coming around more to help me try to get back on track with studying. Often, we are disturbed when I have to attend to Jeremy's needs. Scott never seems frustrated, and he and Jeremy are actually civil to each other. Jeremy even shook his hand once, and thanked him for coming over to help keep me on track.

The night of the incident, I stayed up all night with Jeremy, wiping his head with a cool cloth as sweat poured down his face. He shook almost uncontrollably, his teeth clattering. He moaned in pain most of the night, only stopping for short bursts of sleep.

The second night after the incident, Scott had come over to study with me, when we heard a knock on the door. When we answered it, I was aghast to find the weasel faced boy, standing as if everything was fine on my top step. He had the audacity to come looking for Jeremy at my house! Scott told him in so many words that if he ever showed his face around Jeremy or I again, he better pray Scott simply would call the police, because jail would be the least of his worries. Weasel-face ran off after that like the coward he is, and I don't expect we'll hear from him again.

Jeremy seems to be coming back to his normal self as time goes on. He's able to sleep more and more with each night, the pain in his muscles and stomach subsiding. I enjoy being with him, happy to see him in less pain. We laugh together, snuggle, watch movies, and cook dinner, just like it was before he left for his tour. We made love again, finally, last night. In that respect, he's definitely recovered.

I didn't realize how having him around me could be so distracting until I bombed my first exam in one of my classes. Okay, I didn't bomb it per se, but I got a C+. In my mind, that may as well be an F.

Looking at the C+ on the computer screen in the library, I can't believe my eyes. Scott, who is standing by me, pats me on the shoulder. "Want to go out for a drink?"

I'm trying to hold myself together. *A 'C'? Me? Oh my God, oh my God…*

"Yeah, that sounds really good actually. But," I pause, sighing, "maybe I should get home to him."

"Come on, Dylan. He's fine. He's doing better and he's a big boy."

I look up at Scott's hopeful face. "Okay," I agree. Since we took all the alcohol out of my house when Jeremy moved in I haven't had a drink in a long time. But after seeing my grades, I need one.

Scott takes me to a little bar not far from campus. It's filled with students, even though it's two in the afternoon. We grab a table and sit, and he orders us two beers. I've never been a beer drinker, but right now it seems like a really great idea.

"So, is it safe to say Theresa is officially moved out?" he begins, trying to make casual conversation.

I sigh. "I guess so. Things seem to be going really well with her and Sean. She's moved most of her essential items. I think she really loves him." And she's blissfully happy all the time. And passing school. And can eat at a restaurant without getting photographed or called a cow. And doesn't have to worry Sean will die in the night...

Scott frowns at my forlorn expression. "Dylan, you have to concentrate on your grades more. I know you've been, uh, distracted. But this is serious now."

"I know, I know," I say. At least I can always count on Scott to be painfully honest.

"I want to tell you something," he says. The tone of his voice makes me look up at him, my heart picking up speed. His expression is serious. The waitress puts our beers in front of us and, with a thank you, she walks away.

I wait patiently for him to begin speaking.

"I think you need to leave him, Dylan."

I give him an exasperated look. This again?

He holds his hands up in surrender. "Seriously, jealousy and personal gain aside." He puts his hands down. I listen intently.

"Dylan, I'm not sure if I can phrase this correctly. So just bear with me."

I nod.

"The man has a lot of issues. You have some things you seem to be working on too. I only know so much as you've told me, and it's not a lot but it's enough to know there's something."

343

I glare at him. Nice, so now I'm crazy?

"Just stop, okay? You know what I mean. You've just gotten out of your home, really, for the first time. For a long time you've been defining yourself based on others and their expectations. You can't define yourself by other people."

"I know that," I snap. "Where are you going with this?"

"What happens if he starts using again, Dylan?" Scott says, leaning over the table. "He said, he's only quitting for you. And I know you, if he starts using again you're going to think it's because you're not enough for him."

Duh.

"Right..." I say, as if that should be obvious.

"But he shouldn't be quitting because of you. He should be quitting for himself. That way if he starts using again, you'll know it's because he doesn't feel like *he's* worth anything. And you'll be able to work on yourself and not have to carry the burden of him around. You don't need more burden in your life. It's enough you have to deal with the press, but basing your self-worth on a drug addict won't help you, either."

I look down at the table. We sit in silence for a long time, as Scott allows me to reflect. He's right, of course. Absolutely right.

"I don't know how to be without him," I whisper. Anxiety rises in my throat.

"Well, that's a problem." Scott's caring voice caresses me. "He's addicted to the drugs. The drugs are a tool for him. They create false feelings in him. They make him feel things he can't feel on his own: happy, relaxed, self-confident, and peaceful. They're a constant distraction from dealing with his past. Don't you realize you're using him in the same way?"

I look up at him, my eyes tearing.

"It isn't healthy, Dylan. This relationship. You need to get out, even if it's just until you can both deal with things on your own. You can't help each other if you're both dealing with your own issues."

I've never been much for prayer, but I've been praying a lot lately. I beg God, silently in that moment, to give me the strength to know what to do.

When I get home, I'm surprised to see Jeremy up and around, washing dishes in the kitchen. The most famous rock star in the world washing dishes in my kitchen. I'm almost over the strangeness of it. Almost.

"Hey, you're late," he says, smiling at me, putting a dish in the dishwasher. He walks over to me and kisses me lightly on the lips.

"I grabbed a drink with…" I paused for a nanosecond, "some friends." I don't know why I feel so guilty about being around Scott when it comes to Jeremy. Maybe it's because of our topic of conversation today.

Jeremy looks at me suspiciously, but lets it go.

I put my bag down by the kitchen table as Jeremy closes the dishwasher. He's humming a sad, lovely tune. He slinks over to me again, just like he used to, his hair messy and sexy. I smile, my heart skipping as he grabs me around the waist. I put my arms around his neck and we dance, right there in the kitchen.

"What are you humming?" I ask, quietly.

"A new track I'm writing," he says, smiling down at me, his navy eyes close to mine. He begins to sing to me, "*And she says 'Drown me in you,'/ And how can I resist?/ With her love so perfect, so sweet/ that even I can barely breathe./ I've lost myself to you/ so you want to lose yourself in me./ That's alright, baby, that's alright.*"

I recognize the words I spoke to him the first night we made love. I smile widely, embarrassed by the idea of a song written about me. I kiss him passionately, my love for him overwhelming me. He tightens his grip on me, pulling me even deeper into the kiss. I reach up, unbuttoning his shirt, as he pushes the blazer from my shoulders. His shirt falls to the floor, and I reach down for his jeans, undoing his belt. His hands caress my back, undoing my bra.

Soon we find ourselves naked on the floor, his comfortable weight on top of me. He kisses me softly on my forehead, my cheek, and my neck before entering me. He fills me almost to the point of pain, but it's always amazing. I moan in relief. I didn't know how much I needed him, needed this.

He begins to move slowly, the heat of our bodies magnified by the coolness of the floor on my back. As he makes love to me, he whispers softly in my ear. "I love you, Dylan. I'll never want anyone else. You're everything to me, my reason for living. Nothing's ever meant anything to me before you." He repeats those words, over and over again, while I I burry my face in his shoulder, silent tears running down my cheeks. I cherish this moment, locking his words into memory, locking his body into memory, until he finishes and collapses on top of me.

I wake up Tuesday feeling very well rested. My eyes wander up to the clock on my bedside table, smiling when I realize it's the afternoon. Oops, I guess no class today. I had promised Sean that I would be returning to work tonight so he no longer needed to cover me. That gives me a few hours at home to rededicate myself to studying.

I turn my head to the left, and see Jeremy sleeping peacefully. The light covers his bare chest like a blanket, illuminating him like an angel. His face has returned to its normal color once again. He looks healthier than I've ever seen him, and very beautiful. It makes my heart ache. As unhealthy as our relationship may be, it doesn't make me love him any less.

I creep out of bed, careful not to disturb him, and make my way across the hall. I take my time with my morning routine and have three generous sized cups of coffee before I finally sit down at the kitchen table, laptop ready and books in hand.

A few moments after I've begun to read from one of my books, I hear footsteps coming down the hallway. I turn, seeing Jeremy rubbing his eyes, wearing only boxers. He's breathtaking. I smile at him. "Hi," I say.

He looks at me, running his fingers through his messy hair. "Hey," he says, yawning. He sits down in the chair across from me, stretching his muscles.

"How are you feeling?" I question, returning my gaze to my textbook.

"Better. My muscles ache a bit."

"Hmm," I say. We're silent for a moment. I think he catches on to the fact that

I'm distracted, so he gets up from the table and flops down on the couch instead. He turns the TV on and flips through the guide.

About an hour goes by, and I'm proud of myself for getting so much work done. I pause for a moment to rub my aching eyes, looking over to where Jeremy is in the living room. He fidgets, readjusting himself every few seconds, tapping his foot.

He looks over towards me, as if sensing I'm staring at him. I give him a forlorn smile. He looks like a caged tiger, trapped in a small space and uneasy.

"I'm bored," he complains. "I think I'm going to go out."

My heart sinks. He did finish his detox medication this morning, and the nurse felt okay to leave, saying she would be returning only during the night.

"Okay," I say in a small voice.

He stands, walking past where I'm sitting and into my bedroom. I try to continue reading, but after I read the same sentence in my book seven times, I give up and try to concentrate on not hyperventilating instead.

He comes out of the room and stops in front of me. I look up at him, trying to make my face emotionless. He's wearing jeans and a black hoodie.

"Aren't you going to call Rich?" I ask, gingerly. I'm trying to disguise the panic in my voice.

He smiles lovingly at me. "No, I just want to be alone for a while. I'll be careful, promise. I have my cell on me. I'll get out of your hair for a while and I'll be back soon."

He strokes my hair for a moment. I'm scared to even get up and hug him goodbye.

"I love you," he says, leaning to kiss the top of my head.

"I love you…" I say, my voice trailing off.

He turns, grabbing the keys to my car and opening the door. Once the door is closed, I run to the window, peering through the curtain so he can't see me. I see him lope down the steps and start walking down the street.

The hyperventilation begins as soon as he's out of sight. I drop down to my knees in front of the window, turning to sit on my floor with my head in my hands. Where is he going? Why wouldn't he volunteer that information?

Do I follow him? What do I do?

He didn't take my car, so I figure he can't be going far. I get up from where I'm sitting and return to the table. I try to continue studying, but I can no longer concentrate, my chest filled with anxiety. After about an hour, I give up and walk over to my TV. I flip mindlessly through the guide. I look over towards the wall, where we set the mirror he had broken to be put out with the trash later. The pressure on my chest increases.

Four hours later, I'm a mess. I'm pacing the floor, running over to the window by the door every few seconds to see if I can see him coming. My car is still there, unmoved since this morning. I call out of work, much to Sean's dismay. I'm constantly checking the news to see if any reporters have spotted him around the city.

About a half hour later, after I become a useless hysterical lump on my bed curled up into the fetal position, I hear my front door open. I perk my head up and hear it shut. I scramble out of bed and run down the hallway into the kitchen, where I'm met with Jeremy carrying plastic bags.

He cocks an eyebrow at me, "Hey, babe."

I can't talk. I frantically look him up and down, my eyes lingering at the crook in his arms trying to see if there are new track marks. He sighs and puts the bags on the counter, extending his arms to me. They're clean.

He gives me a wary look and starts taking the groceries out of the bag. "Did you get your work done?" he asks.

I'm silent for a moment. "Where were you?" I finally whisper.

He puts down the jar he was holding and walks over to me. "Hey," he says, soothingly. He rubs the back of my head, pulling me into his chest. "I went for a walk, and then I stopped to get us some groceries. That's all."

That's all for six hours? I don't think so.

"Jeremy," I say, my tone serious. He pulls away from me, holding my hands in his. I look up into his eyes, expecting an answer.

His face looks sad. "I went to see my mom."

Oh.

I let that sink in. "How did that go?"

He shrugs. "She's happy to see me clean, but I didn't go there to make her happy. She's one of the reasons I use so I wanted to start facing my demons. Tell her I don't want to be in contact with her in any way again. And that I wouldn't be helping her with the store anymore. So I picked up a few things I wanted from her home and that was that."

One of the reasons he uses? I assume he means because she forced him to be a child star. And because of his brother, Jonathan.

I suddenly feel like a major jerk. "I'm sorry," I say, both for his mother and my reaction.

"It's okay, Dylan. I don't blame you for worrying. But, if you were going to be this much of a mess over it, you should have talked to me about it."

I nod. "What's for dinner?"

He smiles, walking over to the groceries on the counter. My anxiety is quelled as we start cooking and laughing with each other, as if the whole thing never happened.

Chapter 16- Facing the Music

The next morning, I wake up early for school, determined to get there today. I'm sore and satisfied from a night with Jeremy. I look over towards him, seeing him stir as well. He opens his eyes and looks at me. We smile at each other.

"You're so beautiful, especially in the morning," he whispers to me. "You make my heart ache."

I gently run my hand down the side of his face before getting up and walking towards the bathroom. I shower and dress, and before I know it, it's time to leave.

Leaving Jeremy for the first time without the nurse being home makes me extremely nervous. I know eventually, if this relationship is going to work, I have to trust him.

When Rich knocks at my door, I'm still waiting for my coffee to brew. I invite him in just as Jeremy walks into the living room. They smile and hug each other, talking about how things have been. Rich tells him how good he looks, and Jeremy thanks him.

After I put my coffee in my thermos, I tell Rich I'm ready to leave. Rich nods, and finishes his conversation with Jeremy. They had been talking about when Jeremy plans to resume the tour. Jeremy had told me he would be meeting with his executives today, which helps quell my fear. At least he'll be kept busy.

After a kiss and a hug from Jeremy, Rich and I head out the door and to the car.

I get to my Criminal Law class and find Teresa. I'm so happy to see her. We hug and talk about how much Jeremy has improved. After a few moments of talking, Scott sits beside me, giving me a quick hug. I'm proud to inform both of them that he went out yesterday alone and came home sober. Theresa looks thrilled, Scott sour.

After school is done, Theresa asks me if I want to grab a coffee in the shop a short walk from campus. I agree and text Rich to pick me up at the shop in thirty minutes.

I love coffee shops. The smell of the intoxicating liquid surrounds us as we walk in the door. After getting a cup and finding a table, I ask her about Sean. "How are things going?"

She beams. "Really, really well. Actually, we've been talking about marriage."

I gape at her. "Marriage? After only a few months?"

"We'll be engaged for a while, of course. But, yeah."

"Wow," I say, astonished. This is the girl who only a few months ago didn't even know the meaning of a second date.

"Especially since I won't have to worry about paying my half of school, thanks to Jeremy." She smiles happily at me, thinking back to that time. I smile at her. Jeremy is kind of a big, generous softie.

I see Theresa glance at the table next to us, and then quickly glance back at me. She glances once more at the table.

"What?" I question her, my brows furrowed. I look at the man at the table next to us, reading a paper. I squint to read the headline. I gasp as I read, *Is Jeremy Mason a Single Man?*

"Dylan, you know you shouldn't read that nonsense," Theresa tells me quickly, as I stand to walk to the front of the shop. I grab a paper from the wire stand where they sit, and head back to our table. When I sit, I throw open the paper. Theresa sighs, defeated.

The picture under the heading of the article is of Jeremy, in the clothes he wore yesterday. He's leaning over the table, giving a professional-looking young woman a kiss on the cheek. Another picture shows him handing her a velvet bag, and her placing it in the pocket of her pants.

My heartbeat is in my throat. He lied to me. Lied! After everything I've done for him, after everything he put me through, he lied to me!

I try to calm myself enough to scan the article. I get the general gist. *Everyone will be thrilled to hear he's no longer sick…Where is Dylan Ackhart…who is this new mystery woman…what is in the bag…*

I fold the paper back up and place it under my arm. I take a long sip of my coffee. I'm shaking with rage. Theresa has been silent the whole time I was skimming the article.

"Anything you want to talk about?"

How can I talk to someone who's never had their heart broken? Who is blissfully happy with the love of her life? No way.

"No, I'm fine."

She nods at me, sadly. "I wish you would talk to me like you used to."

I swallow hard. "Me too."

Just then, my phone vibrates. I read the text from Rich, telling me he's outside. I say a quick goodbye to Theresa, trying not to lose it until I can get back to the house. I jump in the back of the black car, simply nodding to Rich, who can tell by the look on my face not to bother me.

When we pull up to my house, I get out of the car and thank Rich quickly. I shut the door and walk up the steps as Rich pulls away. Entering, paper still in my hand, I walk into the living room. Jeremy's there, watching a football game, smiling up at me.

"Hi," he says, giving me a loving smile. I try to ignore the burning it causes in my heart.

You lying, backstabbing asshole. Liar, liar, liar!

"You…" I start, my voice angry. His eyebrows furrow.

"What?" he asks me, surprised.

"You…you lied to me!" I scream at him. He jumps from the couch, rounding it to stand in front of me.

"What?!" he asks again, astonished.

I throw the paper at him so that it hits him in the chest. He catches it awkwardly, adjusting it in his hands and looking down at it. I see his face darken.

"Oh shit," he says, under his breath.

That's right! Caught, Jeremy!" I'm frantic. My heart rate increase and my rational brain shuts down.

"No, Dylan. I know these pictures look…really bad. But it's not what you think." He almost makes it sound like I think he's cheating on me. Oh, if only our relationship was that simple, to fight over something as petty as cheating.

"I don't think you're sleeping with her, Jeremy. But I do see you're handing her a bag. Is she your mule, now?"

He looks at me, mouth gaping open.

"Is she? You know what? Let me see your arms. And in between your fingers and your goddamned toes. I'm not an idiot!" I scream, walking over to him and ripping his sleeve up to the top of his arm.

He rips his arm away from me. "Dylan, stop! I'll show you okay, just don't grab at me."

When he rips his arm away from me, I lose it. I just, lose it. There's no other word for it.

I start hitting him. Not just hitting him, but beating him. I punch his chest, his arms, and his stomach, over and over. I push him and he stumbles backwards. The whole while, I hear myself screaming at him, "You bastard! How could you? How could you lie to me? After everything I've done for you! How? Tell me how you can do this?!"

It is like all of the anger, resentment, fear, stress, and exhaustion has bubbled up to the surface. I feel my limbs beginning to tire, but I pull my hand back, preparing for one final blow. He's so busy trying to protect himself; he isn't concentrating on what I'm doing.

I let my hand fly fast through the air, coming in contact with his face. The slap is deafening. The sting of his skin on my hand brings me back to reality. I gasp, backing away. Jeremy stumbles backwards, grabbing his face. I see blood trickling out from under his fingers.

"Oh my God," I say, my voice shaky.

Jeremy wipes the blood away from under his nose. He glances at his hand, and looks up at me, his eyes calm. "It's okay, baby," he comforts me, wiping the new blood that falls. "I'm alright."

"No!" I shout. "I hurt you. You're bleeding!" I say, hating myself.

He comes towards me but I back away. I don't want him to come near me; I'm scared of hurting him again. He pauses.

"Dylan, I hurt you too. It's okay. I would have been angry, too. I understand. I've put you through a lot."

I look at him, my eyes wide. "Jeremy, this is not okay! This is not normal. This is not healthy…"

The blood from his nose has stopped, but it does nothing to quell my guilt. He walks over to me again, and this time I stand still. He wraps me in a hug.

"I don't trust you," I whisper, the sad truth leaving my mouth. Tears stream down my face.

I feel him shake his head. "I know you don't. I know. It takes time, Dylan. I gave up the drugs for you. But you don't need to worry because I don't need them as long as I have you."

I remember the conversation Scott had with me at the bar. I sigh. "Jeremy, I don't want you to not use for me."

Jeremy takes a step back, looking down at me in humor. "What?" he says, laughing. He moves a strand of hair out of my face.

"I want you to not use for you. This has to be something you want regardless of if you're with me or not, or you won't stay clean. What if we have a fight and you go out and use? Do you know what that will do to me?"

His face turns serious and he looks into my eyes. "That won't happen."

"But you didn't stop because you wanted to, you only stopped because I left. I think you need to find out why you started using in the first place. You need help understanding why you want to use."

I see panic hit his eyes. "I am, Dylan. I am doing those things. My mom...that's why I went."

My chest is tight. I try to keep my breathing even. "I know, Jeremy. But until you deal with those demons, I don't think you can promise me you'll stay clean. I mean, you're going back on tour, seeing all the same people and places. I can't sit here worrying you'll turn to drugs again. I'll blame myself."

He opens his mouth to interrupt me but I continue. "I have things to deal with, too.

Things in my past. Plus I have school I need to concentrate on. This is my dream, Jeremy."

He looks at me silently for a moment. Tears spill over his cheeks. "What are you saying, Dylan?" his hands caress my back.

I sigh, my heart so heavy I can barely stand. "I'm saying…that we need to let each other go."

He shakes his head, "No!" he cries out. "No."

"Just for now," I add, the tears spilling again. "We can't keep doing this. We need to deal with our issues separately first. Then we can come back to this relationship as two healthy individuals. You need to stay clean for yourself, and I need to deal with my trust issues and anger problems."

He looks down at me, his eyes pleading. Tears run down his cheeks. "Dylan, we can do those things together. And we'll grow and become closer."

I run my hand down his cheek. "It doesn't work that way. Jeremy, we'll just continue to hurt each other. And you have a yearlong tour you'll be on. How can we deal with it together if you're gone?"

"I'll cancel. I will. I won't leave. I gave up everything for you. I changed completely for you."

I know he means it, which makes me feel even worse. "You can't cancel. And you shouldn't have changed for me, that's the point. It's not healthy."

He's hyperventilating now. He drops to his knees in front of me. "Don't, Dylan. Oh my God. Don't, please." He releases one of his hands from my legs and clutches his chest. Alarmed, I kneel down in front of him.

I can see he's alright, just in emotional pain. "I'm hurting too, Jeremy. I am."

He sobs, his face towards the floor. "That woman…" he chokes out. "I got my grandmother's ring from my mom. I didn't want you to have just anything, I wanted it to be special. The woman in the picture…she's a jeweler. She's going to size the ring. A wedding ring. I didn't want to cause a frenzy walking into a jewelry store to get it sized."

Oh God. Oh no.

A wedding ring. For me. He was going to ask me to marry him.

"You said…" he barely continues, "you said you would hold me together. That you wouldn't hurt me."

"Oh, Jeremy," I cry.

We sob loudly for a few moments, holding each other. He puts his head on my shoulder and cradles me in his arms. "You're it for me Dylan. You're the only one I want. The only one I want to call my wife. No one else."

Over his shoulder, I see blood splatters on the floor from his nose. My resolve hardens. "I know, but still..."

He sighs. "You'll come back to me?"

I nod. "Yes, when we've dealt with our issues and you've stayed clean. If we can do that, then we know it's meant to be."

He tries to calm his breathing. We're still grasping each other. "Do you know what I thought when I saw your face in the crowd? That first moment I laid my eyes on you?" he whispers in my ear.

I smile, my chest hurting. "I've often wondered. I thought I saw you continue to look at me during the show, but then I thought I was just nuts."

He nods his head on my shoulder. "I did. I couldn't take my eyes off you. When I saw you, it was like the world stopped. Time stopped. It took everything in me to remember what notes to play and what lyrics to sing. I knew, right in that moment, I was staring at my wife. You've always been my wife, since the moment I saw you. You're the woman I'll spend the rest of my life with."

I squeeze him tighter. "My husband," I whisper to him. One day, if not in reality, then always in my heart.

Epilogue

"Yes!" I shriek, throwing my fist in the air. Straight A's for the semester. Straight A's for my first semester at Harvard.

A strong arm smacks me on the shoulder. "Great work, Dyl!" Scott congratulates me as we look at my laptop screen. He kisses me on the cheek and I hug him around the neck. "Text Jeremy," he reminds me. "He'll be so proud of you."

I try to remember where he'll be. I don't want to text him if it's too early. I forget, he's always somewhere different, but I know he always likes to hear from me no matter what.

Me: Jeremy, straight A's!
Jeremy: Babe, that's wonderful. Knew you could do it. Keep it up. Call you later.

I smile. Even Scott smiles. Scott's been a lot more accepting since Jeremy and I broke up.

The night of the breakup, after Jeremy packed his stuff and left, it was really hard. It was a dark time for me, and I'm sure for him. We had agreed it would be better to not speak for a while, and he left for his tour a week later.

We just started speaking again, but the pain of hearing his voice is still very raw. I know he's in more pain then he lets on. Rich fills me in on his depression over e-mail from time to time. For now we've agreed to talk over text message and call each other only twice a week. I still love him and still see myself being with him, but I'm glad we've had this time away from each other to grow.

I've been working with a therapist of my own, just as Jeremy's therapist has followed him on tour. I'm finally dealing with what I saw with my Dad, what happened with my Mom, and my anger issues. My Dad even flew out to have a session with me, and I told him everything that happened with Jeremy. Talking about it helps.

Scott looks over at me, pride in his eyes, and wraps his arm tightly around my shoulder. Scott makes me feel so centered and normal. He gives me strength to get through all of this. He was my saving grace when I left Jeremy.

But between therapy, school, work, and planning Theresa's wedding, I'm way too busy to date. Being a maid of honor is hard work.

I think of Jeremy constantly. Every day that passes, it gets easier to be without him. But it doesn't make me want him any less. I hear him often on the radio when they play the new track "Drowning In You." That's both amazing and excruciating.

Sometimes I'll catch him on the news, or see him in an article, and so far it's all been good things. I'm surprised he's kept himself out of trouble.

Just yesterday, news blew up about him doing something to his famous guitar. At first, I was scared he had smashed it, but when I noticed my name mentioned in the article, I was confused. Since Jeremy left months ago, I hadn't been bothered or mentioned almost at all by the reporters.

They showed a picture of him performing, back in his prime: arm in the air, back arched, his graceful body out towards the audience. I smiled, seeing a glimpse once more of the man I fell in love with, back from the dead. The article showed a closer up shot of his guitar underneath the picture, and in green letters engraved on the bottom, the name "Dylan" was written in beautiful calligraphy.

It took everything in me at that moment to not call him and beg for him back. I know he would have come back to me, too. But as I sit here, relaxed, looking at my straight A's, my friend by my side, no reporters or screaming fans, I know I made the right choice. At least for now.

I still hope that one day, it won't be so complicated. Maybe one day, it will be as easy as it is now with Scott- with Jeremy wrapped around my shoulders, congratulating me on my grades. But right now, it's not that way and can't be, so we're living our lives the best we can without each other.

Scott squeezes my shoulders once again. "Come on," I say, staring into his eyes, surprising him with a wink. He raises an eyebrow at me. "You're taking me out to celebrate!"

Look for book two in the Rock Bottom Series:
Trials.
Coming soon!